guard I

Dear God, he's c

Breanna staggered in
resounding with the c
She made it halfway across the orchard before
realizing the sounds were growing more distant,
heading in the opposite direction. Whirling, she
looked behind her and saw the distinct shapes
of three men diving for cover at different
angles.

An unnatural quiet filled the night. *They're all
around me,* she thought. The cabin wasn't that
far, but it seemed to take forever to reach it. She
clawed her way over the retainer wall, pulling
herself flat on the ground until the black
shadows from the oak tree shielded her. Even
then she didn't feel safe. There could be more of
them in the yard. She stumbled forward,
flattening herself against the cabin to guard her
back. Crab-walking, she inched sideways
toward the corner.

Then someone grabbed her hair....

ABOUT THE AUTHOR

Catherine Anderson has always wanted to write. Ideas come to her from everywhere, and stories laced with mystery and intrigue are her particular love. *Reasonable Doubt* sprang from her own background in the Pacific Northwest. Her ancestors pioneered Oregon, settling there to make their living mining for gold. Her hometown, Grants Pass, Oregon, and the nearby settlements on Lower Graves Creek were a veritable "gold mine" of inspiration for her first Intrigue. Currently she lives in Everett, Washington, with her husband and two sons.

Reasonable Doubt

Catherine Anderson

Harlequin Books

TORONTO • NEW YORK • LONDON
AMSTERDAM • PARIS • SYDNEY • HAMBURG
STOCKHOLM • ATHENS • TOKYO • MILAN

To Robyn and Sarah
And to my mother, who inspired me

Harlequin Intrigue edition published June 1988

ISBN 0-373-22092-8

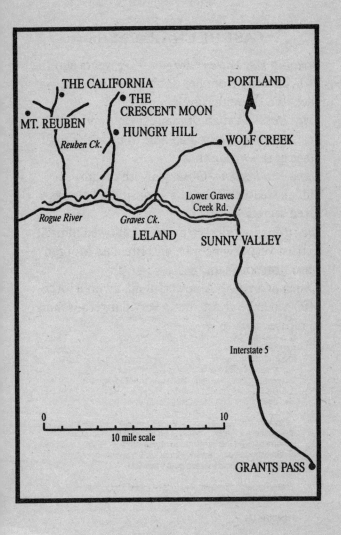

CAST OF CHARACTERS

Breanna Van Patten Morgan—Ten years ago she had run away from her doubts, but now she was back and through running.

Tyler Ross—A man of many talents and no past, who always seemed able to be in the right place at the wrong time.

Dane Van Patten—Obsessed with dreams of hidden treasure, Breanna's cousin had always loved secrets.

Jack Jones—Tyler's "partner" allowed himself to trust very few people, and Breanna Morgan wasn't one of them.

Chuck Morrow—A powerful man with a lot to offer when he chose, but a very dangerous man to refuse.

Prologue

The cold in the room cut bone deep, dank as a grave. A lantern perched on a wooden shelf, its flickering sphere of light overwhelmed by the shifting shadows that played upon the earthen walls. Four men stood near the door, three together, one alone, the air between them crystallized with tension.

The heftiest of the threesome unrolled his T-shirt sleeve and lifted out a pack of cigarettes. When he tapped the pack against his ink-stained forefinger, the sound echoed around him. He smiled as he reached for his lighter. With a flick of his thumb, he rasped flint against steel and dipped his head toward the spurt of orange flame. The glow from it rippled over his face, emphasizing his coarse features and cold, flat eyes.

"It's like this," he whispered, exhaling smoke. "You get rid of her, or I do. It's your decision."

"How?" Desperation rang in the lone man's voice. "What do you suggest? That I tell her to leave the second she gets here? She won't go. She inherited the cabin in the will. It's hers and the mining claim's filed in her name."

"If you'd filed before she got here, the claim would have been yours. We could have taken the cabin by default. You screwed up. How you undo it is up to you. The way I see it, if she stays, it's her or us.''

"Just what the hell do you mean?''

Letting his cigarette dangle from the corner of his mouth, the older man leaned against the wall. Lifting his hand to his throat, he made a slashing motion across his Adam's apple. "That clear enough for you, pretty boy?''

"You aren't serious! A move like that would bring every cop in the country down on our heads.''

"Not if it's done right. No one knows we're here, remember?''

"You miserable bastard,'' the younger man hissed. "How much time do I have? She doesn't scare easy.''

"We can hold off production a few days. Meanwhile, we'll watch her so she doesn't poke around and find our equipment. Sound reasonable?''

"Reasonable? You don't know the meaning of the word.''

Chapter One

Hypnotic regression. Those were the only words to describe the feeling that washed over Breanna Morgan as she climbed out of her silver Honda and gazed at her grandparents' small cabin. In the dusky light, its yellow logs and tin roof looked postcard perfect against the tree-studded backdrop of Hungry Hill. Flashbacks buffeted her, some sweet, some nostalgic, others painful. She stood rooted until her mind could assimilate the shock.

With a determined lift of her chin, Breanna strode to the aluminum driveway gate and swung it wide. The night wind whispered, a decibel louder than the gurgle of Graves Creek, following the stream's course as it twisted and turned through the canyon to spill into the white water of the Rogue River five miles west. Above Breanna, a clapboard sign dangled by one corner from the arbor that formed an entry arch. Its rhythmic, forlorn squeaking underscored the surrounding gloom. Glancing at the encroaching laurel and oak trees, she drew in a deep breath and slowly exhaled. After spending most of her twenty-seven years in the mountains, as a child playing in the surrounding woods, as an adult doing wildlife studies, the remote location of *The Crescent Moon* mining claim shouldn't bother her.

But it did. Vague unease wrapped itself around her and refused to let go.

Turning back toward the Honda, she saw her black dog, Coaly, had exited the car. He seemed bent on exploring everything, and that was a mighty big order when miles of Oregon forests stretched in all directions.

"Come on, old man," Breanna called as she slid back behind the steering wheel. "It's time to get settled for the night."

The mostly Labrador mutt led the way down the drive, his incongruous plumed tail waving like a flag over his back. Some of his excitement spilled over to Breanna. She had always loved it down here. Once she settled in, maybe a little of the magic would return. It was a perfect environment for writing, much better than living in town with all the distractions that neighbors inflicted.

Parking near the retainer wall steps to facilitate unloading her hatchback, Breanna fished in the pocket of her faded jeans for her cabin key as she slid out of the car. Coaly ran circles around her for a moment, then veered away to sniff the foundation of the old barn. As she ascended the steps to the overgrown yard, Breanna could see the ravages of neglect everywhere. Weeds flourished in her grandmother's rose beds beside the house. The cement edges of the stone walkway were beginning to crumble. She didn't know what her cousin, Dane, had been doing during his visits here these last seven years, but it was clear he hadn't been caretaking. No wonder their grandmother had given the cabin to Breanna.

Four paces up the walk, Breanna froze, her gaze riveted on the front door. It hung awry on its hinges, swinging slightly as if someone had bumped against it only seconds earlier. The door frame was split and gouged where the sturdy dead bolt had been forced inward. Myriad emotions rushed through her. Disbelief turned to outrage, and both were quickly smothered by fear. Intruders caught in the act could be dangerous. Standing here, she blocked the only exit as effectively as a cork in a narrow-necked bottle.

The door swung slowly shut, then yawned open again, creaking on its hinges. Breanna jumped. Then she realized it was only the wind. Coaly lumbered up the steps behind her, tongue lolling, tail whipping against her leg as he passed. With no apparent presentiment of danger, he bounded onto the porch and gave the swinging door a nudge with his nose.

Trusting her dog's keen sense of smell, Breanna relaxed a bit. He'd be raising a ruckus if anyone was in there. Straining her ears for any unusual sounds, she advanced on the cabin. As she stepped onto the porch, her well-trained eye zeroed in on a footprint in the soft dirt next to the walkway. She leaned over to study it. A man's boot, judging by its size, one with a waffled sole. A hiking boot? It gave her an eerie feeling looking at it.

"Coaly, wait up."

The canine's response was a happy bark as he frolicked into the dark entry hall. Pausing on the threshold, Breanna pushed the door wide. No growls from Coaly yet. That was a good sign. She'd need her flashlight, though. It was black as a tomb in there. Hurrying back to the Honda, she dug into the glove box until her fingers curled around the cylinder of plastic.

"Coaly?"

Breanna switched the flashlight on as she entered the short entry hall. Glossy log walls burnished with age, just as she remembered. Gramps's hand-carved coatrack hung to her right. On her left was a— She came to a dead stop and stared. A white face glowed back at her. For an instant that seemed like eternity, she couldn't move. Her blood pounded in her ears, a loud, rhythmic swish that deafened her. Then she recognized her own distorted image, reflected by an old mirror. She laughed, the sound squeaky and tremulous. If she didn't stop this, she'd have cardiac arrest before she reached the living room.

"Coaly? Come here, boy."

The hall spilled into the main living area. She eased forward, then fell back, waving her arms. Cobwebs. She sputtered, shining the light on her shoulder. Gray wisps clung to her sun-streaked brown hair. She brushed them away, then played the light over the river rock fireplace, the battered kitchen table, the lime-green gas stove. A thick layer of dust covered the sheets on the studio couch and sofa. More cobwebs were draped from rafter to rafter.

"Brother! Talk about a hard day's work; this is it." Her voice rang hollow in the room. The heavy smell of aged pine mingled with moldy dampness, making her shiver. "Gives me the creeps to think of sleeping in here."

First things first. For now, her major concerns were dealing with the broken lock on the front door and clearing a place to stretch out for the night. When she pushed through the curtained doorway to the bedroom, the tarnished brass bedstead gleamed back at her. It was the only valuable antique in the house; she'd been half-afraid it would be gone.

But when she came to think of it, nothing seemed to be missing. Breanna returned to the living room, flicking the light around. Gran's oil paintings of the creek hung above the oak mantle. The mahogany tables stood in their respective corners, the tops littered with Gran's odds and ends. A thimble. A short piece of fishing line. A garden trowel. Nothing disturbed, nothing stolen. A slight frown settled on Breanna's brow. It didn't make sense. Usually if you found your front door kicked in, your house was either vandalized or stripped of its valuables.

"Maybe someone got stranded out here and needed shelter," she said to Coaly. "Polite houseguests. They even left the sheets on the furniture."

The dog didn't respond with his usual bark, but she could hear his claws clacking on the planked floor. Training her flashlight on one of the paned windows, Breanna sighed. Night was closing in fast. She wouldn't sleep a wink unless she could lock up tight. Her earlier feeling of unease had escalated into a full-blown case of edginess. No phone, no electricity. Worse yet, no lantern. Where was it?

Fanning the light along the rafters, she spotted the old Coleman hanging on a hook above the stove. Red clay dust coated its base. It had probably hung there untouched since Gran's first stroke seven years ago. She could almost see her grandmother in the kitchen, flour streaking her apron, her salt-and-pepper hair swept back with tortoiseshell combs. The cozy picture accompanied her as she returned to the Honda to get her can of kerosene.

Forty-five minutes later, Breanna jammed a chair securely under the doorknob and knelt before the hearth to light a fire. Now that the car was unloaded, she could try to relax. Flames licked up the crumpled tufts of old newspaper she had found on Gran's closet shelf, blue tendrils curling hungrily around the sticks of kindling. Mesmerized, she stared at the smoldering newsprint. Then she noticed the date on the right-hand corner.

August twenty-third, ten years ago. Only a few days before the—

Her throat tightened and she grabbed the poker, shoving the newspaper into the flames. Why on earth had Gran kept papers that old? And from that particular month?

Forcing the tension out of her shoulders, she glanced around. The yellow glow of flame and kerosene light cast the rooms into flickering shadow. How many times had she sat in this very spot, knees hugged to her chest, eyes trans-fixed on her grandfather's face as he told stories about John Van Patten's ghost and his legendary gold? Those were the memories she should dwell on, the wonderful ones that were the essence of her childhood.

Smiling, she rose to double-check the door. If someone wanted in, her makeshift barricade might slow him down, but that was the best she could hope for. Breanna tugged on the knob to be sure the chair was angled under it to the best advantage, still wondering who had broken in. The most likely explanation was treasure hunters. Gramps had sounded so convincing when he talked about the Van Patten gold that most people in this area thought the story was gospel. Even her cousin, Dane.

Dane.

She hadn't spoken to him in years, but it wasn't beyond the realm of possibility that her cousin had given the house one last search before Breanna moved in. It would be just like him to come down here on the sly, thumping the walls for a hidden panel, checking the stones in the fireplace to make sure none were loose. Yes, it could have been Dane. On the other hand, it might not have been. Goose bumps rose on her arms.

As she reentered the living room, she noticed smoke es-caping through the fire screen. Hurrying to the hearth, she grabbed the poker and shoved it up the flue to check the draft lever. Wide open. The chimney was blocked. Just what she needed. "I don't believe this!"

Coughing and waving her hand to clear the air, she stepped to a French window and threw it wide. Then, kneeling on the hearth, she again seized the poker and shifted the wood so it would burn more swiftly. Dousing it with water would only create more smoke.

The wood was laurel, deadfall from Hungry Hill. Its scent and the searing of hot smoke in her nostrils catapulted her mind into the past—to another night, another fire. *August, ten years ago.* Her knuckles went white as she tightened her fingers around the brass handle of the poker. Images flashed with Technicolor clarity, faster and faster until they came together in a hot, kaleidoscopic amber glare. Sweat popped out on her forehead, triggered by the panicky shiver of nausea that still swept over her whenever she thought about it. Arson, death, suspecting someone she loved. Guilt roiled within her. She wasn't sure which ate at her the most, believing Dane capable of such treachery or keeping silent about her own inconclusive suspicions.

Memories of that violent night lingered in Breanna's thoughts as she turned out the lantern and unrolled her sleeping bag on the sofa. She sank wearily onto a cushion, drawing her legs beneath her and propping an elbow on the couch arm. Her nerves were strung so taut that she couldn't lie down and rest.

The open window made her feel vulnerable. It would be so easy for someone to creep up on her. At least she had Coaly. She gazed out at the shadows in the moonlit yard. Just shadows, not an intruder. A rafter creaked above her. The lantern gave a final sputter, sending a prickle of alarm up her spine before she realized what had made the sound.

Seconds dragged into minutes, minutes into hours. Nothing but the usual noises. Breanna pulled the sleeping bag close, watched the window, blinked herself awake when her eyelids drifted shut. As exhausted as she was, she didn't dare sleep. An owl hooted. The sound of its call faded into silence, mournful, lonely. It was the last thing Breanna was aware of as she slipped into an uneasy doze....

It seemed only moments later that birds were singing her
awake. She slipped off the sofa to stand at the open French
doors, gazing out at the golden shafts of sunlight that spilled
through the oak leaves. *Home,* she thought. *This is how I
remember it.* The sweetness of Gran's roses perfumed the
June morning, lightly blended with honeysuckle and the
lingering fragrance of withered lilac blooms. Coaly slept on
the lawn, warmed by a circle of sunshine.

Turning, she directed a speculative glance at the dusty
stove. Breakfast would be short and simple. Her work was
cut out for her if she wanted this place livable by nightfall.

BY EARLY EVENING, Breanna had given the last screw on her
new front door lock a final twist. She had been busily
working since morning, scrubbing the cabin, unpacking her
things, driving to town for a lock and wood to replace the
splintered door frame. She stood back to survey her handi-
work with a sense of satisfaction. Not only had she accom-
plished a lot, but staying occupied had diverted her thoughts
from last night's uneasiness.

Tossing her screwdriver into the toolbox, she leaned her
head back and stretched. As tired as she was, it comforted
her to know she would be able to sleep tonight, safe behind
a locked door. Then a troubled frown pleated her forehead. Dropping her outstretched arms, she glanced over her
shoulder. If she had felt it once today, she had felt it a dozen
times. Eyes following her, making her skin crawl.

Was someone out there? Or had her nerves shoved her
imagination into overdrive? She scanned the thick brush
that bordered the creek. Nothing, not a sign of movement.
Smiling at her own silliness, she bent to close her toolbox.
Even if someone was there, it was probably a local from
Wolf Creek or Leland. Sunday was a day for campers.

"Nice evening, isn't it?" a deep voice boomed.

Breanna gave such a start that she slammed the lid of the toolbox on her thumb. Pain ricocheted up her arm. She sprang to a standing position and turned with a muffled cry. A dark-haired man wearing jeans and hiking boots was striding up the steps. His shirt was such a brilliant red that she couldn't believe she had missed seeing him a moment ago.

"Where did you come from? Don't you know it can be dangerous, sneaking up on someone like that?"

He paused midway up the walk to study her, his steely blue eyes alert to her every move. "I wasn't sneaking. I'm sorry. I didn't mean to startle you."

She gave a shaky laugh and dropped her gaze to his boots. Hiking boots, suede with red laces and waffled soles. She felt the blood drain from her face as she focused her attention on him. If this was her intruder, she could be in serious trouble. He was well over six feet tall with a good two hundred pounds to back up his height, every ounce hard, lean muscle. A camera hung from a braided strap around his neck, a Leica, the type only a professional photographer or serious hobbyist might carry.

"Well, for not trying, you sure did a good job of it. I about jumped out of my skin. I didn't hear you drive up. Are you on foot?"

He nodded. "I'm Tyler Ross. I have a cabin about a mile up the road. Been down by the creek working and when I saw you moving in, I thought I'd better stop by and check on things. You do realize this place is a mining claim? It belongs to the Van Pattens."

"You say you were working? Doing what? How long have you been watching me?"

"I wasn't exactly watching you. I just noticed you up here." He shrugged one shoulder, an offhanded gesture that belied the distrust she saw in his eyes. "I'm a photographer. I was getting a few shots down in the orchard."

"In my orchard? Of what?"

"Deer. A doe and fawn."

Breanna tensed, watching his face for any sign of deception. His eyes met hers without wavering. If anything, she read suspicion in them, not guilt. This time of evening, deer usually emerged to feed. The apple orchard would be a likely spot to get pictures of them. "You say you live up the road?"

"Look, I didn't mean to frighten you—"

"I'm not frightened." Her voice rang a little too sharply. A flush of heat spiraled up her spine. "Well, maybe I am, just a little." She managed a smile and extended her hand. "I'm Breanna Morgan, Alicia Van Patten's daughter."

Expecting him to relax, Breanna kept her hand extended, but he ignored it.

"Then you're related to Dane Van Patten?"

Why the question sounded like an accusation she didn't know. "Yes. He's my cousin. Is there a problem with that?"

"No, of course not."

Feeling ridiculous with her hand held out, she dropped her hand just as he reached out to shake it. By the time she could react, he was drawing back.

A sudden smile creased his tanned cheeks. "We'll get this right sooner or later. I'm pleased to meet you, Miss Morgan."

"Likewise, I'm sure." She placed her palm across his. His callused fingers tightened around hers in a firm grip, pleasant, not crushing, the kind of handshake Gramps had called trusty.

"It is Miss, isn't it?" He loosened his hold slowly. "Or should I say Ms.?"

"Miss is fine."

With a nod toward her porch, he said, "I see you've fixed the lock."

"You knew it was broken?"

"Noticed it late yesterday afternoon. I planned to repair it, but I haven't been to town since to get a dead bolt and molding. Nothing disturbed, I hope?"

Tipping her head back to watch him, she said, "There were a few things stolen, but nothing I can't replace."

She braced herself for a reaction to the lie, a twitching muscle, a flicker of surprise, but all Ross did was nod. He either had rock-steady nerves or was innocent, she wasn't sure which. While she studied him, she caught herself admiring the striking blend of his irregular features. His nose was a bit too large, jutting sharply from between his thick eyebrows with no indentation at the bridge, but it suited him, enhancing his high cheekbones while it offset the squared angles of his jaw.

"So, Miss Morgan, how long do you plan to stay?"

His eyes caught and held hers, a much deeper blue than her own, smoky, darkened with flecks of cobalt and outlined by a sweep of black lashes. Magnetic, direct, the kind of eyes that hid secrets well. She would be wise not to forget that.

"For good. My grandmother passed away recently and willed me the cabin. One stipulation was that I file on the claim and keep the assessments done so it can stay in the family. Her biggest fear was that strangers would take it."

"You mean you plan to live here?"

"Why shouldn't I?"

"On a permanent basis? Mining, part-time or full-scale, is heavy work."

"I'm not afraid of work. And I come from a long line of miners. My grandfather worked in the *California* mine for a number of years."

He glanced toward Mount Reuben. "The *California*, that's up Reuben Creek, isn't it? Funny name for a mine in Oregon."

"My grandfather claimed it was named for a Californian, and other miners said it ran so deep, it went clear to California. I don't think anyone knows now for sure."

"So you're going to be a prospector? Having no electricity will get old in about a week. Same for no indoor plumbing. It'd take a lot of mettle to stick it out down here." The breeze lifted a lock of his ebony hair, waving it across his forehead. "Take some friendly advice. This is no place for a woman alone. You'd be asking for trouble."

"I avoid trouble."

"I hope so. Wouldn't want you getting hurt."

Breanna's earlier distrust mushroomed again. She tensed and shot him a glare. "Hurt? I played in these woods as a kid, know them like the back of my hand."

"It's not as peaceful down here as it used to be."

The night wind picked up, cool, raising goose bumps on her arms. "Is that so?"

"Look at your door. If that's not trouble's calling card, I don't know what is. If you plan to stay, I wouldn't go wandering if I were you. And I'd steer clear of those old outbuildings. You don't want to end up a statistic."

"You have an interesting way of turning a phrase, Mr. Ross. I could almost believe you're trying to scare me."

"Maybe I am."

"Why?"

"Could be I'm a concerned neighbor. I realize it's a dying breed, but there are still a few of us left."

Shoving her hands into her jeans pockets, she nudged a pebble on the walk with the toe of her sneaker. "Well, I don't scare easy."

"I hope I haven't offended you."

"Not at all." Breanna gritted out a smile she felt sure looked set in concrete. "I do have a lot of work to do, though, and it's nearly dark."

One of his eyebrows shot up, but he didn't argue. "I'll get out of your hair then. Nice meeting you." He turned and struck off down the walk.

"The pleasure was all mine," she replied evenly. Then, as a parting shot, she called, "Oh, and watch out for my dog. He's not one to be friendly with strangers. I'm afraid he's an incurable biter."

Ross slowed and glanced back at her. "A little black fella?"

"Not so little."

Another smile curved his mouth. "He and I already tangled down by the creek. The only thing he seemed interested in biting was my lunch. Be seein' you, Miss Morgan."

She stood there watching until he disappeared around a bend in the road. "Not if I have my druthers, you won't."

Silence settled around her like a cloak. Sighing, she nudged the pebble with her shoe again, then kicked it. She wasn't quite sure what to make of Tyler Ross, but for now he was her number one suspect. It would take a big stretch of her imagination to believe his visit this evening had been sheer coincidence, especially after the ominous little warnings he had given her. The word statistic conjured up ugly newspaper headlines.

Shifting her gaze to the weathered old barn, Breanna mulled over their conversation. A treasure seeker, perhaps? Maybe he was one of a group. She could almost see them, armed with maps, metal detectors strapped to their shoulders. Ross didn't look the type, but one could never tell.

Her eyes trailed to the boot prints near the porch that she had found last night. Waffled soles. Did Ross's hiking boots leave a similar impression? Unfortunately, he hadn't stepped off the walk onto soft dirt so she could check. Even if he had, and she could be certain the prints were his, it would prove nothing. He had admitted to having seen her broken door. He might also have walked onto the porch to examine the damage.

Exhaustion weighed like an anchor on Breanna's shoulders. A flash of black at the corner of the barn drew her notice. Coaly. Dirt flew from beneath his paws. He was probably after some animal. She gave a sharp whistle and waited for him to reach her. An early night sounded tempting. First a bath, then a quick dinner, and the last order of business was bed.

After gathering fresh clothes and toiletry articles, Breanna struck off for the creek with Coaly tagging behind. The bathing hole was a deep pool, surrounded by a privacy screen of thick foliage. On the opposite bank, the eroded earth was rust red, with gnarled tree roots reaching like clutching fingers into the stream. She stripped near a bush, dumping her clothes in a pile, then carried her bathing things to the diving rock, a low bank of shale that curved out into the water. As she poised to dive, she hesitated.

Eyes. Instinctively she hugged her breasts with one arm and crossed her lower body with the other. Then Coaly came into view, tail wagging, nose to the ground. That was her cue to stop being paranoid. She lifted her arms and pushed off the rock, slicing deep into the water.

Breanna emerged in a spray, gasping for breath. She had forgotten how icy Graves Creek was. Doing a breast stroke to the rock, she grabbed her shampoo, did a quick job on her hair, then seized the soap. This would be one quick bath.

Coaly, drawn by her splashing and sharp gasp of surprise, came bounding onto the rock, barking furiously. Breanna tried to reassure him, but he seemed convinced she would go under and never come up. In his frenzy he managed to muddy her towel, knock her razor into the pool and slip partway off the rock to douse his hindquarters.

Breanna heaved herself out of the water, fended off the dog, and extracted her towel from beneath his feet. The fabric was nearly as wet as she was and smelled of...dog. By the time she had used her clean clothes to dry off, and then struggled into them, she had had it with dogs, and even without using the doggy towel, she felt pretty sure she was wearing enough dog hair to pass as one if someone didn't look close.

And someone *was* looking. It hit her as she finished tying her sneakers. Coaly, elated to have her safe on shore, paused in his prancing to curl his lip, his liquid brown eyes glinting.

Chapter Two

An eerie creaking noise drifted to Breanna from the brush.
It had no sooner stopped than Coaly barked, throwing his
ears forward. Then off he went into a thick growth of manzanita. Apprehensive about what he might find, she held
back for a moment. When no snarling erupted, she struck
off after him. Ten feet into the foliage, she found her pet
sniffing the ground. Pushing him aside, she spied footprints. Waffled soles, like the impression she'd found by her
porch.

Impotent rage. Now she knew exactly what it meant.
Coaly, hot on the scent, plunged through the brush toward
a low-hung copse, but Breanna had seen enough. It had to
have been Ross. Graves Creek wasn't exactly teeming with
people.

Returning to the stream for her things, Breanna then
strode for the cabin. She made short work of getting ready
for bed, then sat on the edge of the mattress to brush her wet
hair, glaring at the floor. Ross was cool, she'd give him that.
He hadn't batted an eyelash when she baited him. Well, she
wasn't leaving, if that was his game plan. It would take a
whole lot more than silly warnings and lurking in the brush
to make her break her promise to Gran and leave the place
to claim jumpers.

Going to the kitchen, Breanna hugged her arms around her against the evening chill. Her long flannel gown did little to warm her, especially with her hair hanging wet on her shoulders. Putting a pan of soup on the gas stove to heat, she cast a determined glance at the fireplace. Cleaning the flue was the next chore on her list. Next time she bathed, she could dry her hair by the fire. She would need a chain, though, to knock the blockage loose. If she remembered right, Gramps had kept some in the barn.

Her lips thinned to a grim line. If Ross showed his face tomorrow when she was armed with a chain, she'd be sorely tempted to throttle him with it.

EN ROUTE TO THE BARN the following morning, Breanna was brought up short by the low rumble of a powerful car coming around the bend. A blue Corvette? A fancy automobile like that was as out of place down Graves Creek as a San Francisco trolley car. She knew instantly who must be at the wheel. Less than two months ago her mother had mentioned how well Dane seemed to be doing at the accounting firm, and that he had recently purchased a fancy new sports car.

Breanna walked toward the approaching vehicle, debating how to handle this meeting. Dane undoubtedly resented the stipulations in Gran's will that gave Breanna first option of owning the cabin. With much less enthusiasm than she would have liked, Breanna watched her cousin climb out of the driver's seat. The sunlight glanced off his blond hair as he straightened his gray sport coat and gave one leg a shake to get a wrinkle out of his slacks. Same old Dane, fussing and primping.

"Hello, Dane. It's good to see you." The lie left an acid taste on her tongue.

"Hi, Bree."

His eyes met hers, large, sky-blue Van Patten eyes, right down to the thick fringe of his gold-tipped lashes. Looking into them, Breanna could no more deny her kinship with him than she could her own brother. Memories of their childhood drifted into her mind, of long, lazy days of summer when they had run wild together, catching salamanders in the creek, romping in the hayloft, sharing secrets. What had happened to them that they could stand here today, eyeing one another like enemies?

"It really is good to see you," she repeated, truly meaning it this time, hoping he'd do nothing to spoil it.

"So you said." His tone was curt. "I wish I could say the same. When I drove in, you were headed for the barn. What for?"

"Some chain. I have to sweep the chimney."

"Yeah. Well, who promised you a rose garden?"

"Dane, there isn't much point in being antagonistic."

"Isn't there. I've put my sweat into this place these last seven years. Have you? No, you just get it handed to you."

"It was Gran's decision, Dane. I tried to make her change her mind and she refused."

"Because you were her favorite, always were."

"Oh, come on. Be fair. Of the four grandkids, I was the only one who could really make a go of this place. You're an accountant, Jason's a lawyer, Deanna's a teach—"

"You could have refused, Breanna. The word no *is* in your vocabulary. I've heard you say it enough times."

"Are you questioning my right to be here?"

"You swore you'd never come back. Then, bingo, you walk in and take over. Why, Bree? That's all I want to know."

"I was seventeen when I said that. I realize now that I have too many memories here to let the place go to strangers."

"Are you implying I'd let claim jumpers come in? Watch what you say. My mood isn't the best."

The thin thread of Breanna's patience snapped. Before she could stop herself, she gestured toward the neglected yard. "The truth is that you don't give a fig for the claim, Dane. Look at it, then tell me Gran should've left it to you. For seven years she paid you to keep it up—out of her social security, mind you—and in all that time you squeaked by, doing as little work as you could. The walks are disintegrating. The outbuildings are rotting away. The fences have tumbled down. For the time you've spent here, you've done precious little sweating. What have you been doing, anyway? Lounging under a tree, daydreaming?"

"What I do down here is none of your business unless it somehow affects you, which it doesn't. Too bad I can't say the same. You come sailing in, taking over, to hell with the gossip it will cause. It doesn't even occur to you that I've stuck it out, lived through the stares and nasty whispers until people started to forget." A grimace crossed his face. "All that is beside the point. What bothers me worst is you don't stop and think how I feel. I've spent years searching, never giving up on the gold. With my luck, you'll stumble over the treasure and keep it yourself. It isn't fair, but you don't care, do you?"

"You know better than that. If there is a treasure, and I stress the *if*, I'd divide it equally among all us kids." Breanna felt the color wash from her face. "It isn't the treasure at all, though, is it? That's not really what's troubling you."

"Don't be ridiculous."

She didn't miss the way his gaze shifted, as if he were afraid she'd read too much in his eyes. "It's the fire," she said softly. "Admit it, Dane. What really concerns you is that my return may start people talking again."

"And why not? You're not stupid, Breanna. We got off by the skin of our teeth on a fake alibi. Don't you realize how shaky our position is? Another investigation could land us both in jail."

"Not if we've nothing to hide." Breanna shoved her hands into her jeans pockets, watching, analyzing his expression. She knew him so well, perhaps too well, this man who had been her childhood chum. "And we don't. Do we, Dane?"

The question drifted into the air; hung there unanswered. Dane's sudden pallor alarmed her.

"Dane." Breanna stepped forward, lifting a hand to touch his arm. "Dane, I love you like my own brother, you do know that? If there's something you haven't told me, you can trust—"

He jerked his arm away. "I'm so sick of you suspecting me. What kind of a person are you? We used to be best friends, and you believe I'd murder somebody? You know better."

"Yes . . . yes, I do. And knowing you is what has kept my mouth shut. But you're hiding something. I see it in your eyes. What happened that night, Dane? What *really* happened?"

He stepped back, leveling a finger at her. "Fair warning. Don't go stirring up gossip. You got it? And don't go poking your nose where you shouldn't. That goes for the gold *and* the fire. Is that clear? You screw around with me, and I'll—"

"You'll what?" Every muscle in Breanna's body tensed. "You'll what, Dane? I want to hear it. Don't threaten me. It won't work this time. You're not the only one who's fed up. You're hiding something from me. I'm going to find out what it is."

"There's nothing."

"And I think you're lying."

"You think I murdered a man?"

Breanna couldn't speak. She could only stare at him.

"That's it, isn't it?"

"Yes! Does that satisfy you? I think you lit that fire, Dane. I think you killed Rob Thatcher." The words came with such difficulty that she trembled. Ten years, and she had finally accused him to his face. She hadn't planned on that. A sob ripped its way up, ragged, hollow, turning her throat raw. "I think you were involved. When I woke up that night, you were just returning to camp. You *said* you'd been out in the bushes, but you had been running. You were sweating and breathing hard."

"Sure I was running. For God's sake, the whole damned mountain was on fire!"

"How far did you go into the bushes? A mile?"

"I was scared. That's why I was out of breath. Panicky."

A surge of anger swept through her. "If I knew for sure that you were lying...if I had any proof whatsoever, I swear to heaven, ten years ago or not, I'd turn you in."

"Oh, is that right? You remember one thing, *Saint* Breanna. We were *both* camping on the mountain that night. If it hadn't been for Morrow giving us an alibi, we'd have both hung for it. So go ahead, tell the whole world. When you put a noose around my neck, you'll put one around your own as well."

Breanna knocked away his accusing finger. "I told you, don't threaten me. One thing keeps me silent, just one thing, and that's not knowing anything for sure."

"And you never will." His voice grated as he spoke.

"That remains to be seen, doesn't it? I need to get supplies in town. Maybe I'll do a little research, too. Go to the library, read the old news stories. Will I find something, Dane? Something I didn't notice then?"

"Let me give you a little advice. If you ever decide to tell the cops we weren't with Chuck all night, that I had left camp, you remember one thing. You'll be stepping on toes. You might end up real sorry someday, *real* sorry."

"For someone with nothing to hide, you sure rile easily. Get off my land, Dane. Now, before I forget you're my cousin."

"Gran wouldn't want me to feel unwelcome here, remember?"

"Maybe Gran didn't know you. Maybe none of us really did. Get out of here."

"Oh, I'm going," he said with a laugh. "And, uh, take care of yourself. It's rugged country. Fact is, I'd think twice about staying. A lot of folks around here might not like having an arsonist for a neighbor."

Breanna had an unholy urge to draw back her arm and hit her cousin. Dane's gaze dropped to her tightly clenched fist. "What's happened to you?" she whispered. "There was a time I trusted you with my life. Now you threaten me? Me, Dane? Look at me. Really look. I'm not your enemy."

Something other than anger crept into his eyes, another emotion, long lost, almost forgotten.

"Take care of yourself." He looked over his shoulder. "No matter what you might think, I never meant to hurt anyone. I sure as hell never meant to hurt you." His voice dropped so low that she could barely discern the words. "Leave here, Breanna. Please. Don't stay here."

"Why? What are you saying?"

He clamped his mouth shut and shook his head, his expression pleading. Then he turned and strode toward his car.

"Dane!" Breanna started after him.

Just then she saw a streak of black coming from behind the lean-to garage. It was Coaly, running low to the ground, neck extended, going so fast he was almost a blur. The dog skidded to a halt, lifting his muzzle to bark, circling Dane. Breanna wasn't alarmed. Her pet usually greeted strangers in a threatening manner and her cousin had never met Coaly before.

"It's okay, Coaly," she called.

Her words didn't have their usual calming effect. The dog drew closer to Dane, sniffing, snarling, his eyes glinting. Dane stood stock-still.

"Call him off, Bree."

At the sound of Dane's voice, the dog crouched, then leaped forward. Too late, Breanna managed to scream. "No!"

Coaly cannoned into Dane's chest and knocked him backward against the automobile fender. Man and dog rolled in the gravel. Dane yelled, fingers entangled in the animal's black ruff, arms shoving him away. Breanna couldn't believe what she was seeing. As cantankerous and protective of her as Coaly was, he had never launched a flying attack before. His fangs snapped the air.

"Coaly, no...no...!" Breanna rushed to drag the dog off her cousin. Coaly was so intent upon biting that he nearly turned on her before he recognized her touch. "Bad dog." Never before had she hit her pet, but now she raised her hand. "You bad, bad dog!"

"Don't!"

Breanna hesitated. Blood streaked Dane's cheek. His expensive jacket was torn at the lapel.

"Don't," Dane repeated more quietly. "He's just trying to protect you. Don't punish him for it."

"But he..."

Dane staggered to his feet, keeping his face averted. He turned toward his car, straightening his coat with a shrug of the shoulders. "Think about what I said, Bree. You shouldn't stay here."

"Dane, how bad are you hurt? You're bleeding. Dane?"

He stopped beside the car, fishing in his slacks for his keys. Breanna wanted to go to him, but didn't dare release Coaly. Dane threw open the door and swung himself into the car. A moment later he was reversing up the driveway to the road. When the Corvette disappeared around the curve, Breanna was still standing there.

Several seconds passed before she could straighten her frozen fingers to release Coaly's collar. Then, as she turned to go back to the barn, she saw something green on the ground, right where Dane had stood. A neatly folded twenty-dollar bill. He must have pulled it out with his keys. She hurried to pick it up, snatching it from under Coaly's nose.

"You start eating money, fella, and your compulsion to devour paper could get expensive." Breanna stuffed the twenty into her pocket. The next time she visited her folks, she'd leave twenty dollars with her mom to pass on to Dane's. Better that than seeing Dane herself to return it. "Come on, troublemaker," she called crossly to her dog.

As she walked up the drive toward the barn, she held off scolding Coaly until she calmed down. Lifting her eyes to the mountain, she paused. It was beautiful, silhouetted as it was against the powder-blue sky. The burn area was on the other side of the ridge. By now, any significant clues would be overgrown with new trees, grass, underbrush. After all these years, was it worth it to dredge it all up again?

Yes. Once and for all, she wanted to get to the bottom of it. Rob Thatcher had lost his life in that fire, one that had been deliberately set. Whether it had been premeditated murder or a prank gone awry, she had to know if Dane had been in any way involved. There was something her cousin had never told her, something he *couldn't* tell her.

Breanna propped her hands on her hips. Perhaps Dane had found the entrance to *The Crescent Moon*. The Van Pattens had stopped working it after the second collapse at the opening, and that was before Gramps was born. It was too dangerous, Gramps had said. Over time, with the help of several rock slides, even Gramps had forgotten exactly where *The Crescent Moon*'s entrance was supposed to be, and he had forbidden Dane to look for it. Had Dane disobeyed? Had he found the underground tunnels that honeycombed the property?

A lump of dread congealed in the pit of her stomach. What if Rob Thatcher had also found the entrance? She couldn't believe Dane would hurt someone over a fictitious treasure, but maybe she had never really known him. Her stride lengthened. As soon as she finished cleaning the flue, she was making that trip to town.

As she drew near the barn, Breanna remembered her dog. "And you! You're on my blacklist, old man. Dane is family, understand? You act like that again, causing a big ruckus, and I'll have to chain you. I can't have you making trouble."

She had the distinct feeling she wasn't alone as she walked up the entrance ramp. Turning, she checked behind her, but there was no one in sight.

THE WOMAN'S VOICE TRAILED across the orchard, clear as a bell as she climbed the rickety ramp into the barn. The two men watching her glanced uneasily at one another. "Call Ross. We gotta get her out of there. The last thing we need is her snooping around and finding our equipment."

"You warned him."

"Call him," the older man growled. "Tell him to get down here on the double."

BREANNA GAVE THE HEARTH a final sweeping and carried the last bucket of ash out of the cabin to dump it behind the garage. On a scale of one to one hundred, she rated chimney sweeping at about zero. She was black from head to toe. A bath was in order before she drove to Grants Pass, no question about it.

"Hello there."

Breanna whirled, nearly upending her bucket. Tyler Ross was walking up the drive. "Well, well," she said. "Fancy meeting you here." Taking quick stock of his fresh brown shirt and denims, she added, "Not crawling in my bushes today, I see?"

His eyes touched on her face. Breanna couldn't see her reflection in them, but she didn't need to. She knew her face was soot-streaked.

"Have I caught you at a bad time?"

"Not at all. Last night was a bad time. Today's a mere irritation."

Oblivious to her sarcasm, he gestured at the bucket. "Cleaning the fireplace?"

"The chimney." Her nose itched. She resisted the urge to scratch. "Mr. Ross, let's get down to brass tacks, shall we? I know you were spying on me last night, and to say I'm furious would be an understatement."

"I thought I explained—" He broke off, apparently at a loss. "Look—uh—I dropped by to apologize. I'm afraid I got off on the wrong foot with you last night, and I didn't—"

"The wrong foot? If you think an apology can undo it, you're very much mistaken. You violated my privacy."

He raked a hand through his hair. "Come again?"

He was either a consummate actor, or he hadn't the faintest idea what she was talking about. "Last night, down by the creek. You spied on me while I bathed."

"Someone was spying on you while you bathed?"

"Not someone...you. I found hiking boot tracks all through the brush. And please don't insult my intelligence by denying they were yours."

"Why would I deny it? My prints are all up and down the creek."

"They are?"

"I traipse all over down there." His voice rose. "Listen, it wasn't me. I drove to Wolf Creek right after leaving here. If you want to check, ask Charley at the gas station. I filled up before I went to the store. Are you okay? Did they hurt you?"

"They?"

"The men."

"What makes you think it was more than one?"

Irritation flickered in his eyes. "A figure of speech. Are you all right?"

Uncertainty stilled her tongue. He looked so sincere that she found it difficult to believe he was lying. Charley. It would be easy to check his story. Surely he realized that. "I'm fine. Angry, but fine. I'm sorry for jumping to conclusions if it wasn't you. I guess I put two and two together and came up with five. You do have on hiking boots."

"So does anyone else down here who has good sense." His eyes dropped to her sneakers. "Present company excluded, of course."

A smile tugged at the corners of her mouth.

"I'm batting a thousand, aren't I? Look, Miss—could I call you Breanna?—I stopped by to apologize for being so negative last night. After I had time to mull it over, I realized I didn't even welcome you back to the neighborhood. I'd like to do that now."

He proffered her his palm, his gaze meeting hers so directly that she would have felt petty refusing the handshake. She peeled off her sooty glove. "Thank you. A welcome is a nice change of pace after the last two days."

"That sounds discouraging. Problems?"

"Nothing I can't handle. You know how it is when you're moving. Murphy's Law and all."

She eased her hand from his.

"You know, I don't live but a mile from here by road. If you need anything, anything at all, I'd be happy to help."

For the second time since meeting him, she found herself admiring the handsome blend of his features. "I appreciate the offer."

"I'd like to know you'll take me up on it. Don't get me wrong, but what I said last night still stands. It's not safe down here nowadays. A woman alone…well, it worries me. I'd rest easier, knowing you'll come pounding on my door if trouble pops up. And please stay out of that barn. The floors in there are about to rot through. If you fall and bust a leg, you could lie there for days before anyone found you."

She had to agree. The floors in the barn had seemed a little weak. "I'll bear that in mind."

With a nod at her bucket, he said, "Well, it's obvious you're busy. I'll be on my way so you can finish up."

Breanna wiped the soot off her watch crystal to check the time. "You're right. I'd better get cracking if I'm going to town."

Striking off up the drive, he lifted a hand in farewell. "Catch you later."

"Yes, later."

Breanna strode to the ash pile and dumped her bucket, then gazed toward the brush along the creek where she had seen Ross's footprints. Worrying her bottom lip between her teeth, she turned toward the house. Then she realized what was bothering her. Tyler Ross had mentioned the barn. How had he known she'd been in there? And why did he care? Breanna shrugged and went on into the house.

Before bathing, she wanted to check the flue. A small fire would come in handy. She could dry her hair more quickly by the heat of the flames. She hurried to the bedroom closet where Gran had stacked the old newspapers. Pulling one down, she crumpled a sheet as she returned to the living room. Tossing it onto the freshly cleaned grate, she tugged out another.

Just as she was about to crumple it, she noticed a circle of ink around a tiny news story. Frowning, she smoothed the paper and sat down on the sofa to scan it. A fatal car accident on Mount Sexton, a man whose name she didn't recognize, a resident of San Diego, California. A single-car wreck. No alcohol level in his bloodstream. The police assumed the lone driver had lost control in a curve and plunged through a guardrail.

Puzzled, Breanna crumpled the paper and tossed it into the grate, following it with another sheet. Why had Gran circled a story about a stranger? Breanna stared at the front page. August sixteenth, the year of the Reuben Creek fire. Recalling the date of the newspaper she had used on her first night back, she returned to the bedroom. She lifted the entire pile off the shelf, throwing them onto the bed. Shuffling through them, she checked date after date. All were August releases.

Sifting through them, she searched for headlines about the fire, hoping to save herself a trip to the library. That seemed strange. Gran had saved papers up through August twenty-fifth, the day before the tragedy. After that, nothing.

Glancing at her watch, she started. If she was going to bathe before going to town, she'd have to hurry. She'd need to make copies of the newspapers on file at the library, speed to the courthouse for maps, buy No Trespassing signs, then go grocery shopping. And she wanted to be safely locked in the cabin tonight when the sun dipped behind the mountain.

EIGHT O'CLOCK. Breanna looked at the darkening sky. She had a good thirty minutes of light left. She had made record time going to town. Despite a dead end at the courthouse, which had forced a detour to the mini-storage facility where Gran's papers were stored, she had obtained everything she needed, including copies of maps of *The Crescent Moon*, which the court clerk had maintained didn't exist. She was pleased she had time for a walk before dinner and bed. A little exercise would help her sleep.

Her sense of accomplishment faded a bit as she strolled with Coaly through the lower orchard. She had photocopied several reports of the fire, but hadn't yet had time to study them. Later. For now, she and Coaly deserved a romp. Dragging in a breath of air, she broke into a jog. After making three circles around the orchard with Coaly at her heels, Breanna headed upstream toward the house.

The orchard made a lovely picture this time of evening. No wonder Ross took photos here. The old barn, weathered gray with age, sat to the left. As Breanna passed it, a thumping noise echoed through the dusk. She swung around to stare and saw a flash of movement angling from the barn across the road to disappear into the shadowy woods. A man? Gramps's tales of John Van Patten's ghost filtered into her mind. One of his favorites had been that he had seen John inside the barn one evening.

Sheer, black fear surged through her for an instant and her knees turned to water. Then sanity flooded back. Of all the ridiculous—*I don't believe in spooks,* she scolded herself. *And even if I did, this particular one would never hurt me.* Breanna watched the woods. Her unwelcome visitor had vanished. As much as she hated to admit it, she preferred the idea of John Van Patten's company. Ghosts came and went without reason, but flesh and blood specters didn't appear in a remote area like this without motive.

She might find something if she followed the man's trail. Her tension rose a few more percentage points at the thought. Not in the dark. Whoever her uninvited company had been, she wasn't chasing after him. Nope, not this lady. She'd do the smart thing, which was to go home and lock the door. Tomorrow she'd get busy on those fences and tack up the No Trespassing signs.

Chapter Three

The door to Tyler Ross's cabin was opened with such force that it hit the interior wall and resounded like a rifle shot. Tyler jumped, slopping hot water from the kitchen kettle onto his hand. He swore under his breath, grabbed a towel off the counter and swiped at the water.

"What in hell's wrong now?"

Jack Jones stomped into the room, trying to shake mud and globs of pine needles off his boots. "What isn't?"

"Do you mind? I don't have a maid to do the floors."

Jack lifted his dark head, brown eyes glaring. "That broad's a pain in the butt. You were nowhere to be found, so I went into the barn to make sure she didn't mess with any of the listening devices when she was in there, and she damned near caught me. Had to make a quick exit through the woods, ran into a tree, fell in a stream. I wish we could arrest her and get her out of the way until this is over."

"Do it. I'll come with you. She'll be safe that way, at least."

"Don't start that again," Jack hissed. "I told you. If we make a move on her, she could blow the whistle. It's not much longer now. We can't screw things up this late in the game."

"And I told *you* . . . I'm not convinced she's in on it."

"You can't be sure of that."

Tyler walked to a window and gazed at the trees along the road. "Call it a gut feeling."

"I don't trust gut feelings, not with women. Your hormones are doing your thinkin' for you."

It was an accusation Tyler couldn't deny. The Van Patten woman was pretty with those vulnerable eyes of hers. If Jack was right, she could probably smile like an angel and knife you in the gut, never changing expressions. "Okay, I concede the point. She appeals. But, Jack, what if I'm right? What if she isn't involved? She could end up dead if she makes a wrong move. That scares the hell out of me."

"*You* ending up dead is my worry. I'm tellin' you, watch your back. She's tied into this. She has to be. Just do your job, man, and make like her shadow, beginning tomorrow morning. Keep her busy. Keep her entertained. *And keep her out of that barn.* It's no skin off my nose if you take advantage of a few fringe benefits, but don't forget who and what she is, not for a second."

Tyler turned toward his boss. "Fringe benefits? You know that's not my style." Bracing a hand against the wall, he sighed. "If she's clean and something happens to her, maybe you can live with it. I'm not so sure I can."

"Sometimes that's part of the job."

BREANNA QUICKLY DISCOVERED the most difficult thing about hanging No Trespassing signs was the fence repair they necessitated. She had been working since seven, it wasn't yet ten, and she was already worn out from digging and hauling sand from the creek. Planting posts that stood up straight was no easy chore. The morning was half gone, and all she had to show for it were three leaning railroad ties. She had helped Gramps do this a dozen times, but knowing how and doing it alone were two different things.

She had just stepped back to survey her last attempt at a vertical line when she heard a vehicle approaching. A dusty red pickup appeared around the curve and slowed. Putting a hand up to shade her eyes, she tried to see the driver, but the windshield reflected the sun. The truck pulled onto the shoulder and the engine sputtered to silence. The driver's door swung wide and denim flashed as a man climbed out.

Tyler Ross. On the one hand, she felt glad to see him, even a touch excited. She wasn't completely immune to a nice-looking man. But could she trust him? If he was a treasure hunter, his friendliness could be a ploy.

He gave her crooked fence posts a long, rather puzzled look as he passed them. "Havin' some problems?"

With her hands riding at her waist, she regarded him with a weariness she was unable to hide. She knew she must look a mess in her dirt-smudged pink blouse, with her hair falling from its clasp. She lifted one arm, checked it for dust, then swiped at her cheek. "A few, yes."

He dug in his heels to descend the bank. "Need an extra pair of hands?"

At this point Breanna felt so hot and dusty that several extra pairs would have been welcome. There were limits to pride, and she had reached hers. "That's a slight understatement. What I need is a whole crew. Supposedly, my cousin was caretaking here. As you can see, he did his best work sitting on his laurels."

He came to stand beside her. Another look at her posts had him laughing. "Looks like we had high wind."

"It might help if I had a level or a plumb."

"Maybe we can jury-rig something. I don't have anything pressing to do. I'll pitch in if you'll pay off with lunch. Fence building is a two-person job."

Breanna gave him a thoughtful glance. It couldn't hurt to give him the benefit of the doubt, at least for the duration of the job. "You're on."

Coaly came charging from behind the barn, his barking interspersed with snarls. Tyler cast an unconcerned glance over his shoulder as he strode toward his truck. "I'm fresh out of roast beef, you old codger." The dog cocked an ear and slowed to a walk. Tyler paused to give him a pat.

It was a rare stranger that Coaly liked. In her book, the dog's unreserved acceptance of Tyler on the property was an imprint of approval. "It looks like you two are old chums."

"He just likes me because I gave him chocolate chip cookies." Flashing her a quick, completely artless grin, he added, "And my napkin. And my sack. Sure he's not part goat?"

"I've had cause to wonder." She met his gaze. *Windows to the soul,* Gramps had told her. *When you size a man up, honey, look him dead in the eyes.* Approaching the truck, she asked, "Have you ever set posts?"

He pushed back his sleeves and raised a challenging eyebrow. "You're asking a born and bred Oregonian if he's ever set a post? You're lookin' at the best posthole man this side of the Cascades. You don't have any rope, I'll bet." He rummaged in a large toolbox. "Luckily, I always carry some. We'll stretch a length between two posts and rig up some kind of plumb line."

Dubious as she was, within ten minutes he had one rope tied off level and had made a makeshift plumb from another piece, with a rock looped in its end.

"This'll work," he assured her. "Won't be perfect, but it's better than a kick in the rump, right?" He positioned the plumb. "Okay, you hold the post straight, and I'll shovel and pack."

Grasping the upended tie, she held it in position. Tyler moved with loose-limbed grace for so tall a man, precise, quick, well balanced. Muscle rippled in his arms and shoulders, clearly visible under his shirt. She relaxed a bit. He made short work of fence building. Maybe she would have perimeter posts to keep out trespassers, after all.

She felt silly now for thinking he wanted her out of here. A man didn't go this far to be neighborly if he didn't want you around. "I really appreciate your help."

He glanced up and caught her scowling. "Penny for them? What's bothering you?"

Inclining her head toward the barn, she said, "I had company last night. Some man. Saw him run out of my barn and take off into the woods. That's why these fences are so urgent. I want to put up some No Trespassing signs."

"A man, you say? Did you get a good look at him?"

"No. Have you any idea who it could have been?"

He helped her brace the post while he stomped the encircling ground. "Sure you're not jumping at shadows?"

A tingle of irritation crept up her throat, but she quickly swallowed it back. She couldn't blame him for being skeptical. *The Crescent Moon* wasn't exactly a metropolis; the story sounded a bit farfetched. "I guess it could have been the ghost," she said lightly.

"The ghost? What ghost?"

His wary glance at her made her smile. "My great-great-uncle, John Van Patten. You haven't heard of him? How long've you been living down here?"

"Three years."

"And you've never heard of John Van Patten? He found the mother lode, you know, then died without telling where he hid it—a very selfish man, from all accounts. And now a selfish ghost. Get too close to his treasure and he appears to frighten you away."

"Uh-huh. Next, you'll gladly sell me the Brooklyn Bridge, right?" He chuckled and stepped on the blade of the shovel, burying it to its hilt. "One thing's sure, though. Ghost or man, he's not too smart. If a brisk wind comes up, that barn'll topple like a card house."

"It's not that bad. I went in yesterday and the floors didn't give way."

"Well, I'm telling you, don't trust them. I went in there once to see if I could find a wrench to adjust my tripod. Those planks gave with every step. Stay out of there. Okay?"

Breanna decided to be gracious. "I'll be careful. But it *is* my barn, you know. There are things in there I'll need now and again."

"Tell me what and I'll get them for you."

"And have my fence builder disabled? Not a chance."

Tyler laughed. Easy, relaxed laughter. It cleansed the last traces of uneasiness from Breanna's mind.

Three fence posts later, Tyler was as dusty and sweaty as Breanna had been upon his arrival. The afternoon sun glared down on them, mercilessly hot, making Breanna's nose feel parchment dry. "How about a lemonade break in the shade?" she suggested. "I'll make some sandwiches."

He wiped a shirt sleeve across his forehead, squinting down at her. "You won't have to twist my arm on that offer."

IT TOOK A VERY CAREFUL balancing of the tray to walk from the cabin to the barnyard without spilling liquid from the pitcher onto their sandwiches. Tyler was sitting in the shade of the fruit cellar, his back braced against the shake siding, arms propped on his upraised knees. "Man, that looks good."

She placed their tray on the ground, cast Coaly a glance to warn him away, then poured Tyler a brimming glass of lemonade and handed it down. "Better be. It's fresh-squeezed."

He tipped back his dark head and took several long swallows. Breanna filled another tumbler and lowered herself cross-legged beside him, proffering the pitcher. "More?"

"Mmm-mmm," he replied, putting his glass to the spout.

She gave him a refill, then settled back against the shakes, taking slow sips while he made short work of a sandwich. It had been a while since she had fed a man, two years, in fact, since her breakup with Richard. She had forgotten how big their appetites were. She felt almost guilty reaching for her share on the tray, but was too hungry to resist. "Does that revive you a bit?"

"Delicious. And there's nothing like lemonade to quench the thirst." Tyler looked over at her, trying his best to remain objective. She was a pretty woman; straight nose, a sensitive mouth, her sun-streaked brown hair escaping the twist of braid atop her head in wispy curls. Her eyes were cornflower blue, expressive and easy to read, the kind that gave a guy's heart a twist if he had any conscience at all. His stomach tightened. "Tell me something. Do you really believe in ghosts?"

She shifted her gaze to the barn. After a thoughtful moment, she swallowed and replied, "To say I didn't would be to call my grandfather a liar. He saw John Van Patten with his own eyes. Gramps never fibbed. He exaggerated sometimes, but never fibbed."

Tyler watched her closely. "Aren't you scared?"

"Oh, yes, terrified." Her smile dimpled her cheek, so mischievous that he nearly laughed and ruined her punch line. Her voice, when it came, was low and impish. "I don't have a bridge to sell you. How about a good used car?"

Now he did laugh, the kind of laugh that came from deep inside and erupted without effort. If she was a criminal, it wasn't any wonder she was still on the loose. With her personality as a front, nobody would ever believe— The thought jerked Tyler up short, and he sobered. He was doing exactly the opposite of what Jack had told him, letting down his guard, trusting her. If he wanted the last laugh, he'd better watch his step.

Breanna saw the sudden seriousness cross Tyler's face. She wondered if she had said something to upset him. Swallowing the last bit of her sandwich, she asked, "Is something wrong?"

"No. Why?"

"You look like somebody stepped on your grave."

"Not as yet." His eyes met hers, searching, then veering away. He glanced at his watch. "Could you hold off on the rest of this until I can help? I do have a couple of errands to run this afternoon."

"I don't expect you to do the entire fence for me," she protested.

"Hey, what are neighbors for? They used to have barn raisings. We're having a fence raising." He gave her a slow wink. "Besides, there are fringe benefits."

His smile told her she was the attraction. "Oh, really? What might those be?"

"The fantastic lemonade and good sandwiches, of course." He rose to his feet in one fluid movement, hauling her up with him. "We'll hit it for another hour, then call it a day. You're getting sunburned."

"I tell you what. I'll accept more help on the fence if you'll come to breakfast tomorrow morning. I'd like to repay you for all the work."

"I'll be here. What time?"

"Sevenish?"

"Sounds great."

Two hours later, Breanna put away the last of the lunch mess and dried the dishes, stowing them in the cupboard. Tyler had just left. She wiped the table, then rinsed the rag and folded it neatly over the antique pump handle. Then she stepped to the window to gaze out at the rose trellises framing the glass. All in all, it had been a good day, exhausting, but nice.

Only one thing troubled her. Off and on she'd noticed a certain reserve in Tyler's manner, subtle, but there, almost as if he held a part of himself in check. Not once had he offered any information about himself, nothing about his family, his marital status or if he had children. She guessed him to be in his mid-thirties. A man that old had to have a past. Yet Tyler gave nothing of his away, not even by a slip of the tongue. It was fanciful, but she had the impression his identity began and ended with Graves Creek. Perhaps she would get to know him better over breakfast tomorrow.

Stifling a yawn, Breanna went to the bedroom to retrieve her newspaper photocopies she'd made at the library. She stretched out on the sofa, determined to stay relaxed. If she planned to investigate the fire, she had to stay objective.

She read until the cabin's interior was swathed in shadows. Read, reread. And found nothing new. But discouraged though she was, she felt better because she was actively seeking answers. If she kept searching, the truth would come out sooner or later. When it did, perhaps Dane would be as relieved as she was to have it in the open.

Digging in her cooler, Breanna pulled out the fresh vegetables she had purchased yesterday. A salad with slices of roast beef from the deli sounded just right after a hot day. After a sponge bath at the sink, she would settle herself in bed with a cup of herb tea and her glitzy novel. She deserved a bit of pampering if the sore muscles in her back were an indicator.

THREE A.M. Breanna squinted at the luminous hands on her travel alarm clock, unsure why she was suddenly awake. She flopped onto her back and groaned. The dog. He was whining, running from window to window. Throwing her legs over the side of the bed, she staggered to her feet. "All right, already, I'm coming."

Coaly's low snarl brought her up short. She knew that growl. Someone was outside. Clammy sweat filmed her palms as she braced herself against the bedstead to look out the French windows. The fruit cellar blocked her view of the orchards beyond.

"What is it, boy? What do you hear?"

Breanna tiptoed to the kitchen, peering out the paned glass at the moonlit drive. Nothing. She glanced down at the dog. His growl deepened, as if to assure her he knew what he was talking about. There was somebody out there, no question of it.

"I've had all I'm going to take of this nonsense. What the devil's going on around here?" She hurried toward the bedroom. "A man in the bushes, a man in my barn. Well, I think it's time I found out why." Tossing off her night-gown, she bypassed underwear, dragged on her jeans, zipped up, and leaned over to shove her feet into sneakers. "Don't look so worried, I'm just going to look. I won't get caught."

Coaly whined again. Breanna had to agree with him. It was risky going out there, but she couldn't continue living here with her nerves stretched like a tightrope, either.

"Nope, you can't go. You'll bark." Yanking on her green blouse, she quickly buttoned it. "Now, you stay." Leveling a finger at the dog's nose, she said, "Quiet, understand? You raise a fuss and you'll give me away."

Coaly's whines trailed off into miserable squeaks. She gave him a consoling pat. "Hey, old man, trust me to take care of myself, huh? If all else fails, I can outrun him."

As quietly as she could, she slipped out the front door, straining her ears for noises. A faint clanking sound rang in the night. *Someone on the other side of the fruit cellar.* She sneaked to the retainer wall steps. Fearful images crept into her mind, but she quickly banished them. This was her property, and if she didn't come out and check on it, no one else would.

If she darted across the drive she could make it to the outhouse, where she would have an unobstructed view of the barnyard. Not giving herself time to chicken out, she bounded down the steps, stooping low as she crossed the opening.

"Whoa, did you see that?" she heard someone bark.

"What?" a fainter voice asked.

"I thought I saw something."

Breanna did a third-base skid behind the outhouse, her heart pounding. She hadn't expected someone to be so close. Especially not two someones. Thirty miles out in the middle of nowhere, she had envisioned at most a lone prowler. *Ouch.* A sharp rock gouged her ribs. She crawled to her knees, grasping the rough wall of the outhouse to help herself up. Inching her head around the corner, she searched the moon-silvered darkness. A hollow thumping sound drifted to her, like footsteps on a wooden floor. A shadow moved from the front of the barn, cutting through the field toward the road. A man. All she could distinguish about him at this distance was that he wore dark trousers and a white shirt.

Another man appeared on the road, a mere shadow in his dark clothing. He stood waiting until the other man reached him, then gestured toward the outhouse. The fellow in the white shirt stepped across the road, pivoting to see her cabin. There was something familiar about his walk, the way he kept his legs stiff and held his arms curved out from his body. She had seen him before. But when? Where? Breanna flattened herself against the planks, suddenly afraid.

The sound of their low voices drifted faintly through the night toward her and from their tone, she felt they were arguing. She glanced uneasily at the house. Coming out here had been a dumb move. A lone prowler was one thing; two were quite another. If they spotted her, she could end up in big trouble.

Remembering Tyler Ross's warnings, Breanna dashed behind the garage and ran its length, carefully skirting the ash pile. At the far corner of the lean-to she paused to get her bearings. If she worked her way through the brush to the upper clearing, she could cut across and double back to the house with the building blocking her from the men's view. Tensing for a burst of speed, she pushed off and plunged into a thick growth of waist-high manzanita. Every snapping twig resounded like a rifle shot. She knew they couldn't fail to hear her. The branches scratched her arms, but she was so frightened that she barely noticed.

The bushes hindered her. Her spurts of speed were taken in lunges as her hips and legs pushed through the maze. Throwing a glance behind her, Breanna sent up a silent prayer she wouldn't see anyone following. She burst into a tiny clearing, and the sudden lack of obstacles increased her forward thrust. She saw something on the ground in front of her, but it was too late to stop. Before she could register the fact that it was a man, she stepped right on top of him.

"Son of a—!"

A whoosh of expelled air cut off the rest of his exclamation. Her shoe sank into his flesh with a sickening squish. And then, to her horror, the man pushed up, catapulting her into a helter-skelter somersault.

"I don't believe you, Jackson!" he grunted.

She tried for a tumbling tuck, but gymnastics had never been her forte. Landing in an ungraceful back flop, she hit a clump of manzanita, plunging through it to the ground.

She didn't know if it was the impact or the sheer incredulity she felt that dazed her, but she couldn't move. The network of branches above her formed a crisscross pattern, so the man's silhouette as he peered down looked like an apparition out of a horror movie. There were small protrusions over his ears and a piece of wire looped around the side of his face to his mouth. *Headphones.* Her every nerve leaped and shuddered.

"I swear to God, Jackson," he whispered, "you'd screw up a sexy dream if we gave you half a chance. Can't you do anything right? Why the hell are you running? Do you want the broad coming out here?"

Jackson? The man leaned farther forward to offer her a hand.

"Get on a loudspeaker, why don't ya? Tell everyone we're out here. You damn near broke my back."

The urge to scream was so strong that Breanna held her breath. She stared at the extended hand. Just another few inches and he would touch her chest. And when he did, it wouldn't take him long to realize she wasn't his friend Jackson. With a trembling arm, she reached up and grasped his palm. Prepared for his startled reaction, she took full advantage of it. With all her strength, she gripped his fingers and pulled. He pitched forward and, as he did, Breanna slammed her right foot against his chest. With a mighty heave, she launched him over her into the manzanita. He landed with a grunt, then yelped with pain.

Springing to her feet, she vaulted the bushes. Her legs felt numb. She staggered into a run, her head resounding with the crashing noises behind her. *Dear God, he's chasing me.* She'd made it halfway across the orchard before she realized the sounds were growing more distant, heading in the opposite direction toward the creek. Whirling and looking behind her, she saw the distinct shapes of three men diving for cover at different angles. Her eyes fastened on one in particular, a tall, broad-shouldered one.

Tyler? Breanna stared in disbelief. No, it couldn't be. An unnatural quiet filled the night. Breanna hugged herself and turned in a full circle. *They're all around me.* She had known fear in the woods before, but never such an icy, eerie dread. In the distance, a coyote wailed, long and low, the last notes of his moon call rising to a mournful crescendo. Panting in terror, she threw one more glance at the brush and turned to flee.

The cabin wasn't that far, but it seemed to take forever to reach it. She clawed her way over the retainer wall, pulling herself flat on the ground for a few feet until the black shadows from the oak tree shielded her. Even then she didn't feel safe. There could be more of them in the yard. She stumbled forward, flattening herself against the cabin to guard her back. *Please, God.* Crab-walking, she inched sideways toward the corner.

Then someone grabbed her hair.

For a wild, frenzied moment, Breanna fought, flinging her head, flailing her arms. Then she realized her attacker was a rose-entwined trellis. Thorny vines snaked around her. Her hair was caught in the trellis slats, tangled in the thorns. She threw herself away from it. Her skin tore. Her scalp exploded with pain. But all she could focus on now was getting inside.

With a sob that cut through the silence around her, she pelted forward, careening around the corner, shooting for the porch. The door jammed, and she shoved on it with all her weight till it gave way and spewed her into the entry hall. Breanna slammed it shut behind her, pressing against it with her back, quivering legs braced before her. Whimpers erupted from her that she couldn't control. Reaching behind her, she grasped the dead bolt and shoved it home.

Coaly leaped at her, whining, licking. She collapsed to her knees, wrapping both arms around him and making fists in his thick wavy fur. He was solid, warm. She clung to him and sobbed. Then hysterical laughter bubbled in her chest. She clamped a hand over her mouth. She had to get ahold of herself. *Think. Panic won't do a bit of good.*

Taking long, deep breaths, she willed herself to calm down. When strength returned to her legs, she rose and ran to the living room. Her skin crawled at the thought of someone staring at her through the uncurtained windows, but she forced herself close enough to double-check the latches. If someone tried to come in, at least he would make a racket breaking the glass. At the table she sank into a chair, staring first at one window, then the next, glad the embers of the fire didn't put off much light.

What will I do if they break in? How many of them are there? Do they know I'm here alone?

Tyler Ross had told her to come to him if there was trouble. Should she make a run for her car? Or would she be safer right where she was? A vision of the tall man running through the bushes sprang to mind. She didn't want to believe it had been Tyler, but what if it had?

No, if she was going to get help, the wisest course would be a police station. The nearest one, as far as she knew, was thirty miles away in Grants Pass. Breanna looked out at her car. Without a phone, it was her only link to the outside world. In the moonlight, its silver paint glowed like phosphorus. If she went anywhere near it, she'd be spotted. They might try to stop her, and that was a chance she couldn't bring herself to take.

The haze of panic slowly cleared from her mind. There were five men on her property, possibly more. The question was, why? She walked over to a front window. The guy in the manzanita had been hiding to watch something. It hadn't been her, obviously, or he wouldn't have stayed where he was so she could step on him. She had a clear view from here of the upper and lower orchards. From where the man had been lying, it was a straight shot to the barn and the road.

Prowlers didn't spy on prowlers. The police would think she was crazy if she went to them with a story like this. Nothing was out there but a ramshackle barn, an old fruit cellar and an outhouse. Why would anyone be out there? That would be their first question. And it was one she couldn't answer. She could almost see the skeptical look on their faces if she started talking about ghosts and hidden gold. And what if it were someone who blamed her for the fire, as Dane had said . . . ? She certainly didn't want to talk to the police about that.

Returning to the table, Breanna sat down again and propped her elbows on its edge, cupping her chin in her hands. Before she went to the authorities and made a complete fool of herself, she had to have something concrete to tell them.

She had no idea how long she sat there, so tense that her muscles ached. Her body felt as if it were on fire and at the least movement, pain shot up her back into her shoulder.

She twisted, trying to feel what she had done to herself. Her fingertips came away sticky with blood.

She folded her arms on the table to pillow her head, still staring watchfully at the windows. With her nerves stretched so taut, she knew she wouldn't sleep. A minute in dead of night lasted an hour, an hour a lifetime.

Morning might never come.

Chapter Four

Breanna woke to the sound of knocking. Blinking in confusion, she pushed herself up from the table, recoiled at the pain in her back and stared at the window. Sunshine. What a welcome sight. Coaly raced to and fro, barking at the door.

"Who is it?"

"The Fuller Brush man," was the good-natured reply.

Tyler. Breanna got up from the chair, weaving on her feet, and dragged her tangled hair from her eyes. She didn't know what to do. Images from yesterday slipped into her mind, but those were quickly pushed out by flashbacks from last night.

"Yo? You in there?"

"Yes, I'm coming."

Quick glances out the windows showed nothing had been disturbed in the yard. She went to the entry and drew the dead bolt. Tyler stood on the porch, casually dressed in jeans and a chambray shirt, his dark hair tousled by the breeze. Coaly squeezed past her, greeting him with an enthusiasm Breanna was far from sharing.

"Oh, it's you."

"Breakfast, remember? I do have the right morning?"

"Yeah, I guess you do."

"My God, what happened to you?" He took a step toward her. "You're hurt."

Breanna didn't think she could possibly look that bad until she glanced down at herself. Her arms were scratched. Her jeans were torn. There were drops of blood on her left tennis shoe. From the horrified expression on Tyler's face, she knew the rest of her looked even worse. "I'm all right . . . I think. Just took a spill."

"Do you have a first-aid kit?"

"Yes."

He grasped her elbow, taking care not to touch lacerated skin as he steered her down the hall. "Let's get it. Some of those cuts should be cleaned before they get infected. I thought we agreed you would come to my place if anything went wrong?"

She lifted her other arm to survey the damage. "I can handle it. It's just a few scratches."

"A few scratches? You haven't seen the back of you yet. Were you afraid of bothering me? When a person's hurt, they should be able to count on neighbors. Look at you. You've let this go so long, your blouse is stuck to you."

Somehow she had ended up on the defensive. She lowered a shoulder, trying to see. "It can't be that bad. I just took a tumble in the brush."

"Manzanita is a tad sturdier and sharper than regular brush. You're sliced up like a salad tomato."

She braked to such a sudden stop that Tyler nearly ran over her. His chest bumped into a sore place on her back, making her stiffen. With her heart slamming so hard she felt sure he could hear it, she glanced back at him. "How did you know it was manzanita?"

Tension crystallized the air between them. Her breath caught in her throat as she waited for his answer. If he knew where she had fallen, then he was also the man she had seen running in the brush. There could be no other explanation.

"It doesn't take a genius to figure it was probably manzanita. Nothing else would cut you up like that."

Dogwood and rosebushes could cut a person, too. Maybe not so deeply, but they could still penetrate the skin. She swallowed, the sound a hollow plunk in the pit of her stomach. "Tyler, I think maybe you should leave and come back another time when I'm feeling better. I can handle this myself."

After a long moment, he replied, "If you're not feeling up to guests, that's okay. But at least let me clean those cuts before I go." Settling his hands on her hips, he propelled her to the kitchen table and drew out a chair, turning it so that she could sit astride with her arms propped on its back. His voice was firm. "Where's the first aid?"

There didn't seem to be any way to get rid of him. "In the bedroom, on the closet shelf."

His boots tapped briskly across the room. She heard him rummaging. A moment later, he returned, carrying a white case.

"Tyler, I saw you last night."

Looking down at her scratched face, with those big blue eyes shimmering, Tyler knew he was in for a hard haul. He was never at his best with no sleep, and he had spent all last night pacing, waiting, dreaming up reasons to come check on her, each of which Jack had vetoed as too flimsy. Unless he lied flat out, he'd have to be damned evasive, and right now he didn't feel too witty. She was a bright lady, at this point a suspicious one, and he knew she would pick up on his least slip of the tongue.

He shot her a glance, his mouth curving up at one corner in what he hoped was a perplexed grin. Snapping the kit open, he said, "And so?"

"You mean you aren't going to deny it?"

"Why would I? I was here planting posts. You sure you didn't bump your head?" She made as if to stand and he shot out a hand to touch her shoulder. "First things first. Let's tend that back."

"I'm crazy to let you do this, but I hurt too bad to argue."

"Take a chance on me," he advised. "I'm a good risk."

She glanced over her shoulder to find him contemplating her blouse, a pair of scissors in one hand. "Do you know anyone named Jackson?"

"Should I?" He paused and a slow grin spread across his face. "It does ring a bell. Michael?"

"Somehow, I don't think that's the same Jackson, unless he took a break from making hit records to come out here and liven up my evening." She threw him another questioning look that he deflected by bending over her. "I hope I don't regret this." Dipping her head, she pulled her long hair forward. "I would have sworn it was you I saw diving into those bushes last night."

"And why would I dive into bushes?" He set the plastic kit on the table. *One round from her. Now fire back.* "Do you want to pull your blouse down, or should I cut a bigger hole?" He grasped her collar as if to peel the cotton off her. She reacted just as he hoped, clinging to the blouse, losing her train of thought. He felt her pulse skitter under his knuckles where they touched the side of her throat.

"A bigger hole, of course. In case you haven't noticed, the blouse is ruined anyway."

"Don't wiggle. These aren't exactly what you'd call man-size scissors and I may be clumsy with them. It looks like you did the diving."

Breanna felt the warmth of his large hands where they touched her arm and back, gentle, so careful. In spite of herself, she relaxed a bit. "Coaly woke me up out of a dead sleep last night. When I went out to investigate, the place was crawling with men. I tripped over one and fell. That's all."

"You're lucky that was all."

Releasing her hair, she twisted her neck to see his face. "Tyler...was it you? Tell me the truth."

He leaned forward to put the scissors on the tabletop, the hard flatness of his midriff brushing her arm. "This is a deep cut, lady. It's going to hurt like hell when I pull this material loose. I'm really upset that you didn't come directly to my place when this happened. I think I'll try soaking it with peroxide."

"You haven't answered me. Was it you?" His reply was to uncap the bottle and pour ice-cold peroxide down her spine. She gasped and bolted upright. "Oh!"

"Hurt?"

"No, no, I'm fine. It's just cold. Are you or are you not going to give me a direct answer?"

"No." He bent over her, prying the material away. "There's that," he muttered, soaking a cotton ball. He bent to look through the hole he had cut in her blouse. "You look like a road map."

"No, it wasn't you? Or no, you won't give me an answer?"

"I've just discovered why doctors put people to sleep on the operating table. I'm trying to concentrate back here. Why would I be running around on your property in the dead of night? Give me one sane reason."

"I can give you a couple. Gold, for starters. Are you a treasure hunter? Is that it?" Before Breanna realized what he was up to, he grabbed the scissors and she felt the blades snipping again, this time right up the center back of her blouse. "What are you doing?"

"What do you think I'm doing? Alterations?" He made a final snip through her collar and the cotton garment fell forward. "No, I'm not a treasure hunter."

"Tyler, if I'd wanted to take off the blouse, I would have in the first place."

"Can we argue about one thing at a time? You're leapfrogging so badly, I can't keep track."

Breanna, struggling to keep her blouse in place, threw him an incredulous glare. It seemed to her that he was the one scrambling their communication. And he was doing a good job of it. "Are you going to answer my question?"

"Which one?" Just before he shoved her head forward, she saw his eyes dancing with mischief. "You see, right now, only one thing seems important to me. Your back. So be still while I take care of it."

"It *was* you. Otherwise you'd just say it wasn't." Even as the accusation trailed off her lips, she doubted the truth of it.

He dabbed at a particularly painful scratch, making her wince. "Breanna, use your head. If I was sneaking around your place last night, I wouldn't bat an eye at lying. I guess the reason I'm not denying it is because I'd like you come to your own conclusion. Do you really think it was me?"

She looked up, into his eyes. What he said was true. If it had been him, he wouldn't hesitate to lie about it. "No, I guess I don't, not really, or I wouldn't be sitting here with my back to you when you're armed with a pair of scissors."

He chuckled at that, then began cleaning scratches again. "Imagination, I guess. Scissors in the back? You're right about one thing, though. It was probably treasure hunters. I've never heard of the ghost, but I've sure heard about the Van Patten gold. It's almost legend." He doused her with another measure of peroxide. "Or it might have been poachers. Did you think of that? There are a lot of deer down here.''

"I didn't hear any gunshots. And the man I tripped over had a radio unit of some kind. Sophisticated for poachers, don't you think?''

"Not in this day and age. Anyone with a pickup in this country usually has a CB and hand units. As for shots, they could have used bows.''

"Poachers,'' she mused. "I don't know, Tyler. I suppose it could have been. They had lookouts. Maybe they were watching the road for cars. But why were they in my barn?''

"They were in your barn?'' He grew quiet for a moment. "Maybe they were looking for rope or some rags to wipe their hands. It's messy, skinning a deer.''

"That could be.''

He capped the peroxide, returning it to the kit. "It was foolish of you to go outside. You could have been seriously hurt. What would you have done if they chased you?''

"I could have lost them in the woods.''

"In the dark? Someone would have gotten lost, all right, more likely you. This is no place for you to be living alone. There's too much that can happen that you can't handle on your own.''

She jabbed a thumb over her shoulder. "See that typewriter over there? I make my living on it, writing books about wildlife. I've spent a lot of time in the woods getting material for my books. I don't get lost in the woods, Tyler, at night or any other time.''

"You're angry.''

"Yes! If you had prowlers, you'd go out and check. No one would think that strange. But let a woman do the same thing and she's taking unnecessary risks. I don't understand the thinking behind that.'' She stood up, clutching her destroyed blouse to her chest. "It's a double standard. As for leaving here, I can't. It's out of the question. It's Van Patten land, and it's going to stay Van Patten land."

He smiled slightly. "Listen. Your back should be okay now. Why don't I come back later? We'll deal with the rest of this then."

"That's just it. I don't need your help to deal with it."

He lifted a staying hand. "Get some rest. You'll feel better when you've had some sleep. After last night, those No Trespassing signs are more important than ever. You can't expect to finish those posts alone. Not the shape you're in. And if you're bent on staying here, fences are a must." He opened the door, pausing to look back at her. "Catch you later, say noonish?"

With that, he was gone. She stood there for a moment, annoyed, confused, frustrated. Then she sighed and bolted the door behind him. A man didn't terrify you at night, then take care of you come morning. He didn't prowl on your property one moment, then post No Trespassing signs for you the next. Maybe he was right. She needed some sleep. Her body felt like a battlefield. Her head ached. Sand gritted under her eyelids. Heading for the bedroom, she sprawled across the bed, tugging the corner of the spread over herself. *Just a short nap,* she promised herself. Then she was going to check that barn to see what the big attraction was.

SMOKE SPIRALED from Jack Jones's cigarette. He watched it thoughtfully. "And on that basis, you expect me to risk blowing this case?"

Tyler slammed his fist on the table, jarring the radio equipment. "Dammit, Jack, why won't you trust my judgment? I remember a time when you risked your life on it."

"You've been out of the business too long. You're rusty." Leaning forward, Jack smashed out his cigarette in the ashtray. "You didn't get personally involved back then. And you knew a snow job when you saw one."

"It isn't a snow job." Tyler stood up so suddenly that his straight-backed chair tipped. He reached out to catch it, then shoved it none too gently against the table. "Her willingness to tell me what happened supports my theory. I tell you, she's completely in the dark."

"Tyler..." Throwing his head back, Jack let out a tired sigh. "Look, give it a couple of days. If you can get something solid, some real proof, I'll get her out of there so fast it'll make your head swim. I don't want the girl hurt, you know that. But my first responsibility is to this case. I can't jeopardize all our work on supposition. Do you realize how many false leads we followed before we finally pegged this location?"

"Can you risk an innocent person's life on poor judgment?" Tyler placed both hands on his hips. "All right, if you want proof, I'll get it."

"And you'll clear it through me before you make a move." Jack's tone made it clear it was an order, leaving no room for argument. "These people are sharp. That's how they've stayed in operation so long. It's not beyond the realm of possibility that Breanna Morgan is the slickest little con artist in the business. And just you keep that in mind."

At eleven, Breanna locked Coaly inside the cabin while she went to check the barn. The dog whined when she shut the door on him, but because she had seen him digging holes under the foundation, she wasn't about to take him with her. With her luck he would scare up a skunk.

She had the strangest feeling when she walked up the ramp into the old building. At first it seemed the same inside, dark and gray-walled with age, but when she studied it closely, there seemed to be something different, something not quite right. As she paced down the corridor that stretched by the feed room and stalls, an inexplicable chill ran over her.

When she reached the end of the passage, the tack room seemed tiny. She remembered it as being a much larger room, almost airy. Now it seemed cramped, with barely enough floor space for a few bags of grain. She knew everyone remembered their childhood haunts as being larger then they really were, but she hadn't been that young when she left. The impression that the barn had shrunk made her feel claustrophobic. The slightest sound made her jump, and she found herself checking behind as she paused to peer into doorways.

The floorboards creaked under her weight. Tyler was right; it wasn't safe in here. Old fruit jars. A box of discarded clothing. A pile of rusted tin cans. Breanna kicked one and sighed. It was just an old barn, smaller than she remembered. She had gone through some nasty experiences in this place. Maybe that was what made her skin crawl. She strolled slowly through. Even the corridor seemed narrower. She remembered Gran's milk cows moseying through here with plenty of room to spare.

The loft. It would be a perfect hiding place. She went to the ladder and gripped its sides. The rungs groaned in protest as she ascended them. Either they were much weaker than they had been ten years ago, or she was heavier. She reached the top and peeked over. Just hay. And not much of that. No sign that anyone had been in it either, not recently. She had played in here enough times as a child to know how hay looked if someone walked in it. She sighed and climbed back down. So much for being a sleuth.

Something on the floor by the door caught her eye. She moved toward it, bending over to see in the dim light. Her eyes widened as she realized it was a crisp twenty-dollar bill. Brand-new. She folded it and slipped it into her jeans pocket. If her prowler had dropped it, it served him right. He owed her that much and more for the trouble he had caused.

As she straightened, her sore back panged her. Why couldn't he have dropped a hundred? That might have made up for her fall in the manzanita. She stepped into the adjacent stall, surveying the shelving, a pleased smile on her face. It was nice, the way money kept dropping into her hands around here. Of course, she mustn't forget to return Dane's.

The gold pans. Another pang, this time one of sadness, ricocheted through her, but she quickly squelched it. She would miss Gran, but memories of her were enough to last a lifetime.

"Well, I guess this was a shot in the dark," she mused aloud.

No sooner had she spoken than Breanna heard footfalls right next to her. Or at least that was where they seemed to be located. She froze and cocked her head. In the wall? The hair on the nape of her neck stood up. Under the floor? It could be Coaly snooping outside. No, he was in the house. Some other animal, then?

"Who's there?" she croaked.

The moment she called out the sounds ceased. Then Tyler's voice rang out from the front of the barn. "Breanna?"

She hadn't realized she'd been holding her breath. It gushed out of her. "In the back." She stepped into the corridor, then flinched, batting at a curtain of cobwebs that stretched across the left corner of the doorway. It swept across her face and into her hair, clinging like sticky cotton candy. The musty smell was suffocating and she shuddered. "Oh, yuck. It's all over me." Wiping her mouth with her arm, she added, "You're early."

Tyler sauntered down the corridor, a silhouette against the bright sunlight behind him. He paused to glance around. "Must be I'm telepathic. I thought I told you the floor was rotten in here. You shouldn't take chances, you know. This thing is really old."

"The floor isn't too bad. It's the cobwebs that are the pits." She sputtered, trying to get the taste out of her mouth. "And the acoustics. I thought I heard somebody in here."

"Oh, yeah? Pretty popular place, this old barn." He stepped past her to give the stalls and tack room quick once-overs. "Not many places in here to hide."

It was so good to see him after her footstep scare that she couldn't quite remember why she had been so annoyed with him earlier. It reassured her to realize that the footsteps she'd heard couldn't possibly have been his. He had called out from the front only seconds after she heard the noises in the back.

"Probably a rat in the wall," Tyler commented dryly. "You ever seen a barn rat? They can sound like three-hundred pounders with fangs a foot long."

"It did sound like someone walking." Remembering her own suspicion that it could be a rodent, she added, "But I suppose a small animal could sound pretty loud. It sort of echoes in here. And I've heard John Van Patten can be a noisy fellow."

"I'm beginning to see you've got a writer's imagination," he teased. "Apparitions in the barn, spooks in the bushes, and—" he curled his hands into claws and moaned, low and spooky "—ghosts who guard their treasures."

He looked so silly that Breanna couldn't quite manage anger, though his making fun did rankle. Joking with him about the ghost didn't make her prowlers any less real. "Look, Mr. Ross. Can you explain this?" She dug into her jeans pocket, fishing out the newly found twenty to wave it under his nose. "Do you think a ghost dropped it? Or maybe a rat? Or maybe I'm imagining it." She gave the bill a sharp tug. "The real thing, see? Dropped by a flesh and blood prowler."

His gaze was riveted on the greenback, and he started to reach for it.

Breanna jerked it away. "Nope. Finders keepers, losers weepers. My barn, my twenty."

With that, she strode past him down the corridor to the door. Tyler stood watching her, his mind clamoring. She wasn't involved in counterfeiting, or she would never have flashed that money at him. He had to get his hands on it, have it analyzed, and get it to Jack Jones. The question was, how?

She walked down the ramp, turning to look back at him, her hair shimmering golden in the sunlight as she cocked her head. "Come on, or are you gonna stand there till you fall through my rotten floors?"

He moved to the door, leaning a shoulder against the frame. Her eyes shone up at him like beacons, clear as stained glass. For the first time since meeting her, he could allow the feelings she stirred within him to surface. Jack was dead wrong. Tyler's gaze dropped to her lacerated forearms. Thinking of what could have happened last night made his knees weak. Then anger at Jack hit him, hot and liquid, pulsing through him until he felt his neck flushing. Rusty, was he?

"Hey," she said softly, "I'm only giving you a hard time to get even."

Too late, he realized his face had mirrored his thoughts. He made himself grin, which didn't prove too hard. Looking at Breanna Morgan was great incentive, mainly because of her infectious smile. "I guess it upsets me when you make light of something so dangerous. If you fell through in here, no telling how far you might drop. This is a tall foundation."

"I concede the point. The old mine tunnels run under some of these buildings. Who knows? There might even be one under here."

His nerves leaped. She had a clear, musical voice that carried too well. "So you'll follow my advice and stay out of here?"

"Yessir. The floors *are* a tad creaky. I felt uneasy walking in there a couple of times. Satisfied?" Breanna watched his dark face, waiting for him to lighten up. Then a thought hit her. "Tyler! You know what? When I heard that noise, it sounded like it was coming from under the floor. Do you realize what that...?" Excitement tightened her throat, and she had to pause. "The mine could run under there. And if it does, it could explain— Tyler, what if somebody is down in *The Crescent Moon*?"

Tension shot through Tyler like a bolt of high voltage. "Like who? The ghost?" He strode swiftly down the ramp. She was talking so loudly that she was a regular broadcasting system. He put a finger to his lips to shut her up, did some quick thinking and whispered, "If someone's down there, let's not warn them we know."

Her eyes widened with delight. "Then you agree it's possible?" she whispered back.

Feeling as if he were in one of those bad dreams where everything happens in slow motion, Tyler steered her toward the house. It was like herding a flock of ducks. "Sure it's possible."

She braked. He walked into her. He felt like screaming. "Watch it, I'm sore," she complained. "What's your hurry? It *is* my mine. If somebody's in there, I don't care if they're scared out. Do you realize how dangerous it could be? Why, if there was a cave-in, I could be sued." She reared back to look at him. "I've got to find the entrance to that mine, Tyler. If it's accessible, I need to blast it closed, board it up and post warnings." She broke off, a strange look clouding her eyes. "Of course, it could be just an animal."

"More likely," he agreed. "Possibly a bear using it. But it's more fun the other way."

"It's been closed because of cave-ins since before I was born. If someone's found it, we're talking dangerous, really dangerous. Come on. I'd rather be safe than sorry. Let's go look at my maps."

"Maps?" Tyler wanted to kick himself for being so transparent, but his interest zoomed in on the word like a telephoto lens. Jack wanted maps. Jack didn't have maps. Why Jack didn't, raised a question Tyler couldn't resist asking. "Where did you get them?"

"Well, there weren't any on file that the clerk could find. So when the courthouse was a dead end, I went to the storage building where we have Gran's things and went through her papers. I don't know how accurate they are. I think Gramps drew them. But they show the tunnels in close proximity to where they probably are."

"I wonder why it isn't filed. You'd think any underground mine would be on record, for safety if nothing else."

"That's what the clerk said. But the file on *The Crescent Moon* was an exception. All the other documents were there, but no maps."

"Sounds unorganized." Tyler slowed to let her precede him up the steps. *Suspicious, that's how it sounds, but I can't say so.* He had to see those maps and get them to Jack if he possibly could. To do that, he needed a darned good reason for seeming so interested. "Breanna, on second thought— Don't laugh...."

She glanced back at him. "About what?"

"Well, it just occurred to me that we could possibly find the treasure." He paused to let that sink in, then added, "If your uninvited treasure hunters don't get to it first."

"If there *is* a treasure."

"Your grandfather said there was, didn't he? And he never fibbed, remember?"

"Well, he *believed* there was. Me, I've never thought the story held water. I watched Dane going crazy after it too many years, finding nothing."

"But the underground chambers have been closed since before you were born. *Think*, Bree. No one could have found it if it was in the shaft. I want to see those maps. That gold should be yours, not some treasure hunter's. If the maps aren't to scale, I've got a friend who's a licensed surveyor. He might be able to revise them."

Leading the way into the house, Tyler stood back, watching as Breanna tucked the twenty from the barn into the side pocket of her purse. He almost whooped with relief when she headed for the bedroom.

"I'll be right back. I've got the maps in the closet."

Tyler waited for the curtain to drop behind her, then stepped softly to the counter. *Quickly, quickly.* His fingers were just reaching...almost there...and he heard her coming back. He began whistling and leaned his hips against the sink hoping he looked more casual than he felt.

"Here we go," she said. "Come look. They're really fascinating."

The maps. Riveting his gaze on them, he cautioned himself not to appear overanxious. *Talk about a lucky break! Those maps are it,* he thought. They could be certain there were no undiscovered entrances to *The Crescent Moon* if they could get copies and study them.

Casting one last glance at the purse, Tyler made a silent vow. No matter what, later he had to get one full minute alone with that handbag.

DANE TRIED TO STILL his hands, but they trembled as he strapped a bundle of money and set it on the pile. Too much pressure, not enough sleep. He narrowed his eyes and gazed at Chuck Morrow, who stood beside him. He was so nervous that he felt sick.

"I thought I made myself clear," Chuck said in that soft, menacing way he had. "You were told to get rid of her. You haven't."

"I—I just need a couple a more days. Give me some time. I've got a plan I'm working on. Believe me, she'll leave after tonight, I promise."

Chuck shook his head. "She almost caught us last night. I saw her out behind the shack, spying on us. She's a bright girl, Dane, too bright. At this point she doesn't suspect. And I want to keep it that way. But we can't curtail work forever."

"She won't find out, I swear it. Come on, Chuck, who would ever dream an operation this scale is down here? According to records, the place doesn't even exist. Marcy took care of that when she lifted the maps."

"Cute kid, Marcy." Chuck bundled a stack of twenties, gave them a pat, then turned, lifting an eyebrow. "Too bad her brakes went out and she went over that grade. Damned shame, wasn't it? On the other hand, it does solve one problem. She can't spill her guts. Now, Breanna, she's another story. She finds out about this, and she'll squeal like a stuck hog. I can't let that happen. You get rid of her, Dane. Understood? Or I'll do it myself."

"How? Like you got rid of Marcy?"

"You have no proof of that. It was an accident."

Dane gripped the edge of the workbench. "Breanna's my problem, Chuck. I'll handle her."

"Then do it!"

Chapter Five

That same evening, shortly after Tyler left, Breanna re-folded the maps of *The Crescent Moon* and stretched out on the bed for another nap, promising herself she would clean up their dinner mess later. A smile settled on her lips as she nuzzled her head into her pillow. Sore and exhausted as she was, she had thoroughly enjoyed Tyler's company as they studied Gramps's drawings of the shafts. Tyler had a rare appreciation for the ridiculous that had kept her entertained. Expecting him back in the morning to work on the fence posts gave her something nice to anticipate. Hanging one arm over the side of the bed, she stroked Coaly's silken head as she drifted off to sleep.

It seemed to Breanna that she had just closed her eyes when someone called her name. She stirred, stared at the ceiling and listened. Had she been dreaming? No, there it was again, a low, keening wail. "Bree-ee-a-a-n-n-a...whoo-oo-oo...Bree-ee-anna..."

The eerie call brought her bolt upright in bed. She glanced at her alarm. Midnight? She swung her legs over the edge of the mattress and stood.

"Coaly?" She tiptoed to the bedroom curtain. "Coaly, where are you?"

A low growl drifted to her from the living room. She paused, then pushed through the curtain. The interior of the cabin was dark. The fire had burned low. She inched across the floor.

"Bree-ee-a-a-nna . . ."

Freezing, she stared in disbelief. Outside the French door stood the shadowy figure of a man. His arms rose, so slowly that they almost appeared to float. Then his head burst into light, blinding her. She blinked and threw up an arm to shield her eyes. Coaly lunged at the window, snarling, clawing the wood. Breanna squinted into the brightness.

She couldn't be seeing what she thought she was seeing. *John Van Patten, The Crescent Moon ghost.* The burst of light on his head was a miner's light. He wore old-fashioned slicker pants, heavy boots, a red flannel shirt. There was no question. It was either John Van Patten or someone who had gone to great lengths to look like him.

"Get ou-ou-t," he moaned. "Get ou-ou-out. Or die . . . Get ou-ou-out."

Fear of the unknown writhed inside her. She didn't believe in ghosts, but it was difficult to remember that when one stood before her. The miner's light suddenly went out. The shadowy shape drifted sideways, beyond view from the window. She saw another burst of brightness shortly afterward, then heard the ghost calling to her again, first by her bedroom—light flashed by the windows—then near the front door. "Bree-ee-aa-aa-nna."

A scream clawed at her throat. Her entire body dripped perspiration. She turned, her movements jerky as a puppet's, staring at the door, knowing even as she did that a spirit could come right through it, locked or not. Coaly ran down the entry, sniffing, snarling. The fact that he didn't bark alarmed Breanna all the more. Even the dog sensed something abnormal.

Before she thought it through, Breanna acted, racing for the dead bolt. Since a closed door was useless, the least she could do was get a good look. There was no point in running away or hiding, so she threw the door open, stepped out, pulled it shut, launched herself over the porch and landed, not on the ground, as she'd intended, but on an escaping Coaly, who seemed as eager to nab the spook as she was. The next few seconds were a riot of confusion. Breanna heard Coaly yelp, felt herself falling, and then hit the side of the fruit cellar. Someone screamed. For a moment, she thought it was herself, but the four-letter words that followed soon convinced her otherwise.

Stunned, Breanna sat crumpled on the ground for a moment, fighting to get her breath, which had been very effectively knocked out of her in her collision with the cellar. She heard her "ghost" curse again. Then Coaly launched what was, by the sound of it, a vicious attack. Breanna pushed herself up on her knees and staggered to her feet. "John Van Patten" streaked past, literally a flash of light because his headlamp was still on, Coaly snapping at his heels.

"Coaly!"

If John Van Patten was man and not ghost, Breanna didn't want her dog hurt. After last night, she knew there could be a group of intruders, and Coaly could find himself surrounded. She bounded after him. Coaly, because of his color, was hard to see, but "John Van Patten" was an easy spook to follow. He not only glowed like a beacon, but he was yelling, fighting off Coaly. Breanna broke into a run. To her relief, she saw the miner's light zoom up the barn ramp, beam bobbing. Then the "ghost" paused, turning back to emit one last "Whoo-ooo-oo" at her before he disappeared into the barn and slammed the door shut. Coaly, unable to pursue, barked and snarled, hurling himself at the offending barrier.

By the time Breanna arrived at the barn to collect her dog, Coaly was off the ramp and circling the building, piercing the night with a volley of barking. With the "ghost" trapped inside, the thought of pursuit occurred to her. But she wanted no repeat performance of last night. She seized her dog's collar and ran for home, dragging the protesting canine with her.

Less than a hundred feet away, Tyler Ross and Jack Jones saw everything. Tyler, relaxing now that Breanna was safely back in her house, turned to his superior. "Explain that one. Somebody's trying to get rid of her. Seems a strange thing to do to a co-worker."

Jack grunted with disgust. "Dammit, Ross, get your head on straight. You see, but you don't see. If they wanted to get rid of her, they'd think of something a little more persuasive. What is it about this broad that's got you blind to what's happening?"

Staring toward the cabin, Tyler's reply was to shake his head. He could be wrong. "Explain the twenty, then. She flashed that at me, no qualms whatsoever. She found it in the barn, dammit. You know it's counterfeit."

"Do I? And on the other side of the coin, what if it's genuine? What if, Ross? That's our job, you know, the what ifs? Say you've made a slip. She's suspicious, thinks you're on to them. She could flash a good bill, knowing you'll pull a switch. You have it gone over, it's clean. End of your suspicion. I tell you, she's poison. Hell, she even left it in a side pocket of her purse, making it simple for you. Use your head. It's bait."

Tyler felt sick. He remembered her slipping the twenty into her purse, right in plain sight, then leaving the room. What if? It looked bad. He had to admit it. Until he got hold of the twenty, no one could know for sure. Until then, he had to be careful, very careful. "I'll get it tomorrow. I'm supposed to help her plant fence posts in the morning. I'll pull the switch then.''

"Believe me. She'll probably give you an open invitation," Jack replied.

"What about this ghost business, though? If she's one of them, why would they do this?''

"I don't have all the answers. Maybe she's horning in on this one fellow's cut, taking over his territory. You take a pack of wolves, give them slim pickings, and one always turns on another. Survival of the fittest. Don't give this group too much credit.''

BY NINE O'CLOCK the following morning, Breanna had not only convinced Tyler they should postpone fence building in favor of finding the entrance to *The Crescent Moon*, but had led him over the hill behind the cabin to look for it.

"The way I see it," she informed him cheerily, "is that my ghost last night has heard the legend. John Van Patten is only supposed to appear when someone gets close to the treasure. So, this guy capitalized on it, trying to scare me away. My guess is he's found the old entrance, and now he's afraid I will. Don't get me wrong, I don't believe there's a treasure. But *he* believes there is. If I want any peace, I've got to find that shaft and blast it shut.''

"So you don't plan to search the tunnels?''

Breanna stopped climbing to look back down the trail at him. "Well, we might walk through.''

"Bad idea. It could cave in on us." Tyler looked beyond her to the rock slide. Was the old entrance up there? The closer they came, the more nervous he felt. Was Breanna setting him up. Or was she as innocent as she seemed? "I think caution should be our byword, don't you?''

She shrugged. "It hasn't caved in on the ghost. Why would it give way on us?''

As they approached the rock-strewn hillside, Tyler prepared himself for the worst. He kept close to Breanna. If counterfeiters leaped out from the brush, a certain lady Tyler knew would be between him and their guns. His stomach wrenched at the thought. How could he have been so wrong about her, so completely taken in?

Smoothing the map, Breanna studied it with a frown. "What do you think? Could this be it?" Expecting Tyler to check the map with her, she glanced up in puzzlement to find him scanning the woods around them instead. "Tyler?"

He leveled steely eyes on hers. "What?"

"Do you think this slide could be near the entrance?"

"It looks likely to me."

Perplexed by the strange expression on his face, Breanna carefully stowed the map in her hip pocket. Yesterday he had seemed so anxious to explore, now he was dragging his heels. "Well, unless you want to forget it, let's get cracking and search it out."

Tyler stood back, watching her weave her way in and over the rocks. "If it's a caved-in entrance, your ghost can't be using it."

"Unless there's a narrow opening." She rounded on him, propping her hands on her hips. "He could use a narrow opening, then conceal it with rock. Are you going to help?"

Reluctant and unable to hide it, Tyler advanced on the slide, rolling up his sleeves. He'd have to work with one eye on her, one eye on the brush, and both ears strained for noise, which wouldn't be easy with boulders clunking. He studied her in amazement. She was a sturdy girl with a well-rounded figure that was amazingly toned for a writer. She threw rocks even he might think twice about. "Do you take extra iron or what?"

She glanced up, perspiration filming her forehead and dampening her hair where it formed a widow's peak. "I told you, I'm not afraid of work."

Her tone implied he was. An unbidden smile twisted his mouth. "I know, you come from a long line of miners."

"Hey, don't laugh. There's no harder work. Gramps was one tough fellow. At eighty he could outdo men half his age. A very smart man, too, for one with no education."

"Well, until this moment I would have said you had inherited his brains. Now I'm not so sure." Tyler heaved a rock. "This is a lot of trouble to go to on a maybe."

"Yeah? And if you don't act on maybes, what do you go on? Sitting and contemplating never got anything done."

Tyler straightened. Every couple of seconds, a medium-size boulder flew past him. He saw a small bulge of muscle pop up on her arm as she strained, and he raised an eyebrow. Most women would be babying those scratched arms and that lacerated back. Criminal or not, she was quite some lady.

Two hours later, Tyler led the way down the mountain, unafraid to turn his back on the woman behind him. They had found nothing yet, no trace of an entrance, and, more importantly, no counterfeiters waiting to ambush them. If Breanna was acting, she had moved one hell of a lot of rock to make it convincing. As the trail widened, he slowed so that they could walk abreast. "We'll take a break, then come back," he assured her. "Some of your lemonade will hit the spot." She didn't return his smile. "Disappointed?"

"Yeah, I am."

"Hey, it's not that important." Before he thought, Tyler draped an arm around her shoulders. Once it was there, he didn't want to move it. "It's just a pipe dream, something to chase away boredom."

"To you, maybe. I *have* to find it, Tyler. My gran made me promise I'd keep the claim. I can't break my word. And if I want to stay, I've got to get rid of whoever's bugging me. The mine theory seemed the most likely place to start." A shadow crossed her face. "I have another reason, too. One that's not quite so clear-cut, more a crazy hunch."

"That sounds serious."

"It is." Her eyes rose to his, wavered with uncertainty. "Probably silly, but— It's about my cousin, something that I've been wondering about."

"Tell me about it."

Her lips parted. He held his breath, waiting, hoping.

"I—can't," she whispered. "I wish I could, but I just can't."

When they reached the cabin, Dane's Corvette was parked in the driveway behind Breanna's Honda. Breanna dived for Coaly and nabbed him by the collar. She saw that the cabin door stood ajar.

"Well, it looks like my company invited himself in," she remarked to Tyler. Stepping to the fruit cellar, she opened the door and pushed an unwilling Coaly inside, dropping the lock bar with a click. "It's my cousin, Dane. And Coaly doesn't get along with him."

"Maybe I should leave," Tyler suggested, hoping she'd veto the idea.

"Nonsense. You're my guest. There's no reason you shouldn't be here."

Breanna's irritation mushroomed into full-blown anger when she found Dane in her bedroom, busily looking through the collection of papers on her closet shelf. He didn't even bother to look guilty when he saw her. "Dane, what do you think you're doing?"

Dane, unaware that Tyler was in the other room, threw the maps and photocopies in Breanna's face. She stepped back in surprise, and her cousin advanced on her. "The question isn't what I'm doing, lady, it's what you're doing. First I see you up the hill, looking for the old mine entrance. Then I come in here and find all this. Why are you collecting all these news stories?"

Breanna's retreat ended when she backed into the wall. Fury twisted Dane's face. His eyes were wild, crazy. "Dane, stop it."

"Answer me!" He shot out a hand and grabbed her hair, making a fist in it. Tears sprang to her eyes. "Answer me, damn you! Why are you doing this? Back off, Breanna. I'm warning you. Back off."

Then Tyler came through the curtain. With a low snarl, he pushed Dane away from Breanna, then squared off, fists clenched at his sides. Dane staggered backward, catching his balance by grabbing the bedstead. "You're the one who'd better back off, buster," Tyler warned. "You got something to say to the lady, say it, but keep your hands off her."

Dane straightened, smoothing the lapels of his jacket. "And who, might I ask, do you think you are, Ross? This is family business. Butt out."

Breanna stepped between the two men. "Wait a minute, fellas. Let's not turn a disagreement into a brawl." Turning to Tyler, she managed a smile. "I appreciate you're concern, Tyler, but Dane just lost his temper there for a moment. Right, Dane?"

"No, that's not right," Dane hissed. Glancing down, he ground one of her photocopies beneath his heel. "You see that? Keep poking your nose where it doesn't belong, and next, it'll be you. Do you understand what I'm saying? Quit snooping. Back off. Forget the fire. Stay away from the mine. You're in way over your head. Pack up your stuff and get out of here while you still can."

Leaving that threat to cloud the air, Dane shoved his way past Tyler and left the bedroom. The entire cabin shook as he slammed the front door behind him. Breanna tensed and squeezed her eyes closed.

"What was that all about?"

Ignoring Tyler's question, she knelt to gather up the papers, infuriated all the more when she saw Gran's old newspapers lying in one corner of the closet, crumpled and torn. If ever she had doubted Dane's involvement in the arson, she didn't now. His reaction to those papers was testimony against him. She rose to her feet, clutching the photocopies to her chest.

"I think Dane may have set the Reuben Creek fire," she blurted, "because someone had found *The Crescent Moon*."

Tyler stooped to pick up Gran's old papers. Breanna saw him note their age. He read for a moment, then tossed them onto her bed, turning back to raise an eyebrow at her. "That's a pretty serious accusation."

"And ten years too long in coming." Setting the photocopies back in their place, Breanna clutched the edge of the shelf, fighting back tears. "You don't have to get involved in this. It's not your problem. It's mine. I don't know if you're familiar with that fire. A man was killed." She looked over her shoulder at him. "If Dane was the arsonist, he murdered him."

The bedroom went dead quiet. After a long moment, Tyler reached for the photocopies. "May I?"

Sighing, Breanna nodded her permission. "There's nothing, no clue. I've already read them."

"Who knows? Maybe someone uninvolved will see something that's been missed."

Following him to the kitchen, Breanna said, "Don't use that word. I wasn't involved, period. Not in any way."

Tyler pulled back a chair. "I didn't think you were."

Dragging her hair back from her eyes, she heaved a tired sigh. "I'm sorry. I guess I'm too sensitive. We were accused of setting it, you know, Dane and I."

"No, I didn't know."

"You will once you've read those papers. I'm going to go get Coaly. I'll be right back."

Tyler waited until she went out, then bounded to his feet. The purse, where was it? Not on the counter. *Damn it all.* He ran for the bedroom. There it was, on the closet shelf. He grabbed it, stuffed his fingers into the pocket and pulled out a—grocery list? He pushed it back. A bank deposit stub? Where was the money?

He heard Breanna talking to the dog, drawing near to the porch. Tossing the purse back on the shelf, he dived through the curtain, raced across the living room and landed in the chair. When she walked into the room, he stretched and yawned, smiling up at her.

AN HOUR LATER, TYLER ROCKED back in his chair, folding his arms across his chest. His eyes searched Breanna's.

"Well?" she demanded.

"You want the truth? I see nothing conclusive to implicate Dane. Or you, for that matter. You had an alibi, an airtight alibi, given by Chuck Morrow." He shook his head. "There has to be another side to this story. You don't strike me as the type to make accusations unless you're mighty positive you're right."

"That was my biggest problem. I wasn't sure, so I kept my mouth shut. A man was killed, and I said nothing."

"I don't understand. According to the paper, Dane couldn't have set that fire."

"And the paper is all lies. At least about the alibi. We weren't with Chuck all night. We ran into him when we were escaping the fire. Chuck lied to the police to get us off the hook." Breanna propped her elbows on the table, covering her eyes with trembling fingers. She could scarcely bear the memories, the screams that echoed inside her mind, the vision of Rob Thatcher caught under a tree, burning alive. And with the memories came guilt that cut through her like a knife. She couldn't bring herself to tell all of it. But some of it she had to tell. It was too heavy a burden to keep locked inside her any longer. "Oh, Tyler, why didn't I simply tell the truth?"

"Only you can answer that. Did you suspect Dane then?"

"Yes and no. I woke up after the fire started, and Dane wasn't in camp. By the time he got there the fire was all around us—" She broke off. She didn't want to verbalize the rest, couldn't. "It was all a blur for days after, the trees falling, the fear, the realization we might die. I wasn't thinking. I was just running."

"Go on."

"Then the next morning the police came. They accused us of setting the fire. Arson, they said, started with gas cans placed around the hippie commune. The hippies weren't too popular in these parts. Lots of people, kids and adults, had made threats. Dane and I were just in the wrong place at the right time." She dropped her hand to look at him. "I was terrified. Murder! Rob Thatcher was pinned by a fallen pine and couldn't escape. I envisioned the electric chair. At seventeen, it's pretty scary when police accuse you of anything, let alone killing someone. We swore we didn't do it, but the police were convinced otherwise. They didn't believe anything we said. And they took us to juvenile hall. I think Dane was even more frightened than me."

"I can imagine. That would scare even an adult."

Breanna forced herself to remember. "It's like a fog, those first few days. I was no sooner in custody than they put me in the hospital for treatment. Smoke inhalation. Just a day, for observation. By the time I was released, Chuck Morrow had come forward, saying we were with him all night, that we couldn't have set the fire. Dane and I—we—we were so scared, we said it was true.''

"Chuck was a friend, I take it? According to the paper he was quite a hero, risking his life to save women and children that night."

Tension clogged Breanna's throat. "I've never understood that part. Chuck is—a snake. He'd never put himself out for anybody."

"He did for you, for Dane."

"And demanded his pound of flesh, believe me. A few days after I got home, Chuck started coming around."

"You lived here?"

"Only for a month in the summer. And we visited a lot. We were staying here then, Dane and I, like we did every year."

"And Chuck demanded his pound of flesh?"

She nodded. "Little favors at first, then bigger ones. Dane seemed scared to death of him. That's when I began getting suspicious. I remembered Dane being out of camp. I realized Dane was scared Chuck would go to the police about something. It occurred to me Chuck knew something, something Dane had done that he wasn't telling. But I wasn't sure, and without being sure, I couldn't accuse Dane. Now I regret that. I think—no, I guess suspect is a better word—that Dane has something hanging over his head, something eating at him, even though it's been ten years."

"You had a reasonable doubt. I don't think there's anything so wrong in your not having gone to the police, considering the circumstances."

Breanna straightened in her chair. Her chest tightened. "I knew right from wrong. And I've had to live with my decision ever since."

"And you're on a guilt trip? Breanna, give yourself a break. You were young, scared, confused. If you had gone to the police, what would they have thought? You could have been charged with a very serious crime at that point. I think it's understandable. Not wise, perhaps, but understandable. What kind of favors was Morrow asking of Dane?"

Breanna glanced up at him. There were some things she couldn't yet bring herself to discuss; not with Tyler, not with anyone. "Nothing important."

"So, here we sit with photocopies. Am I to understand you're looking for proof against Dane, that you've returned to set a wrong right?"

"No, I didn't come back with that intention." Breanna told him about Dane's first visit, his warnings. "It seemed suspicious. It set me to thinking. Dane's so paranoid about the treasure, so afraid I'll look for it. And he gets absolutely furious if I mention the fire. I know he's afraid of something. And I want to find out what. It's almost as if it all ties in together. I know it doesn't make sense, but it's as if the fire and the mine are all the same in Dane's mind."

"You're right. It doesn't make sense." *Or does it?* Tyler studied the woman sitting opposite him. Now that she had told him this, the possibilities were endless. Dane Van Patten with a secret. Morrow holding it over his head as blackmail. It had never occurred to Jack or to himself that Dane Van Patten's involvement could be due to coercion. A fire, a death, a kid with a secret. If Breanna had acted unwisely out of fear, why not Dane? "If I were you, I'd let the past be buried, Breanna."

"Dane could have been my ghost last night." She laughed softly. "I know it sounds idiotic, but he's obviously getting desperate. He wants me out of here so badly, he might do something like that to scare me away. Don't you see? I can't forget it. Dane won't let me."

Tyler rocked back in his chair again. "Has it occurred to you he might go even further, that he could be dangerous?"

Her eyes widened. "Dane? No, not Dane. You saw him at his worst today. Dane could never hurt me. And if he hurt someone else, I'm sure he never meant to."

"I saw him trying to bully you around. Sorry, but I think he's capable of violence. It's not worth it, Breanna. I think you should do as he said. Pack up and go."

"I won't give him the satisfaction. No, if it was Dane here last night, he'll have to get more inventive. I'm not breaking my promise to Gran because a ghost is haunting me and Dane made vague threats."

"Vague? I thought he was pretty blatant."

"You don't know him like I do. Believe me, Tyler. Dane would put his life on the line for me. I know he would."

Tyler hoped she was right. Oh, how he hoped she was right.

BECAUSE BREANNA INSISTED, Tyler returned with her to the rock slide to do more searching for the entrance to *The Crescent Moon*. He was more relaxed on the second trip up there, more certain of Breanna's motives. She was off base, thinking the mine and the fire were tied together, but for one guessing in the dark, she was close to the truth. The mine was intertwined with crime, all right, but it had nothing to do with the fire.

The entire time they worked, he tried to think of ways he might get Breanna's twenty from the barn out of her purse.

If he could distract her, he would be able to snatch it and pull a switch. To do that, he had to stick to her like glue until the opportunity presented itself.

After moving what seemed like mountains of rock, Tyler and Breanna found the wooden frame of a mine opening. "Well, nobody's going in through that," she quipped. "Not without several sticks of dynamite."

Tyler nodded, staring at the cave-in. Rock filled the opening. The day wasn't a complete loss. Now he knew for certain the counterfeiters had only one entrance, the one under Breanna's barn. Jack would be pleased to hear it. "Well, that scotches the theory of a bear under the barn," he said lightly. "We're back to rats."

Breanna laughed. "I guess we are, at that. It's a relief in a way. I can stop worrying that Dane found it. It was pretty scary, thinking he might have hurt someone, trying to keep the old mine a secret."

"I'll tell you what. How's about a late lunch in Grants Pass?" He glanced at his watch. "We've got time. What do you say? My treat. We can make a laundry run while we're at it."

"I don't know, Mr. Ross. You might regret the offer. I'm so hungry after all this work, I might bankrupt you. One thing I don't have is a delicate appetite."

"So make it two lunches. I'm willing to pay that price for your company."

As they walked down the trail, Tyler rested his arm over Breanna's shoulders once again, this time intentionally. An ache of protectiveness tightened his chest. Judging by Dane's threats, he knew he had to get that counterfeit twenty to Jack fast. Breanna's life could be riding on it.

Chapter Six

Forty minutes later, Tyler pulled Breanna's Honda to the far right lane of Interstate 5 and entered Grants Pass at the town's north end. As they passed the gigantic statue of a caveman at the city's entrance, he said, "Now, that's my kind of fellow. See that club he's got? Those things saved prehistoric man a lot of lunch tabs when it came to wooing the ladies."

She arched an eyebrow at him, thoroughly enjoying the easy camaraderie that had been established between them during their drive. "Neanderthal are you? You didn't by any chance go to school here?" She pointed to a busy parking lot on their right. "Pull in at the Ninety-Nine Market and I'll get us some laundry soap."

Tyler braked the Honda and shifted down to make the turn. Pulling to a stop, he shoved in the clutch and reached for his wallet. "Here, use this," he said, handing her a twenty.

"I'll spring for the soap. You're buying lunch."

"Well, take it for a roll of quarters then."

She took her wallet from her bag. Flipping it open, she withdrew a ten and exchanged bills with him.

His eyes sharpened as she fitted his twenty into her bill-fold. "Why don't you just take the twenty, Bree, and leave your purse? It'd be less to carry."

"I might want something else. Be right back."

The moment Breanna turned to walk away, Tyler heaved a sigh. With any luck, she wouldn't spend the twenty from the barn, and he could snatch it later.

The store was crowded with customers. Breanna found the laundry soap, then selected two candy bars from the display rack as she passed. The opportunity to tease Tyler about her gargantuan appetite later was too tempting to resist. She stood in line, stepping forward as the clerk finished each transaction. When her turn came, she set her purchases on the counter and pulled out her wallet.

"That's four forty-nine," the clerk told her.

"Oh, and I need quarters. Can you spare a roll?"

"Sure." The woman took a red cylinder of coin from the left section of her drawer. "That makes it fourteen forty-nine."

Handing her a twenty, Breanna opened her grocery bag.

"A brand-new one," the blonde said. "I don't see many."

Breanna, busy fishing for her candy bars so she could hide them in her purse, replied, "Yes, it is, isn't it?"

The clerk counted change into Breanna's outstretched palm. When she finished, she lifted curious green eyes, her eyes friendly. "You have a nice day."

"You, too."

As Breanna approached the Honda, she smiled to herself. After lunch, when Tyler was full, she'd offer him a candy bar. Sliding into her seat, she said "Okay, I'm ready to eat you into bankruptcy."

He flashed her a grin and pulled out into traffic.

FOUR HOURS LATER, BREANNA parked outside the cabin and cut the Honda's engine. The sun dipped behind the mountain, streaking the gray-blue sky with cottony pink. She sat there a moment, absorbing the evening sounds, the swish of pine boughs, the songs of the crickets, the occasional chirp of a bird preparing to roost. She heard Coaly barking from inside the cabin, eager to be let out, but she stole another few seconds of quiet. Leaning her head against the rest, she closed her eyes.

Tyler. What a lovely day it had been. Even doing the laundry with him was fun. There had been only three dryers available, so Tyler had suggested drying their white things together. It had seemed a practical idea until the clothes came out sparking with static, her nylon lacies sticking to his briefs and undershirts. When all the clothes were folded, two pairs of her bikinis were missing. She felt fairly sure Tyler would pull on a pair of shorts one morning next week and find her lavender Tuesday panties inside the garment with him. A mischievous grin slanted across her mouth. It was one way to make a man remember you. And he was supposed to help her dig postholes again in the morning. She found herself looking forward to that with as much anticipation as she might have to a dinner date.

Glancing at her watch, she sat upright. No more time for loafing she decided. She still had to unload her laundry, let Coaly out for a run, and take a bath before dark.

TYLER PARTED THE DOGWOOD leaves, gazing down the hillside as Breanna left the cabin. She had a blue terry robe draped over one arm, and clutched her toiletry items in the other. Glancing at his watch, he noted the time. *Seventhirty.* He had to enter the house, find the twenty and be gone within ten minutes. That creek was too cold for her to lounge around in. A quick scrub, and she'd be out and headed for home. He watched her crisscross through the brush along the creek, checking to be certain no one was there. Someone was watching her, all right, but not for the reasons she suspected.

He waited for her to disappear, then ran out of the bushes, crossed the road and leaped the picket fence that bordered one side of the yard. Pulling out his wallet, he withdrew a plastic credit card and crept to the French doors. Coaly appeared, pressing his wet nose against the glass. *Don't bark,* Tyler prayed. The dog let out a single "Woof," then wagged his tail.

Sliding the plastic card into the door seam, Tyler jiggled the lever lock, lifting it free of its catch. The doors swung open, and he stepped inside, nabbing Coaly by the collar. "No way, pal. If you get loose, the game's over."

Breanna's purse sat on the table. Tyler slid his hand into the side pocket. The grocery list, the bank stub, a tissue blotted with lipstick. Voilà, the twenty. He took it, replacing it with a bill of his own. As he slid his wallet into his hip pocket, he noticed the maps and photocopies lying on the table. His hand hovered over them, then he vetoed the idea. She'd probably let him take them later to have them drawn to scale. No sense in making her suspicious. Just in case, though, he gave the map another quick study.

A growl from Coaly made Tyler leap and toss the papers back on the table. Footsteps. In three strides, he stepped outside and pulled the windows closed. No time to lock them. He vaulted the fence, zigzagged across the asphalt and dived into the bush.

THE NIGHT WIND WAS PICKING UP. Breanna shivered, knowing how chilly the water would feel. She stepped into the copse and shimmied out of her clothes. Draping her robe over a limb, she carried her bathing things with her to the diving rock. She missed Coaly. With him nosing around, no one could sneak up on her. She had checked the brush, though. She was probably safe enough, and without Coaly along to liven things up, she wouldn't smell like a dog after her bath.

The pool felt like ice when she dived in. Clenching her teeth, she surfaced and began scrubbing. She had just finished rinsing her hair and was rubbing the soap from her lashes when she heard a creaking sound, similar to what she had heard that second night when Coaly had growled. Pulling her hair back, Breanna stared at the copse beyond the bathing hole.

The brush still swayed where someone had disturbed it, but she couldn't see anyone. Alarm coursed through her, growing in intensity until her nerves jangled. Not only was no person there, but her clothes weren't there, either.

She gaped in disbelief. Even her towel was gone.

"Tyler?" That scoundrel. She sank in the water to her collarbone, smiling expectantly. She envisioned him dangling her jeans, teasing her. "All right, Mr. Ross, the fun's over. I'll freeze if you don't cut it out."

The scenario was so clearly etched upon her mind that alarm coursed through her when Tyler didn't step out of the brush. Silence weighted the air. Tyler might tease, he might give her a scare, but he wouldn't drag it out like this while she was treading neck deep in icy water.

After several minutes had passed, Breanna could bear the cold no longer. *Modesty be damned,* she thought. She couldn't stay in there and freeze to death. She seized handholds on the diving rock, hauling herself from the pool. Water poured off her as she gained her footing. Hiding her body with her arms, she ran along the rock, reached shore and dashed into the bushes.

Acutely aware of her vulnerability, she didn't stay long in the brush. Working her way through the foliage, she kept her ears strained for the sound of approaching footsteps. Then, taking a deep breath, she ran into the open. Rocks and stickers gouged the soles of her feet, but she didn't slow down as she wove her way between the outhouse and garage and sprinted across the drive. When she reached the retainer wall steps, a horrible thought hit her. The cabin key was in her jeans. She was locked out of the house.

That realization had no sooner sunk in than Breanna froze on the walkway in midstride. Her clothes lay on the porch, slashed to ribbons. The thief had taken a knife to them. Her pulse rate accelerated as she drew closer. If this was a joke, it wasn't funny. It was sick.

Fear and anger knotted inside her, the ferocity of both blocking out all else. She grabbed her tattered jeans, slipping her fingers into the pocket. *The key. Thank goodness.* With trembling hands, she inserted it in the lock, gave it a twist and burst into the cabin, shoving the door closed behind her.

Making her way to the bedroom, she grabbed a towel off the shelf and dried. Then she dressed, searching the floor of the closet for her other shoes. Her earlier fear ebbed, crowded out by rage. Someone was trying to terrify her. There could be only one motive, to force her to leave.

"Well, it won't work," she vowed, shoving the bedroom curtain aside as she went to the kitchen.

Coaly sat back on his haunches and uttered a sharp bark. She shot a glance outside. About twenty minutes of light remained. "No dinner yet, fella. First, we do some investigating."

As she reached for her flashlight, Breanna noticed that her papers were scattered. A tense silence enveloped the room. *Someone has been inside the cabin.* Knowing her home had been violated disturbed her more than the incident by the creek. How had someone come in without forcing the door? The key in her jeans, of course. She reached for the flashlight. "Come on, Coaly. Let's go see what we can see."

With anger as turbofuel, Breanna returned to the bathing hole, armed with her flashlight. Coaly dived into the copse, sniffing the ground where she had seen the brush moving. More interested in where her prankster had gone than where he had been, Breanna made a wide circle around the undergrowth, fanning her light on the ground. What she *didn't* see made her uneasy. There were no footprints coming out of the foliage. She stooped to get a closer look, walking the perimeter three times. Nothing.

Her throat tightened with irrational fear. For a man to enter and leave the brush, he would have to make tracks. The story of John Van Patten's ghost crept into her mind. *I found the mine entrance today,* she thought. *He appears when someone gets close to his treasure.* Breanna tightened her grip on the flashlight. She couldn't allow her imagination to run wild. *A ghost wouldn't leave footprints, though.*

Before searching further, she checked the horizon to be sure she had plenty of twilight left. No way was she getting caught out here after dark. Entering the brush, she trained her light where Coaly was sniffing. There, confined to a two-foot area, were some very real tracks. Boot tracks, similar to the ones she had seen before. Breanna knelt and touched her finger to a print. Definitely not Tyler's boots. His soles had slanted ridges in the rubber. These had a squared indentation, with the pattern angling triangularly outward from the center.

So she had checked Tyler's boots without realizing it. Ah, yes, she remembered looking at his tracks the day he helped her plant fence posts. It disturbed her that she was subconsciously observing him as if he were her enemy. She passed a hand over her eyes, disgusted with herself. Then relief swept through her. Considering everything that had happened, it was normal to be wary. At least these prints proved that Tyler wasn't her prankster.

Coaly ran to a grassy bank inside the copse. Sniffing a tuft of grass, he snarled. His strange behavior piqued her curiosity and she followed, picking up a trail of tracks that led to the slope and ended there. Coaly walked the bank, his nose skimming the ground in erratic patterns. Had her thief climbed up it? Breanna drew closer, leaning forward to shine her light. There were no footprints.

"I wish you could talk," she muttered to Coaly. "He was in here, that much is obvious, but how did he get out without leaving tracks? Human beings don't evaporate into thin air."

It was a question Breanna couldn't answer. As she left the copse, she trailed her light behind her. Sure enough, there were her own tracks, even in the grass. The ground was moist here, so close to the creek, and her weight left its imprint.

Coaly ran ahead of her, then halted to bark. She slowed her pace. He was trying to tell her something. Did he know where the man had gone? "What is it, boy?"

Coaly wagged his tail, then struck off for the barn at a dead run. Breanna followed him. When the dog reached the building, he stuck his nose to the ground, sniffing at the foundation.

"Oh, for Pete's sake. I'm people hunting, you silly beast." Coaly responded with another round of wild barking, running the length of the barn, then back again to do a full circle around her. "He isn't in there," she scolded.

As she turned to walk away, Coaly startled her by lifting his nose to the sky and howling. It was such a mournful cry that she paused to look at him. A shiver of dread crept up her spine. She remembered the noises she had heard under the barn floor, recalled the cave-in at the entrance. No flesh and blood person could be in there. But Gramps had seen John Van Patten in the barn.

Supposedly, she reminded herself. *Gramps was an old man, Breanna. His eyes were bad. Get ahold of yourself, and stop this nonsense.*

Flipping off her light to save the batteries, she made a beeline for the cabin. She didn't believe in ghosts, but facts were facts. Someone had come to the creek, stolen her things slashed them and moved them to her porch, walking a hundred and fifty feet without leaving footprints in soft ground. Ghost or man?

She wasn't sure anymore.

Chapter Seven

Breanna sat on the porch with one foot propped on her knee. In the bright morning sunlight, she had pulled out dozens of tiny stickers that had imbedded themselves in her soles as she ran barefoot in the brush. As she plucked the last of them from her skin, she thought of last night. If her wild musings about ghosts were any indication, it was time she took a break and got her mind off her troubles.

"I thought I'd find you hard at work."

She glanced up with a start to see Tyler climbing the steps. "Hi. You're bright and early."

He carried his camera in one hand, strap dangling. "What d'ya have there? Slivers?"

"I made the mistake of walking barefoot in the grass."

Giving her foot a final inspection, she drew on her sock and shoe, deciding then and there to tell Tyler nothing more. She knew what he would say if he heard about her clothes being stolen and slashed. One word. *Leave.* Since she had no intention of doing that, another argument seemed senseless. At the worst, it might be some misguided local with a grudge left over from the Reuben Creek fire. And besides, scare tactics had never hurt anyone.

"You gonna be able to work? Or are your feet too sore?"

She groaned. "It's almost too pretty to work. Today's a day to loaf, don't you think?"

His steel-blue eyes rested on her face. "I agree. Too pretty to work."

Heat sprang to Breanna's cheeks and she glanced away. It was the first time he had even hinted he was attracted to her, except with his jokes about lemonade and lunch, and she felt awkward, uncertain how to respond. "How about panning? Do you enjoy it?"

"For gold? Never done it. Sounds fun, though."

"Then let's do it."

"I'm game."

After Tyler had put his camera on the table and she had shut Coaly in the cabin, she led the way to the barn. She preceded him up the ramp and stepped into the dim corridor. "I spotted the gold pans in here the other day. We'll have to scrub them, but they looked usable."

"Careful," he cautioned. "Walk close to the walls where the floors have more support." He paused with her to look inside a stall. "Wood stain," he commented wryly, stepping into the room to check out the garbage pile. "Pop cans. Ah, here we go, Breanna. Someone dined on beer and Vienna sausage in here."

"Probably a picnic in the hayloft. Kids from town, hiding out from their folks."

He followed her into the next stall and plucked a pan off the shelf after she did, dusting it on his jeans. "Well, are you ready to teach me the ropes?"

"Just don't get gold fever," she warned. "It happens, you know."

"You sound like we might actually find something."

"Sure we will. But it's called getting color."

"Getting color. I'll remember. Won't do, me sounding like a greenhorn when I'm in the company of a pro."

Laughing, she walked toward the door. "I'm no pro. Now, Gran, she was a miner. I swear, she could get color out of a kid's sandbox. It takes me a bit longer."

"Well, I'm looking forward to learning. I've always wanted to pan, but I didn't know where to start."

Turning at the bottom of the ramp, she said, "We start by finding a cache in bedrock. Or a turn in the stream is good, where the water hits the bank and eddies for a bit."

"Why's that?"

As they walked toward the house, she elaborated. "Gold usually washes downstream with erosion, then settles. You've seen hollowed places in bedrock that catch dirt? Well, that's a likely spot for gold. You put some soil in your pan, and slowly wash the dirt out over the edge. The color settles because it's heavier. It takes a knack, but you'll catch on."

THE DAY WITH TYLER WENT peacefully. They knelt together on the rust-red bank, working their gold pans for hours, breaking only for a quick lunch at the house. They conversed infrequently. A companion who shared her love for tranquillity was a new experience for Breanna. Most of her acquaintances either chatted constantly or brought along a transistor radio and drowned out the more beautiful symphonies of the forest.

The lack of conversation between them troubled her, though. Again she was plagued with questions about Tyler, information most people volunteered. She suspected he was from Grants Pass, but he had not yet confirmed that. She knew his name, and that was all. And because he was so closemouthed, she felt reluctant to share information about herself. She had already told him far too much, her suspicions of Dane, her guilt about the fire. Tyler was a quiet man, but this went beyond that. She wondered if he was hiding something.

It seemed a shame. She sensed something special between them, a rare compatibility, but he held back from her, stifling its chance of growth with a curtain of silence.

"This is therapeutic," he said, holding up his glass vial to examine the gold dust he had collected. "How much do these hold?"

"An ounce. When they're filled, you can take them in and get cash." She gave her pan a final swish, then shook her hands, wiping her palms on her jeans. "It may be therapeutic, but this water's so cold, I think it comes off snow."

"Not snow, just good old mountain springs. No water on earth like it, is there?"

"There's nothing on earth to compare to this place. Gran called it God's country and I think she was right. Now that I'm here, I don't know why I waited so long to come back."

"Sometimes, things we run from get bigger and bigger. It's hard to turn back and face them."

"Yes . . . hard." She looked over at him, and their eyes locked. Shadows lurked in his. Something troubled him; she knew it, felt it, heard it in his voice. "Tell me, do you speak from experience? Are you running too, Tyler?"

He lifted an eyebrow. "What gave you that idea?"

She gazed across the creek. "You never say anything about yourself. It's like—well, as if your life started here along the creek and you left everything else behind you."

He laughed. "I don't have any secrets. What do you want to know? I'm thirty-six. My marriage ended in divorce. No kids. And I'm a photographer. I love chocolate, hate liver, and onions don't agree with me, but I eat them anyway because I have very little willpower. Anything else you'd like to know?"

"Where did you grow up?"

"Right over the mountain. You guessed right, I was a Grants Pass kid, graduated from G.P.H.S., played football for the Cavemen. My folks still live there when they aren't vacationing. My dad's retired."

"Well, I guess that's a pretty fair accounting of yourself." She looked into his eyes again. The shadows were still there. She realized he had told her everything—and nothing. "I grew up in Grants Pass, too. But for nine years, we might have gone to school together."

"So you're twenty-seven?" He shook out his gold pan and set it on top of hers, smiling. "Married, divorced? You've never said."

"I was engaged. It didn't work out. My work, you see. It's a little odd, a woman traipsing off into the hills for days on end."

"Not odd, different. No harm in that." He rose and offered her a hand up. "As much as I hate to call it a day, it's about that time. I need to get my camera and do some traipsing of my own. Can't buy the bacon without working now and again."

She tipped her head back. The expression on his face held her spellbound. He reached out and touched her hair, threading his fingers through it. The blue of his eyes clouded with sudden tenderness. Then his hand tightened. He pulled her slowly toward him, stepping to meet her. When his mouth touched hers, his lips feathered so softly they were like butterfly wings, gentle, questioning, experimenting. She felt breathless. There was a rightness between them she had never dreamed could exist.

When he pulled away, Breanna felt a sense of loss she couldn't explain, a feeling of *almost*, as if he had abruptly put an end to something he felt he shouldn't have begun. A troubled frown drew his brows together.

Bending to get the pans, he said, "I've enjoyed today. It's nice being with you."

"Maybe we can do it again sometime."

"I hope so." He smiled and placed his left hand on her shoulder, giving it a squeeze as they walked up the bank. "We'd better build fences first, though. I'll come back in the morning."

"You don't have to, Tyler. I can get them done. I hate to interfere with your work schedule. I know what it's like, free-lancing."

"I want to help. That is, if you don't mind the company."

"Not at all. I'll look forward to it."

After he'd retrieved his camera from the cabin, Tyler struck off through the orchard. Breanna leaned against the retainer wall, watching until he disappeared. Tomorrow seemed an eternity away on the one hand, too soon on the other. Something special was happening between them. And that frightened her. She knew what her secrets were and why she couldn't share them. But what were Tyler's?

TWILIGHT FOUND BREANNA hunched over her typewriter, squinting to see in the dimness of the cabin. When she glanced up at the windows and saw how late it was, she pulled the dustcover over her machine. If she didn't take her walk now, she wouldn't get one before dark.

As she descended the steps, she called Coaly, groaning when the dog appeared from behind the barn, his muzzle caked with red dirt. If he didn't stop his infernal digging under that foundation, he'd end up sprayed by a skunk or bitten by a snake. Breanna scolded him and headed toward the bathing hole, walking aimlessly until she passed the copse. Unable to resist, she made another circle, looking for tracks she might have missed last night.

When nothing caught her eye, she headed downstream. It wasn't until she drew abreast of the orchard that she realized she was hoping she'd find Tyler working. She didn't, of course, but once the thought had entered her mind, she was curious to see his photo blind.

Keeping to the creek bank where she could see, she watched for footprints. Not far from her starting point, she spied disturbed earth. Making a sharp right, she ran up the rocky bank and pushed through the brush. After several feet, she came to a small clearing that offered a perfect view of her upper orchard and barn. A smile settled on her mouth. It was an ideal place to sneak pictures of deer. She saw where Tyler's knees had pressed into the dirt. He had so frequently parted the brush that it was permanently separated. Imagining him here gave her a warm, comfortable feeling.

Turning to leave, she spied a small, black object in the grass. Stooping, she picked it up. It was round and made of plastic with a mesh face, about the size of a quarter. She knew very little about audio equipment, but it looked like a tiny microphone of some kind. Did Tyler take videotapes, accompanied with sound? She slipped the disc into her pocket.

The light was fading fast. She worked her way out of the blind and cut across the orchard. With every step she took, she had the sensation of being watched. She did a complete circle a couple of times to look around her. Dread filled her as she scanned the woods and brush. A film of cold perspiration broke out on her brow, and she quickened her pace.

Halfway through the orchard, she turned toward the mountain where the deserted *California Mine* tunneled for miles into the earth. She could almost see the night sky as it had looked so many years ago, tinted rose red with fire. Her ears echoed with the shrill screams of horror that had haunted her dreams ever since. Taking a deep breath, she closed her eyes for a moment, remembering the fire, Rob Thatcher's torturous death, her own frenzied attempts to save him. So long ago, but it seemed like yesterday.

As she neared the barn, other memories pelted her, memories of her last day here ten years ago when Chuck Morrow had cornered her in the loft. Waves of nausea rolled in her stomach. Images of him flashed before her. Her footsteps slowed. She turned haltingly, her eyes widening with alarm as she stared sightlessly at the barn. Sudden realization hit her. Chuck, with his cocky swagger—the prowler in the white shirt with the muscle-bound walk. Now she knew why she had felt so afraid when she had seen that man. It must have been Chuck Morrow, and on a subconscious level she had recognized him.

Breanna broke into a run.

By the time she let herself in the cabin door and shoved the dead bolt home, she had to find the lantern in the dark. Holding a lit match to the lantern's fragile mantle, she adjusted the white glow, then hung the Coleman on a rafter hook.

"There," she said aloud to her dog. "That's better."

Coaly curled up on the braided rug before the hearth, watching her crouch beside him to light the small fire she had laid earlier in the day. It was a fairly warm evening, but the crackling of the cheerful flames might chase away the gloom that seemed to hover.

She rubbed her forehead, staring at the multicolored twists in the rug beneath her. How like life those intertwined strands were, all knotted and kinked so that nothing looked as though it could ever be put straight again. She hated remembering the fire and the events that followed, but it seemed the longer she stayed here, the more she thought of it. Ten years had brought her full circle.

Stretching out beside Coaly, she reached up to the end table to turn on her transistor radio. Some music in the room might make her feel less alone. A throbbing drumbeat came over the air, sensual and intense. She closed her eyes and slowly relaxed, allowing thoughts of Tyler to slip into her mind.

The radio station's disc jockey broke in on the music. "A quick news update, folks, and then back to the beat. The Josephine County sheriff's department made an official statement today, warning all local merchants to be on the lookout for counterfeit bills. And keep your eyes open. The woman who passed a fake bill yesterday still hasn't been apprehended."

Breanna groaned and sat up to flip off the radio. She wasn't in the mood for news, not right now. She got up and let Coaly out for a run, watching the fire while she waited for him. About five minutes passed. Then she heard the dog barking. She hurried down the entry hall, opening the door. It sounded as if he was out near the barn.

"Coaly!" Breanna stepped onto the porch, listening. "Coaly, come here, boy!"

She had just turned to fetch the flashlight when she heard a sharp yelp. A few moments later, Coaly scurried onto the porch, favoring one hind leg. "Oh, Coaly!" She closed the door after he'd hobbled inside, kneeling to check him. He whined when her fingers grazed his right haunch. "What happened, boy?"

The dog lifted one ear and stared at the door. The hackles rose on his back. Breanna stood and slid the dead bolt home. Walking back up the hall, she studied the paned glass windows. Inky blackness coated the squares. The cloak of night beyond the room was impenetrable. Did the light from the lantern seem bright from out there? Could she be seen?

She shrank back into the shadows. The log walls closed in on her. Her heart thudded like the suspenseful drumbeats in a horror movie. Coaly dragged himself to his feet, still snarling. He limped to the living room, glaring at the end windows. There was someone out there. She knew her dog. He didn't react like this to other animals.

After several minutes, Coaly finally relaxed. His limp seemed less pronounced, too. Breanna ran her hands over him again, anger welling inside her when he flinched. Kicked, surely, or hit with something blunt. She couldn't feel any punctures on his skin. Smoothing his soot-black fur, she rested her cheek atop his head for a moment.

"Sleep won't come easy tonight," she whispered, giving him a pat. "But I suppose we should turn in."

She turned off the lantern, waiting for it to sputter out so she could see the yard. Nothing moved. Going to the bedroom, she undressed in the darkness, groping for her nightgown. Tugging it on, she folded back her bedding and slid between the cool sheets. Lying on her side, she watched the windowpanes above her, uncomfortably aware of the fragility of the glass partition. What if she slept too soundly? What if Coaly didn't hear the soft fall of footsteps if someone approached the house? What if, before she could react to the noise, a hand shattered the glass and reached in?

TYLER REACHED FOR A SANDWICH. He took a large bite and chewed slowly, watching Jack examine the twenty-dollar bill from Breanna's purse.

"There's no question," Jack finally agreed.

"So what's our next move? Can I get her the hell out of there?"

"Nope."

"Why? You said get proof, and I got it, dammit. What more do you want? Blood? Hers, to be specific?"

Jack strode to the kitchen, pouring himself a mug of coffee. "Tyler, I've got new information on her."

"What?"

"She passed some bad stuff in town yesterday."

Tyler tossed the remainder of his sandwich on his saucer. "Come again?"

"You heard me. She passed a bad twenty when you two were in town yesterday." Jack turned, leaning his hips against the counter. "It's a positive ID. The clerk described her and the Honda."

"It's a mistake!" Tyler leaped up from his chair. "It has to be."

"No mistake. I'm sorry, old friend." Jack gazed into his cup for a moment, then shook his head. "You know, Tyler, it's possible she's been coerced. If it could happen to Van Patten, it could happen to her. I'm not saying she's not a nice gal, just that she's in one helluva situation. If she turns federal witness, we can get her off with a light sentence."

Tyler walked to the window, staring out at nothing. "I tell you, Jack, she's not involved. I don't know how she got hold of another counterfeit bill, but she's not involved."

Silence settled in the room. Jack scuffed the floor with the heel of his boot. "I wish I could be sure of that." After a moment, he looked up. "You fallin' for her?"

"No." The denial came fast, the truth more slowly. Tyler sighed. "Oh, hell, I don't know. What's love?" He laughed and shook his head. "I like her. We're friends, we have a lot in common. And I sure don't want her hurt."

"Friends," Jack said with a snort. "Sounds like a terminal case to me."

"Yeah, well, you're a century behind. Nowadays, men and women *can* be friends."

"We can't tip her off. You do understand that?"

"Yes, I understand, Jack. I don't like it, I think you're wrong, but I understand."

"If she isn't tied in with them..." Jack sighed, the sound heavy, tired. "My advice to you is to convince her to leave, without compromising our position."

"I've tried that."

"Give it another shot. Morrow's an odd one, unpredictable. I believe he could be violent. If she's innocent and steps on his toes, she could be in trouble.

Chapter Eight

When Breanna opened the door the next morning to let Coaly out for a run, she saw a piece of meat lying on the ground next to the porch. She gaped at it for a long while, holding Coaly back so he wouldn't try to eat it. Gingerly she lifted the meat between two fingers. A fine white powder coated the blood-red grain.

Afraid to let her pet wander the yard alone in case there were other pieces, she followed him closely, growing angrier with every step. Unless she missed her guess, this meat was poisoned. And it had been left by the porch for her dog.

Calling Coaly back to the cabin, Breanna shut him inside with her, then stepped to the nearest window to examine the meat in a stream of sunlight. White granules. She took a sniff. The trace of sweetness seemed vaguely familiar. A loud knock on her front door startled her.

"Who is it?"

"Your favorite fence builder. Who else?"

She let out her breath in a shaky sigh. Of course, it was Tyler. Who else would it be? "Come on in. It's not locked."

She heard the door being dragged inward, then the thunk of his boots as he stomped them clean on the entry rug.

He walked into the living room, holding up her lavender bikini underwear, his face alight with laughter. "For some reason I thought of you the moment I got dressed this morning, and I haven't been able to get you off my mind since." His smile faded. "My God, what's wrong? You're white as a sheet."

She held up the meat. "I just found this on the porch. There's a white film on it, Tyler, and I think it might be poison."

He strode toward her, tossing her lacy underwear toward the sofa. Snatching the piece of steak from her, he stepped to the window to examine it. "Wash your hands. Do you have any plastic wrap?"

Breanna indicated a drawer and ran to the sink, pumping on the rusty handle. Water spewed into the washbasin she held under the spout. "What is it? Will it go through the skin?"

Tyler took a smell. "White arsenic."

"Arsenic? Are you sure?"

"Not positive. It's mixed in with something else. I'm not sure what, but it smells like powdered milk."

"Powdered milk, of course! I knew I recognized it. Tyler, arsenic would kill Coaly. Someone tried to poison him."

Tyler scrutinized the dog. "As little as six one-hundredths of a gram can be fatal for a person, so, yes, if he ate all this, it would probably kill him. Are you sure he didn't get any?"

Breanna couldn't help wondering how he knew so much about arsenic. "Yes, I'm sure." Drying her hands, she tried to smother the fear rising in her. "Tyler, why would anyone want to kill my dog?"

He opened her drawer and pulled out a sandwich bag, depositing the meat in it and running his fingers along the zip-lock seal. "God, I don't know." Stepping past her to the sink, he pumped more water to scrub his hands, then took the towel she held out to him. "I'm going out to check the property, just to make sure there's nothing else out there."

She swept her hair back from her face. "I'll put some coffee on and get dressed."

Tyler spun on his heel and left the cabin without a backward glance. Once outside, he let loose a string of low curses. If he could have gotten his hands on the people responsible at that moment, he would have strangled them. As he walked around the yard, his anger turned to fear. They were growing desperate to get Breanna out of the way. What they might do next was anybody's guess. He had to convince her to leave. Fast. And he was forced to do it without telling her why.

BY THE TIME BREANNA had finished dressing, Tyler was sitting on the lawn, basking in the morning sunlight. She poured them each a mug of coffee and went to join him. For a long while he said nothing, just stared at the road with a scowl on his face. She studied each separate angle of his features. The blade of nose jutting from his thick brows already seemed familiar to her. When he smiled, she knew exactly how his lips would quirk up at one corner in that lopsided grin of his. But for all that, she had no more idea what he was thinking than when she'd first met him.

"Breanna, I think you should leave here," he said at last, glancing over at her. "I know you hate to go, but it really would be best. Surely you see that."

"But—" She shook her head. "I can't leave."

"That's poison on that meat in there." He leveled steely eyes on her. "Somebody just tried to kill your dog. It's not safe for you to stay here."

She set her mug on the grass and hugged her knees, gazing at the undergrowth on Hungry Hill. "Tyler...I can't leave. Try to understand. Maybe from your viewpoint it looks foolish, but from mine there's no choice. When my grandmother was dying I promised her I'd come here, and I promised her I'd stay.''

"What kind of a grandmother would ask that?"

Sudden, white-hot anger surged through Breanna. "What does that crack mean?"

"Exactly what it sounded like. Deathbed promises! They're the worst kind of blackmail, manipulating a person from the edge of the grave. She would never have wanted you to stay here at the risk of your safety, not if she was any kind of grandmother.''

"My safety isn't in question here. The threat was to Coaly.''

"Oh, and he's expendable?"

"No, he's not expendable. What's your problem? You've no right to talk to me this way.''

"Oh, I don't? Maybe I care what happens to you. Maybe I'm making it my right.''

"Is that so?"

"Yes, that's so.''

She dug her nails into her knees and refused to look at him. "I'll take care of Coaly. I'll watch him.''

"End of problem? That doesn't take care of the who. Somebody's getting nasty, real nasty. What will they do next? You think you're pretty tough right now, but what happens when the next threat's to you?"

Before she thought, she said, "There's already been a threat to me. You don't see me running, do you?"

The ensuing silence was so frigid that she felt certain a loud noise would shatter it.

"What kind of threat?"

"Nothing. It wasn't important.''

"Breanna, what kind of threat?"

"Nothing! You don't have to know every little thing.''

"Maybe I want to.''

"And that's your problem, Mr. Ross, not mine."

He bounded to his feet, slopping hot coffee down his leg. She saw him flinch. The denim of his jeans was soaked and steaming.

"Are you burned?" she asked anxiously.

"I'm burned, all right," he replied in a clipped tone. "I want to know what happened. Are you going to tell me? There's no crime in caring what happens to you."

"Oh, Tyler, it's not that. It's just—well, if I tell you, it'll make you all the more upset."

"So, upset me."

"It was nothing, really...."

"Bree-aann-aa?"

"Well, it really wasn't. I went down to take a bath and somebody stole my clothes."

"And? Don't stop. I can see in your eyes there's more."

"Well, when I made it back to the—"

"Made it back?"

"Well, yes, I was naked. It wasn't easy, especially without shoes."

He knelt again, being more careful of his coffee this time. "The stickers, ah yes, I remember. So you ran up to the house in your altogether?" A glint entered his eyes. "What else?"

"Well—um—when I got up here, my clothes were on the porch." In a much lower voice she added, "Slashed."

"What?"

"Slashed," she repeated, a bit more loudly.

"Slashed? With a knife, you mean?" He was talking a little more loudly, too, she noticed. Almost yelling. "Let me get this straight. You were in the creek naked. Someone stole your clothes, slashed them with a knife and left them on your porch?"

"Of course I was naked. You don't take baths with your clothes on."

"You are being deliberately obtuse. I can't believe something like that happened and you never told me about it! My God, don't you realize—? Breanna, it could have been *you* someone took a knife to! Why the hell didn't you tell?"

"I didn't tell you about it because I knew you'd act just like you're acting." She stood and glared down at him. "It gives you more ammunition to convince me I should leave. Well, I'm not. This is my land, and nobody, not you or anybody else, is going to run me off it."

With that, she stormed off to the house. Tyler stared after her for a moment, then sat down on the lawn, so angry with himself that he could have screamed. While he sat there, he did his best to calm down. From her viewpoint, things weren't nearly as serious as they were from his. She knew nothing of the counterfeiting. Given that fact, he could understand her thinking. He could also see why she was angry. Just who did he think he was? He had no business pushing her around, no business preaching to her, no business caring the way he cared...."

He clenched his teeth. As Jack would say, he had a job to do. And he was dangerously close to losing all objectivity. He was spouting off, losing control, forgetting who he was and what she might be.

She wasn't leaving. Not that it was any big surprise. His only option now was to try to protect her. To do that, he needed to be with her. And to be with her, he had to make up with her. A humorless grin twisted his mouth.

When Tyler knocked on the door, Breanna was seated at the table braiding her hair. As she twisted it atop her head, she called "Come in!" through the hairpins she clenched between her teeth. She liked the effect, sort of a hiss.

He walked to the end of the hall, resting his shoulder against the logs. "I'd like to apologize."

She pulled one hairpin from her teeth, jammed it in her hair and slurred, "I'm listening."

"I'm sorry for sounding off. I shouldn't have. It's just that I—well, I'm worried, that's all, about what might happen."

Taking the last hairpin out of her mouth, she finished fastening her braid. "Just as long as it's clear. I'm not leaving."

"Believe me, you made it perfectly clear."

"You won't pick at me about it anymore?"

"I don't promise that. But I won't pick at you anymore over this."

She said nothing.

"Look. How about dinner out tonight? A peace offering. Do you accept?" Coaly sat between them, tail wagging, eyes darting to each of them as they spoke. Tyler glanced down at him. "You can't disappoint him. Think how he'd miss me if you stay mad forever."

She smiled. The truth was she would miss Tyler, too. "Dinner sounds nice. One thing, though. Don't say anything derogatory about my gran again. You can say a lot of things, but never about my gran."

"Is that what got you so boiled?"

She shrugged one shoulder. "It was what started it. And once I get started, I sort of escalate. I'm sorry. I guess I overreacted."

"I didn't intend to slam your grandmother. I just think if she were here, she'd be telling you to leave, too. I'm sure she never meant to lock you into an impossible situation."

Breanna shot him a warning glare.

"And I'm equally sure she was a wonderful person," he added quickly.

"Yes, she was. The best grandmother ever."

"Not the best. *Mine* was the best." His eyes began to twinkle. "Truce? How's eight o'clock sound? We'll go to the Wolf Creek Tavern. Over dinner, maybe we can plan some kind of strategy to put a stop to this nonsense."

"That sounds a whole lot more acceptable to me than chucking everything and running."

"Somehow I kinda figured that." He leaned around the corner and lifted the plastic bag of meat from the counter. "I have a friend who can analyze this. I think I'll get it checked."

"You have a friend who analyzes poisons?"

"Yeah, a chemistry teacher at the high school. I grew up with him. See you at eight, then?"

She nodded. "I'll be ready."

Just before the door closed, he called, "Keep close tabs on Coaly in case I missed something out here."

CLOSE TABS, BREANNA DISCOVERED, meant keeping Coaly locked in the house with her while she worked. His whining nearly drove her mad, but she toughed it out, typing, dabbing white ink over her mistakes and muttering. By eleven her nerves were jagged. When she heard someone pull into the driveway, she gave such a start that she jumped up and bruised her knee on the edge of the table. Limping to the window, she looked out. A blue Ford pickup sat beside her Honda, and she glimpsed a man climbing the retainer wall steps. A moment later, a knock came on the door.

Breanna stepped into the entry hall. For a moment, she considered calling out before she opened up, but that seemed so timid that she discarded the idea and turned the knob. She had no sooner done so than she wished she had erred on the side of caution.

Chuck Morrow stood on her porch. Ten years had turned
him to fat around the middle, but otherwise he seemed un-
changed. His deadpan brown eyes slid over her. He smiled
the same sneering smile. And, as before, he managed to
make her feel violated just by looking at her. Breanna's
stomach lurched.

"What do you want?" she asked.

Her heart leaped when he put a boot on her threshold and
braced a shoulder against the jamb. Instinctively she stepped
back, wedging herself between the door and the wall to keep
Coaly in the house.

"I just came to chat." He spoke barely above a whisper,
his tone low and suggestive.

She tightened her hold on the knob. "Get lost, Chuck."

"Forget that. It's time we got down to business. Dane tells
me you've been snoopin', reading all the old news stories
about the fire. That true?"

"What's it to you?"

"The way I see it, you know all you need to know. I put
my neck on the chopping block for you, lied for you. I don't
like it too good, you coming back and rehashing everything
now. The way I see it, if you screw around and get yourself
arrested again for that arson, I'll be sent up as an accom-
plice. That would make me mad. And you don't want to
make me mad."

Breanna looked him straight in the eye. She knew he was
trying to frighten her, bully her, the way he had before. That
was Chuck's style. He tried to control people, using their
fears as leverage. It had worked ten years ago. He was hoping she'd react the same way now, either by leaving or ac-
quiescing to his demands. But she wasn't a kid anymore. She
was a woman who could see Chuck Morrow for the lowlife
he really was.

"To be quite frank, I don't care one way or another if you're mad, Chuck."

"You better care, missy. You owe me. Maybe I'm here to collect."

Anger tightened her throat. "I beg your pardon?"

"If I was to go to the police, even now, and tell them you weren't with me that night, that only Dane was, why you'd be in jail so fast your head'd spin. Way I see it, you wouldn't like that, being locked up. I'm doin' you a big favor. Seems like you'd treat me nice and make it worth my while. Some excitement a couple of times a week, maybe, a little TLC. Keep me happy, make me feel appreciated for puttin' myself out for you."

Breanna tipped her head toward him. "So it's excitement you want, huh? Why, Chuck, you've come to the right lady for that. I'll give you more than you ever dreamed."

She leaned a little closer, winked coyly, and opened the door for Coaly. The dog cannoned out of the door like a bean from a slingshot, snarling viciously. Breanna nabbed him by the collar just in the nick of time, halting his forward thrust. Chuck sprang backward, his attention riveted on the dog. "Is that exciting enough for you, Chuck, or would you like more?"

It gave her no end of satisfaction to see the man scramble to get away from her. "You're crazy. You're a crazy woman!"

"More woman than you can handle, that's for sure. Now you get your slimy little carcass off my place! Is that clear? And don't come back. You do, and I'll let Coaly loose next time."

"That damned dog's a hazard, that's what," he muttered, staring at Coaly. "I thought he was dead. He *will* be. That's a promise you can bank on, sister." He staggered down the steps, jabbing a finger at her. "Sic him on me and I'll shoot the little monster."

Chuck leaped into his truck, gunned the motor and reversed up the drive. A cloud of red dust rose in his wake. Breanna sank onto the porch. Her legs felt like half-set Jell-O.

She stroked Coaly's head, looking into his eyes. A sweeter, gentler dog there never was, yet in the last week she had seen him launch three vicious attacks. He had always been protective. He had always been a growler. But, contrary to what she had told Tyler at first, he had never bitten anyone before coming here. Now, all of a sudden, he had turned mean. There had to be a reason. Could he sense danger here that she couldn't?

Adding up all the facts, she had very little to go on, but it was enough. She had seen Chuck on her property late at night. He had by his own admission been speaking to Dane. And, as he left just now, he had muttered that he thought Coaly was dead. Like it or not, she had to face it; Chuck Morrow was at the root of her troubles.

And she knew from experience that any trouble Chuck Morrow stirred up was bound to be ugly.

Chapter Nine

At five-thirty, Breanna headed for the creek to wash her hair before her date with Tyler. After her last bath, she felt too nervous for anything more than a quick shampoo. This time if anyone crept up on her, she would be fully dressed and able to run.

As she worked her way through the brush, she heard Coaly yelping back at the cabin. She would have liked to bring him along, but it was too risky. Finding the poisoned meat this morning, and hearing Chuck's threats since then, she didn't want him wandering while she wasn't watching.

Kneeling on the diving rock, she unfastened her braid. Her reflection shimmered on the surface of the water, and she turned her face to see it at a different angle. Her blue silk dress would do nicely for dinner, she decided. Her strand of pearls and white heels would—

Her heart leaped into her throat. A face shimmered beside hers on the water. Not a human face, though. The other reflection was straight out of a child's nightmare, black, featureless, with great, gaping holes where the eyes should have been.

For a moment fear paralyzed her. She couldn't move, couldn't scream. By the time she'd collected her wits, it was too late. A hand slammed into her back, launching her headfirst into the water. The blackness of the bathing hole surrounded her. Water seared her throat; burned into her lungs. She flailed her arms, clawing for the glow of sunlight above her.

Breaking the surface, she thrashed about, aiming for the rock, but her attacker still stood upon it, one arm extended toward her, a scythe clutched in his hand. She stared at the long, curved blade, at the gleam of its sharp edge. The man's intention was clear; if she left the water, he meant to kill her.

It *was* a man. Even as she struggled for air, she realized the face she had seen had been human, after all, disguised in a black ski mask. He wore a black overcoat to conceal his body build. She stared up at him. Who was he? And why was he doing this?

The weight of her clothes and shoes was dragging her down. Breanna kicked frantically, making figure eights with her arms to stay afloat. She knew she couldn't stay in the deep pool long. If the cold didn't overcome her, exhaustion would. The man strode along the diving rock back to shore, then stepped into the copse. He had no sooner disappeared into the trees than Breanna swam toward the opposite bank. She could find a handhold in the tree roots and escape into the woods.

She had only moved a few feet toward the bank when a rock splashed beside her. Glancing back over her shoulder, she saw the man had emerged again. He stood at the water's edge, his arm drawn back, the scythe a gleaming arc over his head. He didn't speak, but the threat was clear. If she went anywhere near the far bank, he would come after her.

She was trapped.

The man stepped back into the brush, but she could still see his silhouette. He stood there, watching, waiting. Her blood thrummed in her temples. Even in the freezing water, she could feel sweat break out on her brow. The current tugged at her legs. She fought to keep her chin up, paddling backward, praying her toes would touch bottom. The man leaped from the brush, moving to aim the scythe at her. He wanted her in deep water? She took a mouthful, choking, fighting to get her chin high. Oh, God, he wanted her to drown!

Could he hit her? The stream wasn't that wide. He wouldn't have to throw the scythe far. She imagined the blade sinking into her skull, imagined dying there in the bathing pool where she had played as a child. As long as she stayed in the center of the stream, he didn't threaten her. As terrifying as drowning was, Breanna preferred that to being gaffed like a fish. Again the man stepped back into the copse, barely visible.

He waited like a sentinel standing guard. She realized he was going to wait until she sank....

Stay calm, she thought. "Who are you? What do you want?"

No answer. She trod water, her chin bobbing against the ripples. Her shoes felt like lead weights on her feet, heavier and heavier with each kick. Exhaustion was setting in quickly and still the man stood there. She began to feel cold. *Oh, God, so cold.* It seemed to her that hours passed. She knew she had to find something to hold on to soon to keep from sinking. But she couldn't. The man's profile was clearly visible against the patches of light behind him, a black hulk, staring, not moving.

Shudders began to rack her. Spasms followed. Then after a while, even that passed. Numbness settled in. Her arms and legs felt like stiff rubber.

As dusk settled over the mountains, she panicked. "Go away!" she pleaded. "Go away, whoever you are! Go away, do you hear?"

She couldn't be sure, but she thought she heard low laughter. Why? Who could hate her so much that he would enjoy seeing her die?

Later, when the sky had lost nearly all its light, Breanna heard footsteps approaching in the brush. A low creaking noise drifted toward her.

"Bree? Yo? You down here?" Tyler's familiar voice boomed, ricocheting back and forth along the creek. Nothing had ever sounded quite so good to her. "Bree? You down here?"

"Tyler?" Her voice came out in a wail. "I'm in the creek."

He emerged from the tangle of undergrowth, becoming recognizable as he drew nearer. Neatly pleated gray slacks, a white shirt, a tweed jacket. Breanna sobbed and wind-milled her numb arms, swimming clumsily forward against the current.

"Breanna, what the hell?"

"Watch out! Behind you! He's behind you!" Her feet scraped bottom, and she staggered toward him. "He's got a scythe, Tyler."

Whirling, Tyler crouched to defend himself and the woman behind him. No one was there. He relaxed slightly, then Breanna's sobs reclaimed his attention. He turned to look at her. What he saw scared him. Her face had a blue cast to it. Her lips were purple. But what concerned him most was that she wasn't shivering. Her body temperature must be dangerously low.

"He's in there. He'll kill us."

She ended the sentence with a low whimper and fell sideways in the stream, too weak to stand. He swore under his breath and waded out to her, lifting her to carry her to shore. Water cascaded from her clothes, soaking him from the chest down. Shifting her slightly, he shrugged out of his jacket and wrapped it around her. "It's all right. If someone was there, he's gone, sweetheart. Damn, you're like ice. How long have you been in here?"

Breanna tried to hug his neck, but her arms were dead-weights. She pressed her cheek to his shoulder, so glad for his warmth that she began to cry.

"He came—behind me—out of nowhere, pushed me in. Wouldn't let me out. I was getting so tired."

"My God!" he whispered, pressing a wonderfully hot mouth to her forehead. "I'll kill the bastards for this."

Breanna shrank as close to him as she could get. She was so exhausted, so cold. Knowing he was there, that she was safe, seemed like a miracle. And she *was* safe with Tyler. Just the way he held her told her that.

He carried her to the cabin and shouldered his way through the door, heading directly for the bedroom. Pushing the doorway curtain aside, he stepped in and lowered her feet to the floor, holding her by her arms for a moment to be sure she could stand. There were towels folded on the open shelving. He grabbed one and began peeling her clothes off of her.

Breanna felt no trace of embarrassment, only relief. Limp relief. Her awareness centered on him—the deft touch of his hands, the warmth of them against her skin, the solid wall of his chest holding her upright. She was barely conscious of her nakedness as he dropped her shirt to the floor. Next, he tugged her jeans over her hips, set her on the bed and peeled them down her legs, taking her shoes off with them.

"I thought I was going to die."

He lifted her to her feet again, rubbing her briskly with the towel, taking care not to touch the manzanita scratches on her back. In the dusky light she could see the worry in his eyes. "The main thing is to get you warm. Did he hurt you?"

"N-no."

"How long were you in there?"

"T-two hours, I th-think."

"I swear to God, if I ever get my hands on the creep, I'll kill him."

"T-Ty... I—I'm s-so c-cold."

"There, you're halfway dry, at least." He lifted the bed covers to deposit her beneath them. "I'll go light a fire."

While he was gone, Breanna huddled between the sheets and longed for his warm arms. She was shaking convulsively now. She heard the clatter of kindling and the rustle of paper, then a soft whoosh of flame when Tyler struck a match to it. Amber patterns of light danced on the doorway curtain. He returned to the room, rifling through her stacks of clothing on the shelves until he found one of her flannel nightgowns.

"My l-logger socks. Th-there on the bottom shelf, the g-gray ones with r-red tops. My feet are so cold I can't f-feel them."

"Honey, don't try to talk." He stepped toward her with the gown. "Sit up and I'll get this over your head."

She held the sheet to her breasts, releasing it with one hand while she shoved an arm down each sleeve. That alone was quite a feat, considering how badly she was shaking. The soft flannel felt dry and warm. Tyler pulled one of her feet at a time from beneath the covers, slipping the socks over her toes.

"Oh, Tyler, I'm s-so c-cold, so h-horribly c-cold."

Huddling on her side, she cinched her arms around herself, clinging to what little heat she had left. Tyler's shoes thunked on the floor, and she heard the change jangling in his slacks as he pulled them off. He untucked the other pillow and threw back the covers. She felt the mattress sink with his weight.

"Come here, sweetheart."

Breanna tried to speak, but the moment she did, her teeth clacked. He drew her head to the hollow of his shoulder. Both his arms encircled her, one around her back so that he could rub her side, the other over her hip to massage the backs of her thighs. She rolled toward him, desperate for his heat.

"You're chilled clear to the bone. It's lucky I came when I did. I can feel the cold coming clear through your gown."

Breanna had given up talking.

"Much longer and..." She felt a tenseness sweep through him. "The shaking's a good sign," he whispered. "Your body's trying to warm itself. Damn, Bree, you're so cold it's scary. Hypothermia is no joke. You don't feel numb anywhere besides your feet, do you?"

"Y-yes." Her teeth immediately chattered and she clenched them shut again.

"Where, Breanna? Your legs? Your arms?"

It took an effort to nod.

Tyler swore under his breath and sat bolt upright, flipping around onto his knees. His hands dived under the covers to strip off her socks, then he clutched the hem of her nightgown. Her eyes flew open when he slid the cloth up her body.

"No arguments," he muttered. "It's coming off."

He seized her by the shoulders, sat her up and tugged the gown over her head, tossing it aside. When he lay down again, the shock of his hot skin against her cold breasts made her breath catch. His arms encircled her. It seemed to her his hands were everywhere, rubbing her buttocks, the backs of her thighs, her shoulders, rubbing so hard, so vigorously that her skin burned.

"T-T-Ty-ler!" she protested.

"Hush," he whispered, draping one of his legs over hers to run his foot up and down her calf. "It's okay, it's okay."

"B-but it h-hurts. It b-burns."

"I know. It'll stop after a while. Ssh, sweetheart. Just get close so I can get you warm."

Breanna turned her face into the curve of his neck, breathing in the musky, steamy heat of his skin. *Tyler.* She drifted, sinking ever deeper into the swirling heat that radiated from him. And without realizing it, without knowing exactly when, she finally stopped shaking and slept.

MUCH LATER, SHE WOKE, blinking in confusion, her face pressed so snugly into the hollow of Tyler's shoulder that her lashes fluttered against his skin. Her lips had parted in slumber and when she explored with the tip of her tongue, she tasted saltiness. *Tyler's chest.* Her mind cleared and she stiffened. *God, he's wrapped around me like a sarong.*

"Don't panic. We've been like this for hours." His breath was warm on the top of her head, his lips feathering against her hair. "You've been snoring like a little buzz saw."

She lifted her chin. "I don't snore."

He laughed and rolled with her, coming up on one elbow, his broad chest canopied over hers. "You most certainly do, Miss Morgan. But it's a very appealing snore."

Breanna swallowed and her larynx plunked in the base of her throat like a pebble hitting a still pool of water. Every fractional inch of movement, hers or his, stimulated her nipples. The muscle in Tyler's jaw ticked. She could see it going a mile a minute in the silver moonlight, a shadow, then gone. His eyes met hers, shimmering pools of gray.

"Feeling better?"

"Yes," she replied in a strained whisper.

"Is all the numbness gone?"

"Yes."

He smoothed her hair from her cheek, his touch so light, so slow that she was sure her heart stopped beating for a second. And it seemed to her that his face had drawn closer.

"I was so scared," he whispered. "So scared. I've never felt so..." His face tightened, his gaze delving into hers. A long silence followed, wrapping around them like a warm cocoon. "Bree?"

"Yes?"

Gazing up at his dark countenance, at the now-familiar line of his jaw and his squared chin, Breanna knew what he was asking. Her reply was to touch his cheek, trailing her fingers to his mouth. For a long moment they looked into each other's eyes. Then he lowered his head, brushing her lips with his.

An indescribable sweetness unfurled inside Breanna. It was too late to ask herself questions. Perhaps her narrow escape from death was making her reckless. Maybe it was waking in his arms, feeling his body pressed against hers. All she knew was that she needed him. For now, there was only the moonlight—and Tyler.

He came to her as if in a dream. A slow, languorous dream that slowly built in intensity. Their bodies melded as if they had been made for each other. No shyness, no awkwardness, no sense of strangeness. Only an indescribable pleasure that lifted them on its swells to higher and higher peaks. Joined with him, she felt a sense of completeness she had never experienced before.

Afterward, he held her, stroking her hair, pressing gentle kisses to her forehead. She relaxed against him, feeling blissfully content. The way he touched her made her feel treasured, and that, more than anything he could have said, told her that what had happened between them was as special to him as it was to her.

He curled around her and slept, his dark face buried in the drapery of her hair upon the pillow. She ran light fingers down the length of his muscular arm. His name whispered like a lullaby in her mind until she fell asleep.

WHEN BREANNA WOKE AGAIN, Tyler was no longer beside her. It was still dark beyond the window, but the doorway curtain danced with golden firelight. The inviting crackle of burning logs enticed her from the bed. She found her nightgown and logger socks, slipped them on, then tiptoed to the curtain, lifting it to peek out.

Tyler sat before the hearth, one arm resting loosely on an upraised knee. He wore only his slacks, and the dancing amber of the firelight burnished his skin to bronze. Sensing her presence, he glanced around and lifted an arm to beckon her to his side. Breanna needed no further invitation. When she lowered herself to the rug, he cuddled her close, tracing circles on her arm through her flannel sleeve.

"I've been sitting here daydreaming about murder," he told her with a low laugh. "I wish I could have caught that son of a bitch."

"Didn't you see him?" she squeaked. "He had to have left right when you showed up."

"No, I didn't see a soul. Of course, I wasn't looking for anyone except you on the way down. Which direction did he come from? Do you know?"

"He came up behind me and pushed me in."

"Can you identify him?"

"No, he was wearing a black ski mask and overcoat." Catching her lower lip between her teeth, she stared into the fire. "I can't be sure who it was."

"Something's troubling you. What? This is no time to keep secrets, Bree."

She lifted her face. His hovered a scant inch away, cast into shadow by the firelight. For the first time since she had known him, his eyes didn't have that shuttered look. They ached with readable emotion, his fear for her underscoring all else.

"It's just that—" Breaking off, she sighed, took a bracing breath and averted her gaze so she needn't look at him. "Chuck Morrow paid me a visit today. He was rather unpleasant and I can't help but wonder..."

"If it could have been him? My God, Bree, why would he—?"

"Ten years ago, we had a very similar conversation and I ran away. I think he hoped the same tactics would work again."

"What kind of tactics?"

She leaned against his warmth, drawing strength from him. His arms crisscrossed around her. He rubbed her skin through the sleeves of her gown, massaging her, patting her, his every touch a comfort. "Remember, I told you Chuck came around asking favors? Of Dane? Well, he made demands on me, too. He tried to make me sleep with him. He said he'd tell the police the truth if I didn't do it."

"Oh, damn," Tyler moaned, "that rotten bastard."

"I—I was so scared by then that I went clear up into the loft with him. Dane begged me to do whatever he said. And then he threatened me if I didn't. He was more terrified of Chuck than I was."

"How did Dane threaten you?"

"He said they'd tell the police *I* set the blaze."

"And what did you do?" His hands clenched on her arm. "Up in the loft, Bree. With Morrow?"

The memories flashed in Breanna's mind, ugly, horribly real, as clear as yesterday. "I couldn't bear for him to touch me. He kissed me... pushed his tongue in my mouth. I'd never been kissed like that before."

"Of course you hadn't."

"It made me feel sick. I realized, almost too late, that jail would be preferable to having his hands on me and I ran."

Tyler lifted a hand to her hair, stroking it. "What kind of man would use leverage like that on a young girl?" His whisper was ragged. "Ah, Breanna, no wonder you ran from the memories for so many years. Who would blame you?"

"Dane," she whispered. "We were never friends again. I couldn't forgive him for standing down at the door of the barn, watching to be sure Gramps didn't come. He didn't care about me, Tyler, or about Rob. All he cared about was himself."

Silence fell over them for a moment, then he said, "I have a feeling Dane has paid dearly for hurting you, Bree."

"How has Dane paid? The only thing he lost was my friendship and I don't think he misses it. Dane has everything, fancy clothes, an expensive car, a beautiful home and family."

"If Morrow tried to blackmail you, don't you suppose he's asked similar favors of Dane over the years?"

The thought made her shiver. Knowing how low Chuck Morrow could stoop, it was entirely possible. "What kind of favors, though? What could Dane give him that he would want?"

A tense silence followed. "Who knows?" Tyler replied. "I just have a feeling. How was that fire set? I know I read about it, but I can't recall."

"Cans of gas, stashed in the brush around the hippie commune. Someone put a dynamite cap over the mouth of one, set the fuse and ran. When the fumes in the one can exploded, the resulting fire set off the others."

"A person would need a permit to get a dynamite cap."

"Not if you were the grandson of a retired miner."

"You really believe Dane did it, don't you?"

A faint memory invaded Breanna's mind. *Gas.* She had a vague recollection of driving to town with Dane in Gramps's Jeep, filling the back with red cans. The muscles in her stomach tightened. When had they done that?

She pressed closer to Tyler, suddenly cold. "Oh, Tyler, I don't know. Dane was a good kid. Not mean. He might have set a little fire...as a prank...but I can't imagine him trying to light the whole mountain. He knew how tinder-dry the woods got."

"You may never know the truth," he told her. "Morrow—he didn't hurt you when he came this time?"

"No, I handled him. I don't expect him back anytime soon."

Quiet settled over them, the minutes passing, the warmth of the fire and Tyler's presence soothing her. Breanna stared at the orange embers. *The gas.* Why couldn't she remember? Had it been for Gramps, for Chuck Morrow? Was it the gas used to set the Reuben Creek blaze? Her head began aching again. She had to find out, she had to. The only way to do that was to arrange a meeting with Dane and ask him flat out. Even if he wouldn't tell her, she knew him well enough to read him. If the questions scared him, then she'd know....

"Bree, don't get angry." Tyler's hand tensed, pressing hard against her arm. "I have to say it one more time. *Leave.* Go stay in town, at least for a while. Please. You could have been seriously hurt tonight. Let me drive you to town, your parents' place...anywhere."

"Oh, Tyler. I know you're right. And I'm scared, really scared. But now it's even more important than before that I stand my ground. Don't you see? I ran before. I've lived with it for ten years, never escaping it. If I don't see it through this time, I'll be running from the truth for the rest of my life. Try to understand."

"I do understand. I hate to admit it, but if it were me, I'd stay, too." He sighed. "Okay, lady. You want to stand your ground and fight back? I just volunteered for the infantry."

She smiled. "What does that mean?"

"It means you have a new roommate. Mind? No more baths alone, no more staying alone here nights."

"I *should* say thanks but no thanks. It's an awful imposition on you."

"What are friends for? Besides, you couldn't pry me away from here with a crowbar, not after tonight. I say we check out that brush by the creek come daylight, find out where our friendly scythe carrier came from. Seems like the first move to make. Agreed?"

"Agreed. Oh, Tyler, I'm glad you're here."

His mouth moved next to her ear, whisper light. "Me, too."

She tipped her head back to look at him. "You know, there is another possibility we haven't considered. Last night by the creek it could have been the ghost."

"Old John, guarding his treasure? Come on, Bree, you're just upset, strung out. You can't believe that."

"What if he did find the mother lode?" she whispered. "Is it so farfetched?"

"Honey..."

"I know I'm upset. It did frighten me. It's just that he seemed to come out of nowhere and disappear the same way. You didn't see him, did you?"

"No, but there's so much brush, you can hide quite easily. Remember the evening I met you? I was right at the edge of the property and you couldn't see me. Tell you what. We'll save the ghost theory as a last resort, until after we check the brush. I'm fairly sure we'll find evidence that your friend was a real live creep, not a dead one."

Breanna hoped he was right.

Chapter Ten

Daylight found Breanna and Tyler circling the copse. Tyler walked from the brush to the diving rock, studying the footprints, his face creased in a scowl. "I don't understand it," he said, propping his hands on his hips. "We can see where he stood in the copse. His tracks come out to the rock and go back. So why the hell isn't there any sign showing what direction he came from? It doesn't make sense."

Sinking to a log, Breanna braced her elbows on her knees. "It does if you think ghost."

"Oh, come on. He didn't disappear into thin air. There's a perfectly reasonable explanation. We're just overlooking it."

"What is it then?"

Tyler strode back to the copse, staring at the circle of prints that led to the bank and vanished. The trees there weren't big enough for climbing. "I don't know. It'll come to me. But it wasn't a ghost, that's for damned sure."

Breanna rose from the log, brushing bark from the seat of her jeans. "You're right. I know you're right. But the kid in me is getting spooked. This is the second time!"

"Bree, say it was John Van Patten? Hell, I'm open-minded. Let's say he haunts the place, guarding his treasure trove. If he did, you'd be the last person he'd harm. You're a Van Patten. He'd want you to find it."

"That's probably true."

Their eyes met, and Tyler started to laugh. "I can't believe this. I'm actually standing here talking about spooks as if they're real. Come on, let's go to my place and pack my things."

She threw one last glance at the ground as they left, hoping against hope she'd spy something both of them had missed.

Tyler slowed his pace so Breanna could catch up, draping an arm across her shoulders. "I tell you what. Let's go on this assumption. Say it's treasure seekers, like you suspected before, acting out the ghost legend to scare you away. The only way to put a stop to it is prove there's no gold, right?"

She nodded, not quite sure what his line of reasoning was.

"Okay, so let's do it," he said.

"Do what?"

"Prove, for once and for all, there is no gold. We'll go all out, use the maps, rent a metal detector, dig all over God's creation. And we'll tell everybody we see that we're looking. If it's treasure hunters doing all this, when we find nothing, they'll give up and leave you alone."

"Mr. Ross, I hate to burst your bubble, but whom do we ever see to tell? I mean, it's a good idea, but this isn't exactly a metropolis out here."

"We can start tonight in Wolf Creek."

"Wolf Creek?"

"Yeah, yesterday's dinner, remember? We'll go tonight. Talk loud. Tell everybody we meet. And then tomorrow, we'll go to town, get a metal detector, make a big deal out of it. The treasure hunters will hear. Rumors travel like wildfire."

"I suppose it might work. Okay, let's try it."

A smile settled on Breanna's mouth as she fell into step with Tyler. She wasn't sure treasure hunters were her problem, not after the things Chuck and Dane had said, but going along with the idea would assure her of Tyler's company. After last night, she was running a little short on bravado. With Tyler along as her backup, tonight would be an ideal time to ask Dane about that gas they had bought years ago, too. She would find a pay phone and give her cousin a call. If he wasn't home, she could leave a message with his wife, Nan, saying she would be in Wolf Creek most of the evening and needed to see him.

WHEN TYLER OPENED the front door to his cabin and led Breanna inside, she hid a smile. Natural wood tones and leather. It pleased her that he liked down-to-basics living. It gave them something else in common. The kitchen area was clean. A four-place set of brown earthenware dishes shone on the open shelving. The top of the gas cooking range was scrubbed and shining white. His small dining table was positioned in the center of the rectangular room, flanked by the kitchen and the small living area, which boasted a leather sofa, a matching chair and a neatly made bed.

Coaly flopped just inside the door, and Tyler motioned her toward the ranch-style sofa. "Grab a seat."

Breanna chose a straight-backed kitchen chair instead, drawn by the array of radio equipment that crowded half the tabletop. Citizen band? She didn't know much about shortwave communication, but the paraphernalia spread out before her looked too sophisticated for a simple CB base unit. Propping one elbow on the arm of her chair, she leaned forward. An unpleasant odor drifted to her. Next to the radio she spied a brimming ashtray.

"Tyler, I didn't know you smoked."

"I don't. Oh, that's Jack's."

"Jack?"

"Yeah, my partner. He comes down to work now and again."

"Oh, I see." She pushed the ashtray to one side and refocused her attention on the radio. "Do you mind if I turn this on and talk?"

Tyler glanced up from where he was taking jeans off a shelf. "Yes, I do. Please don't touch it."

His tone was so curt that she jerked her hand away from the power button. "I wouldn't break anything."

"It's for emergency use only." It was so unlike him to speak harshly that all she could do was stare. He must have seen how hurt she was; he shrugged offhandedly and turned away from the shelf where he was gathering clothes. "Someday when we're not pressed for time, maybe I'll teach you to operate it. Would you like that?"

"Are we in a hurry?"

"Dinner out, remember? If we're going, we have to get cracking." He sighed and strode toward her. Tossing down a pair of jeans near the radio, he placed his hands on the chair arms to lean down and kiss her forehead. "I'm sorry, Bree. It's expensive equipment, that's all. I have the frequencies all set and the antenna just so. With no phone, it's a lifeline in case of emergency. You can understand, can't you?"

"That's fine. It's yours. I respect that."

He cupped her chin in his hand. "Accept my apology?"

The sincerity in his expression was irresistible. A smile tugged at the corners of her mouth, and his answering grin brought it to full bloom. "Accepted. With my luck, I'll be the emergency."

"Come help me pack," he said, taking her hand to pull her from the chair.

Breanna stowed his things in a bag while he finished selecting an assortment of clothing off the shelves.

"I'm taking you dancing tonight," he announced. "You do dance?"

"I'll dance you under the table."

"Oh, no, I'm not talking fast stuff." He cast her a teasing grin as he walked to the closet. "I mean romantic dancing."

"Oh, that kind." She picked up a pair of socks and put them in the bag, then strolled toward him.

He opened his closet, and Breanna's eyes widened. On the inside panel of the door, in a very carefully arranged order, was a host of pictures. Her own image stared back at her, some frontal shots, some full-length of herself walking across her orchard. Below them, he had printed *Breanna Van Patten Morgan* on an index card in bold, black letters. There was even a picture of Coaly, with *Bites* scrawled on the bottom edge of the photograph.

Tyler had no sooner opened the door than he tensed. It was so obvious that he had forgotten the gallery of photos that it almost struck her as funny. Almost. It was so strange a collection and so painstakingly displayed that it sent a chill over her instead. Why? What had possessed him to take all those shots of her and her dog?

Her gaze flew to a cardboard poster that stood just inside the closet. Pictures of her claim? Breanna couldn't believe what she was seeing. The layout was extensive, done almost like a map, each photo labeled. Tyler...

He took some clothing off hangers and pushed the door shut with a loud click. The muscle in his jaw ticked as his eyes met hers. "I was fascinated with the subject matter."

Fascinated? He had clearly marked off her land, almost as if he had staked it out. But why? And when?

"Breanna…" He looked down at her for the longest time, then sighed in defeat.

"Why did you take all those pictures?"

"I needed an exact layout of the property for my observations. I use the orchards all the time for my animal studies. You know that. You use maps, don't you?"

"Yes, but—why did you need an exact layout of me?"

"I've wanted an exact layout of you since the moment I first saw you."

"You expect me to believe that?"

"I'm asking you to," he said simply.

"And what if I don't buy it?"

"I know it seems a little peculiar, Bree, but why wouldn't you buy it? I've got no reason to lie, do I?"

"Tyler…" She watched him carefully, trying to gauge his reactions. "I—I'm beginning to care for you, you realize that? You wouldn't use me to cover looking for the gold?"

She relaxed when his gaze didn't waver from hers. "No, Bree, I'm not looking for the gold. The gold? You don't believe that."

"But Tyler, the pictures. Why did you put them on a poster like that?"

He sighed and ran his hand over his hair. "Well, when I put them up, I barely knew you. I took the pictures on a lark, then when I developed them, I thought I might as well use them, so I did a layout. Sometimes I work with a partner. Not often, but I have been doing that here the last couple of months. And since I quite often use the blind in the orchard, I didn't see any harm in doing a spread for him, so he'd know how the land was situated in relation to the cabin." He shrugged his shoulders. "The pictures of you were so he'd know you if he saw you. And the ones of Coaly are pretty self-explanatory. I didn't want Jack getting his leg chewed off."

Now that he had explained it to her, it all made perfect sense. Only moments ago, he had mentioned Jack, his partner. The ashtray was further proof the man worked with him. Tyler was a photographer, after all. He probably snapped pictures of just about anything if the mood struck him, much as she did with her writing, doodling notes and sketching stories.

"Oh, Tyler, I'm sorry. I don't know why I'm acting this way."

He toyed with a stray curl at her temple, his wrist warm against her cheek. "Don't say you're sorry. You had a rough time last night. I understand that. You're not yourself."

"That's no excuse for—" She laughed softly. "I'm sorry."

He touched a fingertip to her mouth. "I just said don't say you're sorry. You know, we'd better hurry. As it is, I'll barely be unpacked before it's time to get ready to go to Wolf Creek."

Breanna nodded and reached for his satchel on the bed. "Do you have everything you need?"

His gaze rested on her for a long moment. "Everything," he said softly.

THE WOLF CREEK TAVERN was a relic of the past, a huge white building in Colonial-style, with tall columns rising from the veranda to support a graceful, full-length balcony. Because of the periodic shutdowns for repairs over the years, Breanna had never visited the inn. She caught her breath in awe when they entered the central hall, gazing appreciatively at the red oak graining on the wainscoting and doors.

"Gorgeous," she whispered.

"I'll second that." Tyler's gaze trailed from her upswept hair to her blue silk dress, warming with appreciation. "You look fantastic."

He looked pretty good himself. In his black slacks and charcoal-gray shirt, he was easily the most attractive man she had ever known. And the nicest one. While they waited for the hostess, he gave her a mini-tour of the ladies' parlor and the men's sitting room on the ground floor, entertaining her with stories about famous people who had frequented the place.

"Ah, here comes the hostess," he said, interrupting himself and taking Breanna's arm. "Now comes the best part, the food."

They stepped back into the central hall, following the waitress to a large, rustic dining room. After they were seated, Tyler ordered coffee, then smiled at her. "The manicotti here is out of this world."

It sounded good to her, so she agreed with a nod, then glanced over her shoulder to check the door, half expecting Dane to appear.

"Looking for someone?" Tyler asked.

"Yes, as a matter of fact. I called Dane's while you were getting gas. I need to talk to him. I told his wife we'd be in town most of the evening, so I'm kind of hoping he'll pop up."

"We should be easy enough to find." Tyler smiled. "In Wolf Creek there aren't too many places we could be. Right?"

When the waitress returned, Tyler placed their order and chose a wine. Before the woman left, he asked, "By the way, is there a rental outfit in Wolf Creek? We'd like to get a metal detector."

The waitress's brown eyes filled with curiosity. "No. You'd have to go clear to Grants Pass, I imagine."

"We're treasure hunting. You know of the Van Patten place, down Graves Creek?"

"Anybody who's lived around here long knows the Van Patten place. Why?"

"There's supposed to be a fortune in gold buried down there." Inclining his head toward Breanna, he added, "She's a Van Patten."

"Sounds exciting," the woman said enthusiastically.

Breanna couldn't help but notice that Tyler's good looks were stimulating a lot more interest in the waitress than his talk of buried gold. Of course, natives of Wolf Creek were accustomed to tales of stashed treasure.

"How sure are you that there's something there?" the waitress asked.

"About as sure as you can get." Tyler left it at that, lifting an eyebrow for emphasis.

"Well, I wish you all the luck."

"Just keep it under your hat," he said in a stage whisper. "We don't want word getting out. You know?"

After the waitress had left, Breanna leaned forward over her steaming cup of coffee. "Now, why did you say that? I thought the idea was to spread the word all over town?"

"That *is* the idea." His eyes twinkled with devilment. "Don't you know the quickest way to get a woman to repeat something is to ask her not to?"

"Oh, those are fighting words, Mr. Ross."

He winked at her over the rim of his cup.

AFTER A DELICIOUS MEAL, Tyler led Breanna through the parking lot to the car. As he opened the passenger door for her, she glanced up to find him looking at her with a strange, almost sad expression on his face. The iridescent glow from the light poles in the parking lot glistened on his dark hair.

"Is something wrong?"

He smiled and ran his knuckles along her cheek. "No. I was just thinking how much I enjoy being with you, that's all."

At a loss for words, she slid into the seat. He closed the door and came around to the driver's side, climbing behind the wheel. "Now where?" he asked.

"Not home?"

"This early? I promised to take you dancing. And it sure couldn't hurt to pass the word at one more place about our treasure hunt."

Trying to recapture her earlier lightheartedness, she teased, "Wanna print up a notice and pass it out?"

"No, I think telling one more woman ought to do the trick."

Breanna groaned at that remark, then burst into laughter.

DANE VAN PATTEN ROLLED DOWN his window to get some fresh air. Chuck smoked one cigarette after another, filling the Corvette with smoke. The smell of chicken-fried steak from a nearby café's exhaust fans wafted through the night air, mingling with the scent of pine from the surrounding hillsides.

"There she is," Chuck whispered, leaning forward to peer through the windshield as a car pulled up near the café. "With some man, dammit."

Dane tensed, focusing on the parking lot across the highway. "It's too far away. I can't tell who the guy is. What should we do? Wait?"

"Hell, no! We don't wait. If she's suspicious, I want to know it."

Dane opened his door to climb out. "Did it ever occur to you that maybe I didn't lose the money at her place? That it might have been some other woman fitting the same description?"

"That's what we're fixin' to find out, isn't it?" Chuck slammed his door and circled the front fender of the car.

"And if it was her? If she's on to us, then what?"

"Use your imagination."

THE SMALL CAFÉ WAS QUIET and its jukebox supplied Breanna and Tyler with the music they needed for dancing. Beyond that, nothing mattered. Tyler scooted two tables aside to provide them with floor space and wrapped both arms around her, nudging hers around his neck. Body to body, hardness cradling softness, they swayed, oblivious to everything around them. Breanna found herself forgetting all about Dane.

Tyler bent his head, pulling Breanna closer. As his eyes drifted shut, a dozen images of her flashed behind his lids. His arms trembled, and he cinched them tighter. Time was closing in on them, and he felt as though he were sinking in quicksand. Each second with Breanna might be the last. If she was involved in the counterfeiting, she would never forgive him when Jack started making arrests. And he couldn't blame her. He had committed the unforgivable sin, done the one thing he had always sworn he'd never do. He was intimately involved with a suspect. When the truth came out, she'd never believe he hadn't intended it this way, that he hadn't used her, trying to get information. And how could he convince her otherwise when he wasn't sure of his motives himself?

Raising his lashes, he studied the curve of her cheek, the soft fullness of her mouth. Like hell, he wasn't sure of his motives. He'd fallen in love with her. And that wouldn't make his job any easier. Was he out of his mind? If Jack was right, she might be a liar, a con artist, a thief, even a killer. How could he forget that, even for an instant?

She opened her eyes, and he found the answer to his question when he looked into those deep pools of soft blue. When he was with her he forgot everything, everything but the tenderness she evoked in him. Maybe Jack was right, but Tyler didn't think so. Even her agreeing to the treasure hunt was testimony to her innocence. If she were a counterfeiter, the last thing she'd want would be someone snooping around on the property.

A slight frown drew her brows together. "What are you thinking?" he asked.

"Oh, just how nice this is, how I wish—"

"What? Tell me, Bree, what do you wish?"

"That it didn't have to end, that the night could go on forever, just like it is right now."

"Well, I can't make that wish come true. But we could do it again." His throat tightened around the words. "Next week, maybe?"

She pressed her cheek to his shoulder. "I'd like that."

The bell above the door jangled and Breanna turned her head to see who had come in. *Dane.* And right on his heels came Chuck Morrow.

"What is it?" Tyler followed her gaze, and she felt his body snap taut. "Your favorite personality. What luck."

"You know Chuck?"

"By sight. I haven't had the dubious pleasure of making his acquaintance."

Dane spotted Breanna. He froze in midstride when he saw Tyler, then continued walking. Chuck didn't seem nearly so big with Tyler in the room. Tyler dropped his arms and a chill ran over her. She'd felt much more secure pressed against him, not so alone and vulnerable.

"Hello, Dane," Tyler said in a low voice.

"Ross." Dane gave a polite nod. "Uh, Bree, that first day when I was at your place, did I by any chance drop something?"

"Oh, yes, you did, but that wasn't what I wanted to talk to you about."

Dane's eyelid twitched. He threw a quick glance at Chuck, who stood nearby, legs spread, arms akimbo, his chest puffed out to show off the physique he didn't have. In his white T-shirt, with one sleeve rolled back over a pack of cigarettes, Chuck resembled a potbellied hoodlum from a sixties movie. Breanna gave him a wide berth when she went to the table to get her purse.

"I have twenty right here," she told Dane, digging her hand into the side pocket of her bag where she had stowed the bill she had found in the barn. She handed it over, forcing herself to smile. "Dane, is there someplace we could talk a minute?"

"I don't want just any twenty," Dane whispered. "I need the one I dropped."

Breanna laughed. "Oh, that should be simple enough. You had your name on it, right?" Then she realized Dane was serious. "Um, wait a sec. I put yours in my wallet, I think." She sifted through the currency in her billfold, handing Dane the worn twenty that was left. "There, is that the one?"

"No. Here, let me see that." Dane grabbed her purse and pulled out her wallet. Leafing through the money inside, he said, "Dammit, it isn't here. Lord, you spent it, didn't you?"

"What's the problem here?" Tyler asked her.

"Dane dropped a—"

Chuck interrupted, smiling and rubbing his chest. "It's nothing really. Dane here, he'd lose his head if it wasn't attached." Glancing at Breanna, Chuck's smile broadened.

"He had a real important number written on it, that's all. You sure you don't have it?"

"Just what are you looking for?" Tyler stepped to Breanna's side, so close she felt his arm pressing against hers. His voice soothed her.

"Dane dropped some money down at the cabin," she explained. "I guess there was an important number written on it, and I spent it."

Breanna stared into Dane's eyes, knowing even as she said the words that she was repeating a lie. He wanted the twenty, all right, but not for any phone number. Her cousin returned her purse and one of the twenties. She tightened her hands on the soft leather, shifting her gaze to Morrow. As she did, she inched closer to Tyler, thankful for his presence. Something was wrong here, very wrong. "I'm sorry, Dane. Tyler and I went to town the other day. Not knowing it was special, I didn't keep your money separate. I planned to leave twenty with my mom so she could pass it on to yours."

Chuck cocked his head. "You don't happen to remember where you went shopping, do you?" He laughed, holding up a hand. "That's a dumb question. What good would it do now?" Patting Dane's shoulder, Chuck shrugged. "Tough luck, old man."

Breanna's gaze wavered and she pressed a hand to her throat. "If it will help, we went to the Ninety-Nine Market...for soap."

The color washed from Dane's face. Then he grinned. "Like Chuck says, my tough luck. Um—Nan said you wanted to see me? What about?"

Breanna had no time to think. She acted on pure instinct. "Oh, nothing important...just to visit. I—I thought it might be fun if you and Nan—you know—it would have been like old times if we could have spent an evening together.''

Chuck stepped closer. ''That's good to hear. When Dane first got the message, he thought maybe you were still—'' Breaking off, Chuck's gaze moved to Tyler. ''But, nah, you wouldn't be that silly. Not after our talk yesterday, right? After me explaining everything so clear to you?''

Breanna flinched when Chuck raised his hand to place it on her shoulder. It was a seemingly friendly gesture, but she knew the meaning that underlined every word he spoke. Dane had suspected her true motive for wanting to see him, that she had wanted to grill him about the fire. Chuck was letting her know his threats of yesterday still held. If she continued to pry into what he considered none of her business, he would be angry. Her stomach lurched as his fingers tightened, digging into her flesh. Pain radiated down her arm, and she lifted her chin in response, refusing to be intimidated.

''Speaking of being like old times, isn't this just?'' Chuck gripped her shoulder harder. ''We go back a long ways, don't we, babe?''

Something flashed before Breanna's eyes. The next second, she realized it had been Tyler's hand. He clamped his fingers around Chuck's wrist. ''The lady is with me, Morrow.''

''Oh, the jealous type, are you?'' Chuck released Breanna, shaking his head. ''No need, man. Me and Bree, we're just friends. Right, Breanna? She owes me a dollar for every hair on her head. When she was a kid, I pulled her out of one scrape after another.''

Tyler's answering smile was deadly. ''Touch her again, and you'll get what she owes you, all right. Breanna's told me all about her *debt* to you.''

Chuck's face stiffened. His brown eyes shot to Breanna's. "Oh, is that so? My, my, aren't we getting cozy."

"That's right," Tyler said softly. "Real cozy. So cozy, in fact, that I'll make this fair warning. Bother her again, and you'll tangle with me, not her. Is that clear?"

Chuck stepped back, lifting both hands. "Hey, man, no quarrel. I didn't realize..."

"You do now."

Chuck's eyes were riveted on Breanna. Their murderous gleam frightened her. "Yeah, I'd say I do. The writing's on the wall. Come on, Dane. I get the feeling we're not too welcome here."

Breanna was shaking with aftershock by the time Dane and Chuck pushed out the door of the café. Tyler's arm circled her shoulders, warm, hard, indescribably comforting. "You okay?"

"Yes, fine." Pressing trembling fingertips to her shoulder, she forced a smile. "I'm not sure you should have done that, but thank you, Tyler. He was hurting me."

En route through the parking lot, Tyler asked, "Why shouldn't I have done that? If I interfered where I shouldn't have, I'm sorry."

"No, it's just—he didn't like it, me telling you. He's mad now. And Chuck mad is like a rattler when it's shedding. He strikes blind."

Once they were in the car, Tyler flipped on the dome light and turned sideways in his seat. With a grim scowl on his face, he gently peeled her dress back to look at her shoulder. Glancing down, she saw ugly red marks coming up where Chuck's fingers had bruised her. Tyler feathered his thumb across them, then bent his dark head to press a kiss there.

"You don't have to be afraid of him," he whispered. "If he ever so much as touches you again, he's going to think he's a mud hole I'm stomping dry."

"If you're around," she interjected.

Tyler touched her cheek. "Oh, I'll be around, lady, you can count on that. If you want me, that is."

The question in his voice was so subtle that she could have ignored it. Tyler, always the gentleman, never putting her on the spot. An unbidden smile curved her mouth. "I think it would be fair to say you have a standing welcome."

During the ride home, Tyler held her hand, releasing it only to shift gears. She twined her fingers into his, tightening her grip without realizing it until he looked over at her.

"What is it?" he asked softly.

"You'll probably think I'm crazy, but I think there was something fishy about that little scenario back there."

Tyler was quiet a moment. "Like what?"

"That story Dane gave me. He was lying. He didn't have a number written on that money. Tyler—" She turned slightly. "Remember your saying Chuck may have been asking favors of Dane all along? Do you think Dane's gotten mixed up in something illegal?"

"Something illegal?"

"I—Tyler, I remembered something this morning. Right before the fire, I went with Dane to buy gasoline, lots and lots of gasoline. But I can't remember why. Or who it was for." She lifted her free hand and passed it over her eyes. "It's all so foggy. But what if we bought it for Chuck? Tyler, what if that gas was used to set the Reuben Creek blaze?"

"Couldn't you have bought it for someone else?"

"Maybe a neighbor. Or for Gramps. But I—"

"Honey, slow down." He raised her hand, pressing his lips to the inside of her wrist. "I told you earlier, you're strung out. You're not yourself. Why don't you think about something nice for a while? Like our treasure hunt, hmm? I know last night rattled you, but I'm here now. Relax. Forget the ghost and the fire and Dane. You're shaking.''

"All right, I'll try."

He leaned forward, flipping on the radio. Static filled the car as he adjusted the dial, then KAJO boomed loud and clear, the disc jockey's cheerful voice resounding all around them. "And now, folks, we interrupt the music for a quick news update."

Breanna shot her hand forward, turning off the radio, her pulse hammering so wildly she felt dizzy. "Oh, my God, Tyler! It just hit me. Oh, my God, how dense can I get? The other night I heard part of a newscast. About a woman who passed a counterfeit bill! I didn't think it was impor— Oh, Tyler, it was me!''

"What?"

"It—it was me! That twenty Dane dropped. It was counterfeit. That's why they were acting so pecul—''

"Breanna, stop it!" he snapped. "You've got to calm down." Reaching to reclaim her hand, he gave it a comforting squeeze. This was one line of reasoning he couldn't let her pursue. "That's the wildest—well, it's just plain ridiculous, that's all. Dane and Chuck? Come on. Counterfeiting is big-time, not Wolf Creek stuff at all. You're going clear off the deep end here, lady, and scaring hell out of me in the process. I'm really starting to worry about you."

"You don't think it's possible?"

"Of course I don't think it's possible." He flashed her a smile. "Come on now, loosen up. Counterfeiting?"

She found herself laughing with him. "I guess it is sort of far out, at that."

"Like clear into the twilight zone. Where's a good place to rent a metal detector? You know of one?"

Breanna cleared her mind, focusing on Grants Pass. "Well, probably most any equipment rental place carries them."

TWENTY-FIVE MINUTES LATER, Tyler pulled the Honda into her driveway. As he brought the car to a stop, she grew rigid in her seat. A dim glow of light flashed within the old barn.

"Tyler, did you see that?"

"Did I see what?"

"There were lights in the barn."

"Nah, it was just the reflection of our headlights."

"It wasn't, I tell you." She shifted in her seat to look at him. "Someone's in the barn."

"Honey, if there *is* someone in there, it's probably kids from town."

"You think so?"

"I know so, and you're not going in there looking for trouble. You're going directly inside and straight to bed. We've both had about all the excitement our nerves can take for one day."

They climbed out of the car and walked up to the house. Tyler unlocked the door and stepped aside, holding it open for her. She waited in the living room while he lit the lantern on the mantle. He rasped a match and golden light sprang onto the walls. It cast his sharply carved features into shadow.

"I think I'll take Coaly out for a short run," he said, turning from the hearth. "Why don't you hit the sack?"

"I think I will. I must be more tired than I realize."

Breanna went to the bedroom and slipped from her dress into her nightgown. Sighing, she pulled back the bedclothes and sank onto the mattress, thinking of Dane and his strange behavior. Was she overreacting? Or was Tyler making light of something serious?

The cabin door was dragged open and she heard Coaly's nails tapping on the floor. Tyler parted the curtain, stepping to the foot of the bed to remove his shoes. When he stretched out beside her, still fully clothed, she smiled and turned to him. "I have a new bedmate, too, hmm?"

He drew the covers over them. "Just to sleep. You're so nerved up, I thought you might like a little company." He curled an arm around her, pressing a kiss on her forehead. "Want me to leave?"

"No," she whispered drowsily.

His hand traced light circles on her back. "Go to sleep. You'll feel better come morning."

For a long while she lay there awake, listening to Tyler's even breathing. Then, at last, her eyes grew heavy and she snuggled close, drifting off into slumber.

TYLER SLID ON HIS BELLY through the brush, stretching out beside Mike Jackson in the blind. Mike slipped off his headphones, smiling. "Hey, man, I didn't expect you here."

"Yeah, well there's been a new development. The Van Patten woman is definitely clean. I need to see Jack. Call him and tell him to get down here. I can't make a move without his say-so, and time's running out. I want her out of here, yesterday if not sooner."

"Gotcha." Mike reached for his handset, keying the mike. "You got your ears on, Jones? This is The Deer Hunter calling Indiana Jones."

Tyler closed his eyes, not sharing Mike's enthusiasm for the silly call names everyone was using in case someone broke in on their frequency. This was no game of intrigue. Breanna's safety was at stake. Losing patience, he grabbed the handset from the younger man, keying the mike himself. "Jones, this is urgent. Get down here, stat."

Jack's voice rasped back, broken with static. "Gotcha. I'll—b—down—about—ten—minu—"

Tyler swore. "Make it five, Jones. Five, not a second longer. I don't have time to wait."

IT SEEMED TO BREANNA that she'd only been asleep a few seconds when Coaly's whining and scratching at the door woke her. She sighed and reached for Tyler. He wasn't there.... His pillow felt cold to the touch, so she knew he had left some time ago. She sat up, listening for movement inside the cabin. The only sounds came from Coaly and, if his anxious crying was any indication, Tyler had gone outside.

Throwing back the covers, she slipped out of bed and tiptoed through the curtained doorway. "Tyler?"

He didn't answer her. Coaly pawed excitedly at the door, but Breanna ignored him, leaving him inside when she stepped out onto the porch. Tyler had probably just gone to the outhouse, which wasn't a bad idea. The moon was bright, so she could see quite well from her position on the top step; it gave her a clear view of the upper orchard and the front of the barn.

Proceeding down the pebbled walk, she wrapped her arms around herself to ward off the chill air. As she approached the second flight of stairs, a movement caught her eye and she turned to look at the barn. A man stood at the top of the ramp, cast in shadow by the doorway. He bent low, as if to lift something, straightened, then disappeared into the corridor.

Remembering the light that she had seen earlier and Tyler's explanation for it, Breanna's first thought was that the teenagers were still inside and something awful had happened. The loft was high and enclosed on only three sides.

A fall from the ladder could have seriously injured someone.

Hurrying down the retaining wall steps, she struck off for the barn, not even thinking about the nettles in the field grass until she stepped on some. She hated to go clear back for her shoes, so she plucked the stickers out of her soles, then wove her way more carefully, trying to stay on trodden ground.

A humming noise greeted her as she slipped inside the barn, so low and indistinct she couldn't identify it. An engine of some sort? Perhaps an airplane overhead or a car on the road?

She braced her hands against the walls, groping her way down the dark corridor. The humming noise grew louder with each step. Horrible pictures flashed through her mind of Tyler carrying an injured youngster out the back exit to a waiting vehicle.

"Tyler?" she yelled. "Tyler, it's me, Breanna. Where are you?"

She had scarcely finished speaking when the humming noise stopped abruptly. Total silence fell around her. Freezing where she stood, she peered into the black abyss that yawned ahead of her, listening for the sound of a vehicle driving away.

"Tyler?" she squeaked.

What if it hadn't been Tyler she had seen coming into the barn? Her heart tripped a beat. Just the thought of meeting Chuck out here made her blood run cold. *Don't even think that way, Breanna. Of course it was Tyler you saw. He's out here someplace. It stands to reason it was him. He probably went out the back door as you came in the front, that's all.*

It was so dark that she couldn't be certain exactly where she stood, but she knew she had walked at least halfway down the passage. There were rooms in front of her and behind her. Inching backward, she held her breath, her ears straining to hear above the pounding of her pulse. Her palms rasped against the splintery boards and the planked flooring beneath her creaked with each footstep. She tensed, ready to run. *Dear God, what if it wasn't Tyler?*

Right on the heels of that thought, hands clamped down on her shoulders like steel vises.

Chapter Eleven

When Tyler spoke her name, Breanna's knees turned to jelly and she sagged in his grasp, so relieved that a sob of laughter escaped her lips. "Tyler."

He clamped an arm around her waist, hurrying her to the doorway. His heart was slamming every bit as hard as hers. "What the hell are you doing in here? I was in the blind when I spotted you heading for the barn."

"I saw you go in and I was afraid something had happened. You must have gone out the back as I went in the front. What were you doing out here? When I found you gone, it scared me."

He guided her to the cabin, never breaking stride. His fingers bit into her waist, hard, relentless. "I was out taking pictures. I just stepped in there to make sure those kids had left. No sense in sitting forever in a blind, just to have someone spook the animals."

"In the dark? Where's your camera?"

"I have infrared lenses," he informed her. "I dropped everything when I saw you. I'll go get it all come morning."

She could feel some of his camera equipment jabbing her in the shoulder as they walked. He seemed upset. Had her hollering spoiled his photo session?

"Did you get any good shots?" she ventured.

"Mmm-hmm, a couple."

"What of?"

"A mother raccoon and her babies."

He propelled her up the steps to the porch and threw open the door. Coaly tried to run outside, but Tyler nabbed him by the ruff. He pushed Breanna into the entry and pulled the dog along, none too gentle with either of them. Coaly yelped.

Breanna spun on her heel, hugging herself while he lit the lantern. When the white glow illuminated the room, she leaned back her head to gaze up at his taut features. His eyes met hers, glassy and expressionless. He looked pale and beads of perspiration glistened on his brow.

"Tyler, what's wrong?"

"Nothing's wrong. I'm just tired, that's all."

"Being tired excuses you for being cranky with the dog?"

As if a hand had passed over his face, his expression changed. He sighed and ran trembling fingers through his hair. "I'm sorry, Bree, I didn't mean to hurt your dog. You just gave me a scare, that's all. When I heard you calling for me, I was afraid you'd been hurt."

He seemed so sincere that Breanna's anger faded, and she glided across the room to put her arms around him. He stepped back abruptly and caught her hands before she could slip them beneath his jacket. "Let me get out of this shirt. I got into some foxtails and I'm itching to death. I wouldn't want you getting them all over you. Why don't you put some coffee on for us?"

"At this time of night?"

"Make it weak."

As she went to the kitchen, she saw him stop at the end of the sofa and shove something down behind it before he proceeded into the bedroom. A moment later, he reappeared, donning a fresh yellow shirt. She couldn't help wondering what he had slipped out of sight behind the couch. Curiosity bubbled up within her.

"You sure do something for flannel," he told her warmly.

Breanna lit the burner and moved the pot onto the flame.

"Bree?" He touched her hair as he said her name and his tone was such that she lifted her chin to look at him. The tenderness in his eyes warmed her clear through. His fingers sifted through her hair, sandpapery and warm on the nape of her neck as he drew her against him. He encircled her with both arms, drawing her close to rest his chin atop her head. They stood like that for minutes on end, saying nothing.

The coffeepot hissed over the flame and he reached to turn it down, then propped his back against the warming oven, spreading his booted feet so she could lean against him. "You look like a little girl in that nightgown with your hair all tumbling down," he whispered.

"Do you speak from experience? Do you have a little girl?"

He ran his hand down her back. "My wife didn't want children."

"Why?" Breanna loved youngsters so much that it was incomprehensible to her that anyone could dislike them.

"My work. It was so demanding that our family life suffered." He laughed humorlessly. "I finally changed fields, but it was already too late. She was in love with another man—a nice, boring accountant with hay fever."

"Oh, Tyler, I'm so sorry."

He smiled. "It happened years ago. No need to be sorry."

The coffee began to perk. He checked his watch to time it. When it was finished, they broke apart to sit at the table.

"What kind of work did you do then?"

He took a sip of coffee before answering her. "Systematic inquiries. It took me into the field a lot."

Breanna had no idea what he meant by systematic inquiries, but she imagined him going into offices, reorganizing their operations to make them more efficient. "And your wife missed you?"

His eyes filled with laughter. "Not too much. I was finding wads of tissues around the house a long time before I caught the sniffler who was leaving them." He shrugged. "To be fair to Karen, I have to say she hung in there a long time. She just wasn't the type to be alone. No career, no interests. Her life revolved around me. I'm not saying that's bad, but—" He flashed her a smile. "Enough of that. It's past history."

Lifting her mug, she suggested, "To the future?"

As he raised his cup to hers, she noticed how exhausted he looked. Had he been losing sleep a lot lately, doing night photography? Before meeting her, he had probably slept in the daytime if he worked at night.

"Let's go back to bed," she proposed, reaching to shut off the lantern.

He nodded, shoving away his half-emptied mug and yawning. The grin he flashed her fell short of being convincing. "I've never turned down a proposition like that yet."

"I think you need an eight-hour battery charge, Mr. Ross."

"Amen. I'm beat."

Breanna pulled him to his feet and led him to the adjoining room, drifting apart from him at the foot of the bed. The lantern glow was fading, obscuring him in shadow. She heard the thunk of his boots, the rustle of his shirt. Then the mattress sank beneath his weight.

Breanna curled on her side, gazing at his profile. She saw his lashes drift closed, heard his breathing change almost as soon as he grew still. Minutes passed. She tried to relax, but it was no use. The coffee, she reflected.

She finally gave up on sleeping and slipped quietly from the bed. Tyler wasn't the only one who could work in the middle of the night. Now would be as good a time as any to do some proofreading.

As she stepped through the curtained doorway, her eyes dropped to the shadowy outline of the sofa and she remembered Tyler shoving something behind it. Hunkering down, she groped along the wall until her fingers bumped into smooth leather. Running her hand over the bulky shape, she recognized what it was. Tyler's camera case. She could feel his Leica inside it. He couldn't have been taking pictures with infrared lenses. He had lied to her....

The realization washed over her like ice water. Her mind stumbled, then stopped short. If he hadn't been taking pictures, then what had poked her in the shoulder when they were walking? She turned to peer through the curtain. Her knees cracked when she stood, and the sound startled her. She suddenly knew what had been under Tyler's jacket. If her conclusion was correct, the last thing she wanted to do was wake him.

Creeping back to the bedroom, she found his jacket and shirt discarded in a corner. There was nothing wrapped in them and no sign of foxtails, either. She knew he wouldn't have hidden anything in her open shelving. There was only one other place to look. She stared at the sleeping man on the bed, listening to his breathing, not knowing what she'd do if he woke up and caught her.

Dropping to her knees, she inched her way to the bed and fanned her arm under it. Her fingers bumped into cold metal and leather. She traced the shape, then recoiled. *A gun. Oh, God!* Now she knew why he hadn't let her hug him earlier. The story about foxtails in his shirt had only been an excuse to keep her away from him until he could hide the revolver.

"Bree?"

Tyler's voice jarred her so much that she gasped and brought her head up, cracking it on the metal bed frame. The springs groaned above her. Large hands encircled her waist. A sudden, breathtaking fear flooded through her.

Tyler must have sensed it, for he lifted her to her feet and wrapped both arms around her. "Breanna...I'd never hurt you. Don't you know that?"

She had so many doubts racing in her mind that nothing seemed certain to her right then.

"You found the gun, didn't you?" he asked.

Should she admit that she had? Breanna drew away from him. "Why? Why do you need a gun?"

"I always carry a gun when I'm working at night. You never know when you'll run into a snake."

Her chest constricted. He hadn't been working. His camera behind the sofa testified to that, unless his work was something entirely different from what he'd been pretending. In the moonlight, his face was a shadowy caricature of the one she knew; harsh, frightening, his features etched black against the bronzed planes of skin.

"You found my camera, too, didn't you." It was more a statement than a question. He motioned her to sit on the bed and when she stood there, frozen in place, he pressed her down onto the mattress, lowering himself beside her. "Okay. Let's talk."

"Talk?"

He leaned forward studying her, his eyes silver, penetrating.

"What's going on around here?" she demanded. "Why are you wandering my property at night carrying a weapon? Tyler, answer me, or I'm going straight to the police."

"That would be a very bad idea," he said softly.

She stared at him, her stomach churning. The set of his mouth told her he was prepared to use force to stop her. The true Tyler Ross had just stood up to take a bow.

"There are things I'm not at liberty to explain to you," he said gently. "I have commitments that I can't walk away from, as much as I might like to, commitments that I made before I met you. That's all that I can say."

"What kind of commitments? I detest guns, Tyler. I refuse to have one in my house."

"Then I'll leave it unloaded."

"You said you were working! You weren't taking pictures out there. So what *were* you doing? That's all I want to know."

"I can't tell you that."

His tone rang with finality. A slow rage boiled up inside her. Had it been Tyler she had seen running in the brush that night, after all? Whatever it was Chuck had been doing in her barn, Tyler had been in on it. Oh, he had been clever, convincing her it had been poachers or treasure hunters. What a fool she had been! And ever since that day he had pretended an interest in her, keeping her occupied, trying to get her involved in treasure hunts, covering for his friends so she wouldn't find out what they were doing. *Oh, God, he even made love to me!* The truth hit her like a rush of cold air. Tyler had been using her.

On the tail of that thought, Breanna realized that everything he had ever told her was suspect. Every smile, every offhanded shrug, every explanation he'd given her for the strange goings-on, all of it had been lies. Even tonight when she'd been upset about Dane's behavior, his concern about her had been a sham. He had very artfully distracted her, bringing up the treasure hunt.

Suddenly it was all so clear, so sickeningly clear. Tyler was committed to something all right; to *Chuck Morrow*. He was a counterfeiter.

Pain twisted her heart as she studied him. "Was it you with the scythe, Tyler?"

A sad smile curved his mouth. "You know better than that. Deep down, you know."

"Lies, it's all been lies, hasn't it?" she whispered. "Tyler, I think it would be best if you left now. You can come get your things tomorrow."

He sat there on her bed like an immovable rock. "Breanna, don't misunderstand this, but I can't do that. I'll sleep on the sofa if you like, but I can't leave you alone here. It's not safe. At least you know I won't hurt you."

"Do I? I think I know precious little. I don't like being lied to, and I like being used even less."

He averted his face, gazing at the floor.

"There's something here on my land that you want, isn't there? You know who spied on me down by the creek. And you're involved in it somehow. Maybe not directly, but you know who did it." It was on the tip of her tongue to accuse him of knowing Morrow, too, but fear held the words back. She didn't want to find out she was right. "Leave, Tyler. And lock the door on your way out."

He dropped his head into his hand, ruffling his hair with tense fingers. "I can't blame you for thinking what you're thinking, Bree. But let's get a couple of things straight. What happened between you and me...that has nothing to do with anything else, nothing. I would have felt the same way at any other time, in any other place. As for the guy with the scythe, if I knew who he was, he'd be mincemeat." He turned to look at her. "How can you think, even for an instant, that I'd let someone harm you? I know you're upset. I know this looks bad. But surely you know me better than that.''

"I don't think I know you at all."

He rose from the bed, pulling two blankets and an extra pillow from the closet shelf. "Don't pass judgment on me until you know all the facts." He glanced down at her. "Think how it was between us last night. How could that be a lie? You're jumping to conclusions . . . all the wrong ones. I may not be able to explain myself satisfactorily now, but I can tell you this. I'm no criminal. There's no need for you to go to the police."

"Don't you dare throw last night at me!" she cried, jumping to her feet. "As far as I'm concerned, it never even happened. Is that c-clear?" When her voice broke, she threw up an arm to hide her tears, trying to step around him. He grabbed her bruised shoulder to stop her and she flinched. "Don't touch me!"

"I'm sorry. . . . I forgot you were sore there."

"It isn't that. Just please, please don't touch me."

He tossed the blankets onto the bed, reaching an arm around her waist to pull her against him. She couldn't bear him to see her face, so she burrowed her head into his chest. "Take your hands off me. You disgust me, do you hear? Lying is one thing. I might forgive that. But I'll never forgive you for using me."

"I didn't use you."

She laughed. "Oh, I see. It's true love, right? I've swallowed everything else you tossed me, hook, line and sinker. Why not one more time?"

"I can see you're in no frame of mind to listen to reason."

"Reason? I think you've reasoned with me far too much."

"Breanna, please..." His voice flowed over her, warm, gentle, filled with concern. "Whatever else you think, don't misunderstand last night, please. I admit, I made a mistake—"

"A mistake?" She tipped her head back. "Oh, Tyler..."

He rasped his knuckles across her cheek, catching her tears. "When I say it was a mistake, I only mean it in the sense that it was bad timing. I should have waited until all this was settled."

"All what?"

He sighed and closed his eyes. "Listen, I'll sack out on the couch. Okay? That far enough away for you?"

"Do I have a choice?"

His gaze delved into hers. "No, not really, I guess you don't. Neither of us does." He pressed a quick kiss to her forehead before she realized what he was going to do. "Good night, Bree."

He brushed past her to pick up the blankets. She swiped at her cheek with her sleeve, watching him. At the doorway, he paused, turning to look back at her. "Sometimes you have to go on gut instinct. What does your intuition tell you about me?"

"If you're not involved in anything illegal, then do as you preach. Go on gut instinct about me. Trust me and tell me what this is all about."

He smiled. "I can't tell you anything more than I've told you. As for the instinct, I already used it. You don't know it yet, but I believed in you when no man in his right mind would have." He nodded toward the bed. "Don't mess with that gun. It's loaded and it has a hair trigger. And don't leave the cabin without waking me. If nature calls, I'll walk down with you."

Breanna climbed back into bed. Sleep still refused to come to her and she could tell by Tyler's breathing that he, too, was restless. Sometime later, she slipped out of bed to get a drink of water. As she swept the curtain aside to tip-toe past the sofa, his dark head turned on the pillow. Even in the dim shaft of moonlight from the window, she could see him watching her.

"Where are you going?"

"To get a drink."

He settled back, but she felt his eyes following her as she went to the sink. The room was so quiet that every time she swallowed, the sound echoed. As she walked back to her room, her skin prickled. She was a prisoner in her own house.

"Good night, Breanna."

She could have sworn his tone was underlaid with laughter. She climbed back into bed and glared at the ceiling. She heard Coaly plop onto the floor, positioning himself in the doorway between herself and Tyler. Even the dog loved and trusted him. Curling onto her side, she wrapped her arms around herself, watching the moon. This was either the first time Coaly had misjudged someone or Tyler was telling the truth, at least in part. Doubt crowded into her mind. Was she jumping to the wrong conclusions? If she was wrong, if Tyler, Dane and Chuck weren't involved in counterfeiting, she'd never forgive herself for running to the police with wild stories, getting Tyler in trouble for something he hadn't done. She knew what it felt like to be falsely accused. There had to be a way for her to find out for sure. All she had to do was think of it.

In the other room, Tyler gazed out at the moonlight, too, his thoughts centered on the woman beyond the curtain. Without Jack's okay, he couldn't remove Breanna from the premises. And now that she had found his gun, he didn't dare leave her alone long enough to persuade Jack to give that okay. One minute with his back turned, that was all she would need.

That thought brought him upright. Swinging to his feet, he went to the kitchen, opened her purse and took her car keys. He couldn't risk her getting away from him. If she made it to a police station, the local authorities would swarm in and ruin everything. Tyler didn't so much care at this point if the crooks got away, but he did care about the men he worked with, and didn't want any unsuspecting police officers hurt, either. As important as Breanna was to him, he couldn't risk dozens of lives. Since he couldn't get her out of here, he'd protect her as best he could and hope to God that Jack didn't waste any time bringing this mess to a close.

Tyler dropped the keys in his slacks pocket and returned to the sofa. From here on in, he was on his own.

Chapter Twelve

When Breanna woke up in the morning, she had a solution to her problem. Or at least to part of it. She could find out if her hunch about counterfeiting was correct by making a simple phone call to the Grants Pass police. How she had come up with the idea was a mystery to her, unless she had concocted the plan in her sleep, but it really didn't matter as long as it worked. And it would. She felt sure of it. If she could just escape Tyler long enough to reach a phone.

That turned out to be the catch. Tyler didn't let her out of his sight. When she made her morning sojourn to the outhouse, he accompanied her and waited outside. Later, when she walked down to the creek for her bath, he sat on the boulder with his back to her and kept up a steady conversation to assure himself she was still there.

By nightfall, Breanna's nerves were not only frayed, but the tension between herself and Tyler was nearly unbearable. There had been no opportunity for her to use a phone, even though they had driven into Wolf Creek to continue spreading the rumor about their gold hunt. Their stops at the grocery store, the gas station and the café were brief, and Tyler stayed by her side every second. Breanna had never spent such a miserable afternoon.

But the worst part about the dragging hours had been the constant ache in her chest, an ache that sharpened every time she glanced Tyler's way. She didn't know when and, God help her, she didn't know why, but somehow she had fallen crazy in love with him. She stressed the crazy every time the realization hit her; insanity was her only excuse. Their relationship, if by any stretch of her imagination she could call it that, was a shambles. She felt helpless, frustrated and angry. How could Tyler look so happy all the time?

"What lovely things are on the agenda for tomorrow?" she called through the curtain as she undressed for bed that night.

The clank of the coffeepot resounded and she heard the pump handle squeaking. "I guess we'll go get a metal detector."

Breanna shrugged. There was no point in getting the metal detector, but no point in arguing about it, either. She slipped into her nightgown and turned to get his bedding off the top shelf. With no undo ceremony, she elbowed her way through the curtain and tossed it onto the sofa. "Don't let the bedbugs bite."

He turned from the stove, placing his hands on his hips. "Am I to understand that you're going to let the sun go down without us settling this?"

She nodded toward the dark windows. "It's already down. And even if it weren't, in this situation it's beyond my control. Only you can rectify the problem. Good night, Tyler."

"Great attitude. If it isn't rectified *your* way, it can't be rectified."

She returned to her room and jerked back the bedclothes with a snap. "Good night, Tyler...."

"Good night, Breanna."

She climbed into bed and pulled the quilt up to her chin, staring at the ceiling. She wouldn't let him put a guilt trip on her. There was a gun under her bed that was still unexplained. He had been up to something last night and he wouldn't tell her what. Oh, no, she wasn't the guilty party here. And she wouldn't let him make her feel that she was.

She heard him making his bed. In a moment the lantern light faded. "If you wake up first, the coffee's ready. Just light the burner," he told her.

Breanna didn't bother to reply. Better just to pretend she was already asleep. Fat chance of that. The way she felt, she'd lie here awake all night. She curled onto her side and tried her best to relax. It seemed to her as if hours passed before she finally grew drowsy and drifted off.

FIRE....

At first, Breanna thought she was dreaming. The amber glow flickered through her closed eyelids and she heard the crackling of the flames. Fear clutched her and she tossed fitfully in her sleep, trying to stave off the images she knew would come. It was the nightmare, just as she had experienced it a thousand times, and she didn't want to give in to it. *Forest fire.*

When she opened her eyes, she knew something was terribly wrong. The fire wasn't a dream. It was real. The flames were outside, beyond the paned windows. She rose to her knees in bed and stared through the glass, horrified. Her fruit cellar was burning. Flames snaked up the siding toward the shingled roof, hungry, hot, eager. Breanna screamed.

"Bree..." Tyler tore through the curtain, making a dive for his gun. He was already crouched beside the bed when he saw what she was screaming about. "Oh, Lord..."

"My house..." Her voice faded to a moan. "Oh, my God, there's no water! It'll catch the cabin."

She leaped out of the bed, and his arm lashed out, catching her around her waist before she could get beyond the curtain. "You stay right here until I'm dressed."

"Dressed? Dressed! You're worried about clothes when my place is burning down?"

He shoved her toward the bed and slipped into his shoulder holster, pulling his shirt on over the top of it. "You're damned right. I don't know who's out there and, believe it or not, *you* are more important to me than this hulk of logs!"

When he ran through the living room, hopping first on one foot and then the other to drag on his boots, Breanna was right behind him. Coaly barked excitedly when they went outside, but Tyler shoved him back as he closed the door.

"A shovel, where's a shovel?" he roared.

Breanna stood staring at the outside of the door. A skull and crossbones were painted on the wood, glaringly white, with LEAVE scrawled below it. When Tyler turned and saw it, he hissed, "Those bastards."

Breanna rounded on him. "You know, damn you! You know who did this, don't you? Oh, God, Tyler, I'll never forgive you if my cabin burns, do you hear? Never...."

"Where's a shovel?"

"In the lean-to!"

He jumped over the retaining wall and ran into the lean-to, returning in moments with two shovels, one of which he thrust at her. "Smother the flames with dirt. It's the only chance we've got."

Breanna dug her blade into the hard soil, heaving on the handle. "I trusted you. I trusted you!"

Tyler's face looked grim as he bent to his work. He threw twice the dirt she did, but she was still panting with exhaustion by the time they had extinguished one corner of the cellar fire. She sagged, leaning on the shovel handle.

"Watch out!"

Tyler cast his tool aside and dived toward her. For a moment she didn't know what madness had come over him. His shoulder slammed into her midriff and carried her backward. They hit the dirt with jarring impact, and he began slapping at her legs. Breanna glanced down and saw flames shooting up her nightgown.

The moment was both nightmare and reality. She was back on the mountain the night of the forest fire, seeing Rob Thatcher's panicky face, hearing his screams. Only this time, she was the victim, and her own screams were piercing the night. Her first instinct was to run, and that was exactly what she tried to do. Tyler was all that prevented it and she fought him wildly.

"Let me go! . . . Oh, my God, please, let me go! . . ."

"Breanna . . . dammit, hold still."

His arms clamped around her and hysteria whirled in her mind. She was pinned by Tyler, just like Rob Thatcher had been pinned by the fallen tree. And the fire would consume her. Her arms were anchored to her sides and her legs were vised in the crook of his. All she could do was scream in helpless rage as he rolled with her.

Rolling . . . screaming . . . rolling. The sky became the ground and the ground the sky.

"It's out, Bree!" he yelled. "Honey . . . do you hear me, it's out, it's *out*! You're okay. My God, Bree, stop screaming like that. . . . Breanna, stop it. Breanna—"

Whack. Her head snapped back and she blinked. Tyler's face came into focus, illuminated by the nearby flames, his expression frightened. She pressed a palm to her cheek.

Even in the flickering light, she could see the anguish on his face. "Bree, say something, say anything. Are you burned? Answer me."

He tried to lift the charred hem of her gown and she grabbed hold of the still-warm flannel to hold it over her knees. "Don't touch me!" she sobbed.

His gaze swiveled from her to the fire and back, as if he couldn't decide which required his attention the most. With an oath, he ran back to the cellar and began shoveling again. Too numb to move, she sat there, watching him battle the blaze. When at last it was out, he staggered back to her and sank to the ground, resting his forehead on his knees.

"Are you okay?" he asked.

For the life of her, no words would come out of her mouth. She turned to look at him, her eyes coming to rest on his soot-streaked face. There was blood on his cheek; she realized she must have scratched him when they were struggling.

"Tyler, I'm sorry," she whispered. "I don't know what came over me. I know you were only trying to help me."

"Do you?" he asked hollowly. "You sure had me fooled. I would have sworn you thought I was trying to barbecue you."

"I . . ." The words to explain died in her throat.

"Come on, let's get you inside and see if you're burned." He helped her up and led her inside.

"I'm okay, Tyler, really I am," she argued as he reached to peel off her nightgown.

"I want to *see* that you're okay." Her arms were snagged in the sleeves of the gown and when she instinctively tried to cover herself, she foiled his attempts to get it off. "Breanna."

His tone brooked no nonsense. She sighed in defeat and let him tug the sleeves off her wrists, then crossed her arms over herself. He tossed another log onto the fire to give them more light, without exposing them to whoever lurked outside, and sparks sprayed up the chimney. When he turned back to her, she felt a flush of shame creep up her neck.

"For God's sake, I've seen everything there is to see. Turn around." He hunkered down behind her, and her skin tingled beneath his gaze. His light touch on the backs of her thighs did nothing to dispel her tension. No matter what he said, being naked when they were making love had been an entirely different thing than standing here, all passion gone, him studying every inch of her. His fingers grazed her back and she flinched. "Do you have any ointment?" he asked.

"In the bedroom, but I don't need it. I wasn't burned, I tell you."

"You might not know it right now, the state you're in. I'll put on ointment, just to be safe." With that, he stomped to the other room. When he returned, Breanna had her nightgown clutched to her breasts, which earned her a disgusted snort from Tyler. "Turn around," he said tonelessly.

"Really, there aren't any—"

"Just humor me, okay? I don't want this beautiful skin scarred, that's for damned sure."

He dabbed a glob of cream onto her bottom and rubbed it in. He was none too gentle, which made her glad she didn't have any blisters. "Well, if I did scar, it's where no one would ever see."

"It's where *I* would see."

"You're mighty sure of yourself," she retorted. "The way things are right now, there's no guarantee you'll ever lay eyes on it again."

"I'm *damned* sure of myself," he came back.

"Sometimes I think God poured cement between your ears instead of brains."

"The way I see it, you're the one who's a little dense. You see to the end of your nose, and that's it."

He stopped applying cream and stood, striding into the bedroom and returning with a fresh nightgown, which he tossed at her in a wad. With that parting shot, he went to the sink and pumped the basin full of water, then dipped the point of his elbow into it. She pulled on her gown, jerking it down over her hips as she ran to him.

"You're burned!"

He clenched his teeth, easing his forearm into the cold water, inch by painful inch. She watched helplessly, realizing that he had left his own injury untended until he had cared for hers.

"You got burned putting out my gown, didn't you?"

"No, I was playing with matches." He stiffened when she tried to look. "Just get back. It's not that bad."

"You're furious with me and I don't blame you."

He swung his dark head around. "Right now, Breanna, I'm furious with the whole damned world! I'd like to kill the idiots who did this, number one. I'm mad as hell that I'm caught in the middle of it. And every time I remember you fighting me out there, I want to shake you until your teeth rattle. I might be guilty of a lot of things in your eyes, but how could you believe I'd hurt you? Do you have any idea the things you said to me out there? Just leave me alone for a minute."

Breanna closed her eyes. She couldn't remember what she had said, but she could guess. "Tyler, let me explain."

"You don't need to. It's picture clear."

"I'm t-terrified of fire." She licked her lips, averting her face. "Rob Thatcher—he died slowly, pinned under a tree. I—I didn't mean anything I said personally. I have bad dreams, that's all, about burning...."

"You were clear on the other side of the mountain. You were, weren't you? You didn't see Rob Tha—" He broke off. The silence in the room crackled with tension. "Why didn't you tell me?"

"I couldn't." Tears blinded her for a moment. She blinked them away. "I knew the fire was near the commune. There were—women—lots of little kids. I went to try to help. And we came across Rob. He—he wasn't even hurt, not that I could see. Just pinned. Dane and I couldn't lift the pine, it was too big."

"My God...."

Breanna took a quick swipe at her face. "He was hysterical, of course. He knew the fire was deliberate. We were there. He said the—the most awful things. Accusing us, screaming he'd kill us, damning us to burn in hell. He was still screaming when Dane dragged me out of there. I can still hear him. Still, after all these years, like it just happened."

"Breanna..." Tyler straightened and reached for a towel. "Come here."

"No, no, I'm going to doctor that arm. Come sit down at the table."

His eyes challenged her for a moment and then he sighed, walking over to the chair. He rested his forearm on the table's edge, looking up at her as she approached him with a tube of salve. "I wish you had told me all of it."

Breanna's fingers trembled as she smoothed the ointment onto his skin. "It's blistered. You'll have a scar."

"I'm sorry," he said softly. "I should have realized you would be scared of fire. I'm really sorry."

Heat flooded her cheeks. "Tyler, please—I told you, it's said and I don't want to talk about it."

"Some things need to be talked about. You can't bury something like that. It eats away at you like a cancer."

"Would you shut up?" She stared down at him, the words hanging there between them. "Just, please, shut up...."

"No." His gaze probed hers. "You can get angry. You can hate me for it. But you can't bottle it up any longer. Something else about that night is tearing you apart inside. I can see it in your eyes. What, Breanna? You can't leave it unsaid."

"Watch me," she told him as she capped the tube. "Right now, I've got no time to talk about a fire that happened ten years ago, even if people around here still believe I set it. The one tonight needs taking care of first. You saw that message on the door. Someone set that fire on purpose, to drive me out of here. Well, I'll tell you this. It won't work. I'll be damned if I'll leave now."

"And what if it's the cabin they burn next? What are you gonna do, pitch a tent?"

"Very funny. And yes, if they burn my cabin, I'll pitch a tent. If you know who did this, I want their names. I'm going to the police."

"We'll discuss that come morning."

"No, we'll discuss it now, because I'm getting dressed and driving to town. Enough is enough."

"No, Breanna, you aren't. I can't let you do that."

"You what? Did I hear you say that you can't *let* me do that? Correct me if I'm wrong, but since when do you have the right to tell me what I can and cannot do?"

"Since right this minute."

She laughed and took a step back.

"Don't jut your chin out at me like that. You're not going to the police and that's final. I can't explain why, but I'm not letting you go."

"You . . . ?" She sputtered, trying to form sentences and saying nothing. "*You* aren't letting me go? *You* and whose army plan to stop me?"

"Don't be ridiculous, Breanna."

"We'll see who's being ridiculous."

He sat relaxed in his chair. "I'm warning you, Bree, I have to do what I have to do. Please don't force my hand."

"Please and a threat, all in one breath? A second ago, you wanted me to bare my soul. I can't believe you." She took another step back. "I'll tell you this. Don't you dare put a hand on me, because if you do, I'll file charges against you, just as quick as anyone else."

"You don't mean that," he told her softly.

Breanna hugged herself, staring at him. He was right; she didn't mean it. But she *wanted* to mean it. And a part of her hated him for dividing her loyalties this way, forcing her to choose between him and everything else that mattered to her.

"My cabin could have burned down tonight. I should have gone to the police when I first saw those men on my property. I won't be that stupid this time. Now I'm going and that's final."

He stood up and began unbuttoning his shirt. "I'm telling you I won't let you go to the police."

She wheeled and went to her bedroom, rifling through her clothes. He came to stand in the doorway, the curtain swept behind his shoulder. When she had her things gathered together, she placed her hands on her hips. "I'd like to dress."

"Go ahead."

"Very funny. Please leave and give me some privacy."

He didn't move. She had her blouse in her hand and she threw it down on the bed. "You have no right to stop me."

He sighed and closed his eyes for an instant. "Breanna, you aren't leaving this cabin."

"Why, will it ruin things for your friends?"

The muscle along his jaw rippled with anger at that remark. "Yes, it will."

"So, you admit it?"

"I admit nothing. You asked me a question and I answered it as honestly as I could. Someday, you'll see that I tried never to lie to you."

"Give me one good reason why I shouldn't go to the police."

"Because I asked you not to," was his simple reply.

"You ordered me."

"I'm sorry. I should have asked you." He shoved his hands into his jeans pockets and pressed his shoulder against the doorjamb. "I was asking for a fight when I didn't and I'm sorry."

He studied the toe of his boot, making scuffing sounds on the floor. She stared at the top of his head, wishing that she could read his thoughts. He straightened and let the curtain fall. Taking a step toward her, he put the heels of his hands on the brass bedstead, leaning forward with one knee slightly bent.

Breanna picked up her blouse again, then let it fall. "I don't understand you; I don't understand you at all. If you care anything for me, how can you let this happen? If this place had burned, I would have lost everything."

He looked out at the fruit cellar's charred siding. "It didn't happen, though, that's what's important."

"It didn't happen? Is that all you can say?"

"Yes."

"Really? Or is it just all you choose to say?"

His eyes met hers for an endless moment. That look was so intense and delved so deep, she felt as if he'd touched her. "Breanna, I know it's asking one hell of a lot. But please will you trust me for just a couple of days?" He held up a hand. "Before you answer, remember what I said about gut feelings. Think about it for a moment. Not about the gun, not about Chuck and Dane, but about me and who I am to you. I know it looks bad. I know it seems to you I'm being impossible. But if you'll just give me two days, I'll tell you everything."

"Tyler..." Her chest filled with an awful ache. How could she say no when he looked at her with such pleading? "Oh, Tyler, this isn't fair...."

"When you were in the creek, who took care of you? Tonight, who put the fire out? When you fell in the manzanita, who tended your back? I'm not saying you owe me. God knows, I can't blame you for thinking everything you're thinking. All I'm asking is that you take a long, hard look at me and ask yourself if you can't give me a period of grace." He gripped the bedstead so hard that she could see his knuckles turning white, even in the dim light. "Please, Bree, a lousy couple of days? I swear I'm not involved in anything illegal."

Full circle; she had come full circle. Her common sense told her to go directly to the police. Her heart was torn with doubt. Looking at Tyler, how could she believe he was guilty of working with Chuck? Of harassing her, trying to harm her?

"Oh, Tyler, you don't know what you're asking." She sank onto the edge of the bed. "Remember when you told me it wasn't so awful that I didn't go to the police with my suspicions about Dane and the fire? A reasonable doubt, you said. It was understandable, not wise maybe, but understandable? Now you're asking me to do it again, to turn my back on what I know is right and wait. The biggest mistake of my life, and you're asking me to repeat it. Do you have any idea how it's haunted me all these years? I know something's going on around here that shouldn't be. If I'm going to be true to myself, I *have* to go."

Again his eyes locked with hers. "I'm asking you to be true to me. Wait for two days, only for two days. That's all I need to put things right. After that, I'll drive you to the police myself, if you still want to go."

The muscles in her stomach knotted. She brushed her fingers across the nap of the bedspread. "Can I think about it?"

"Sure. I know it's a lot to ask."

"And if I say yes, will you let me help you?"

"Breanna, trusting me will be more help than you know."

Trust. It seemed to Breanna she had operated on blind trust all her life. If he just needed "two days to put things right," she owed him that much. But she still planned to make that phone call to the police to see if her hunch about the counterfeiting was correct. She would try to get a description of the woman who had passed the fake twenty in Grants Pass and see if it matched her own. And she would get information on how to identify a counterfeit bill if she saw one. Yes, she would give Tyler his two days, but she would do it despite the facts this time, not because she didn't know all of them.

"I'll give you till tomorrow to decide," he said.

"Yes, tomorrow," she whispered.

Chapter Thirteen

Chuck Morrow slid a partition back and began unloading a crate of money, stacking neatly strapped bundles on the waist-high pile of currency. "The shipment's got to go tonight. We can't hold off any longer. If this stuff doesn't hit Frisco by the weekend, we can't get it laundered for another month. And I'm not sitting on it that long."

"Just give me one more day. I'll get her out of here, I swear it," Dane pleaded. "Come on, Chuck, please. She's family. I can't stand by and see her get hurt."

"Look, pretty boy, I gave you time, plenty of time. If she's dumb enough to stay after that fruit cellar fire last night, that's her problem. I'll burn her out if they're not gone by dark."

"Oh, that's right up your alley, isn't it?" Dane cried. "If someone's in your way, a little gas and a match will take care of them."

"Damned right," Chuck retorted. "And don't you forget it."

THOUGH BREANNA'S DECISION to give Tyler his two days' grace was already made when she woke up that morning, she still held off telling him. She knew it was ornery, but watching him squirm gave her a perverse satisfaction. He hadn't made the decision an easy one for her, after all, by being so closemouthed. The way she figured it, trust was a two-way street, and he wasn't holding up his side of the bargain. When she went to the bathing hole, Tyler followed. She smiled as he stationed himself on a rock, turning his back to her.

"Looks like I traded Coaly for another form of guard dog," she commented as she undressed.

Ignoring her sarcasm, Tyler replied, "Sure is a pretty day."

"Peachy."

"Ah, come on, Bree. Look at this sunshine. It's fantastic."

Breanna gazed at his back, wondering how many topics of conversation he could dream up to keep her talking. Her replies were his only way of being certain she was still behind him.

Her silence spurred him to ask, "Don't you love this time of morning?"

"Yes, Tyler, I love it."

She especially loved the way the sunlight glistened in his black hair, she thought, sliding the soap up her arm. Sinking to her chin, she watched him lean forward to pick up pebbles and toss them aimlessly into the river. Maybe she did owe him the two days he'd asked for, she thought with an impish grin, but she didn't owe him an easy time of it.

"You know what I'd like to do?" he asked. "I'd like to take off right up the side of that mountain, just you and me."

She saw him cock his dark head to listen. Her grin widened.

"We could sleep under the stars. Cook on an open fire. Forget the whole world exists. Wouldn't you like that, Bree?"

Breanna stood motionless in the water and made no reply. Tyler's shoulders straightened.

"Breanna, are you okay?"

Seconds ticked by.

"Bree, answer me."

It was all she could do not to giggle and give herself away.

"Damn!" He leaped off the rock and whirled. When he saw her, he relaxed. "Why the hell didn't you answer me?"

"Just checking something," she murmured demurely.

"What?"

"I thought you were talking to make sure I didn't leave—and I was right."

He lowered himself to the rock, facing her this time. A twinkle of amusement entered his eyes. "Oh, you were, were you? And now what? Here I planned to be a gentleman and let you bathe in privacy."

Breanna smiled sweetly, unperturbed by his veiled threat. "And now you're afraid I'll swim off? Tyler, you're jumpy. If I did swim off, what would I have to wear?"

The laughter in his eyes faded. "Has it come to that? Do you really want to leave?"

"If I did, would you let me?"

"Why should we open that can of worms unless you want to go?"

"I have the feeling that you would force me to stay here if I tried to leave. Am I right? I'm not sure what it is you're so afraid of, but I'm a threat to you now, aren't I? You haven't said it, but I may as well be your prisoner."

"Breanna..." He tossed the handful of pebbles onto the rocks and brushed his palms clean. "Isn't the word prisoner a bit strong? Is that how you feel about me? Because you found my gun, you no longer *want* to be with me?"

She sighed in exasperation. "You are a master at twisting things, did you know that? And it's always in your favor. You answer a question with a question and turn it around until I'm sounding like the bad guy here instead of you.''

"Oho, so now the truth comes out. Because I have a gun, because I fibbed to you one lousy time, I'm the bad guy. Thanks for the vote of confidence. Thanks one hell of a lot!"

Breanna stared at him in disbelief. He *was* a master at twisting things. And where did he think he got off by looking wounded? "Confidence inspires confidence, Mr. Ross. You do a lot of asking and no giving."

"And just what have *you* contributed to our relationship? Tell me that!" he fired back at her.

Breanna lost her footing and took a mouthful of water. She sputtered and coughed. "At least I told you everything about myself. Do you know what you could do with that information? You could destroy me, my cousin, our families. And I trusted you with it. But when it comes to your precious secrets, you clam up."

He turned his back to her. "Just shut up and get dressed. There's no point in our having a huge fight about something I can't change."

"You see? I rest my case." Breanna strode angrily from the water to grab her towel. "I must be out of my mind to give you two days, absolutely out of my mind."

He swiveled on the rock. "You mean you will?"

She made a circle with her hand. "Two days, Mr. Ross, not a peep show."

A boyish grin creased his face. "Breanna, you're a gem."

"Yes. Well, two days isn't very long. And that's it, not a second longer."

He leaped from the rock, ran down the bank and grabbed her by her shoulders to give her such an exuberant hug that he nearly dislodged her towel. "Two days is all I need. You're beautiful. Have I told you that?"

"I'm wet, that's what I am. Turn your back so I can dress." Just as he started to turn, Breanna clutched his arm. "Tyler, did you hear that? That creaking sound?" Chills swept over her. "There in the copse."

He cocked his head. "It's a limb groaning, that's all. See the trees swaying."

"You sure?"

"Of course I'm sure." He presented his back to her, chuckling to himself. "Of course, it could be the ghost. They make noises. Listen...." He glanced back at her, lifting an eyebrow. "Chains rattling, doors creaking. Hear 'em?"

She rolled her eyes and gave him an exasperated push. "Get out of my way. At this rate, we'll never get to Grants Pass."

Two hours later, Breanna held a quarter up to the coin slot on a pay phone and dropped it in. With a shaking finger, she punched out the number of the Grants Pass police, then turned to watch the front of the service station to be sure Tyler didn't walk up on her. He had instructed the attendant to fill her gas tank, then he'd gone around the opposite side of the building to use the men's room. She only had a matter of minutes before he returned.

When a female dispatcher answered the phone, Breanna said, "Hello, my name is Sharon Wilson. I own a small store in Canyonville, a grocery store. And—um—I heard something on the news about counterfeit bills being passed in the area."

"Yes, we had one incident. Have you had a problem, too?"

"No—no—nothing like that. No, the reason I called was more as a preventive measure. I didn't catch the description of the woman who passed the bill and I was hoping you could tell me what she looked like. You can't be too careful, you know, and Canyonville isn't far from Grants Pass. I'd like to be able to tell my clerks what to be watching out for and I'd like to have some idea of the woman's appearance."

"What was your name again?"

"Sharon Wilson."

"Just a moment, Ms. Wilson." Breanna heard paper crackling. "Ah, yes, here it is. Female Caucasian, slender, medium height, middle twenties, with long, frosted brown hair and blue eyes." The dispatcher laughed softly. "That only describes half my friends. Ah, here we go. She drove away in a foreign car—the lady didn't know what make, but it was silver gray. Does that help?"

Breanna leaned weakly against the wall of the booth. She longed to tell the woman the blond streaks in the suspect's hair were not from a frost job, but the absurdity of that thought stymied her. "Yes, that helps immensely."

"Now, as for what to look for. Counterfeit money can easily be detected, but you really should bring your workers in so an officer can instruct them as to what to watch for."

"Oh, well, it may not be possible for all of them to come in. They're on different shifts. Aren't there any simple ways to tell?"

The dispatcher sighed. "Well, one of the easiest ways is to take a suspicious bill and lay it alongside a good one. First check the red and blue fibers in the paper. Counterfeiters can't exactly duplicate the paper used by the U.S. Bureau of Engraving and Printing, not even with the new photocopying techniques some are using. Next, look at the front and back for distinct print. It the portraits look dull, if the numerals are blurred on the edges, you could be in trouble. The serial numbers should be clear, evenly spaced, and counterfeit bills often have the same digits on every reproduction. Like I say, it's hard to help you over the phone.''

"Oh, you've helped immensely. I really appreciate it."

"It would be better if you could come in. Once you know what you're looking for, you could educate your employees.''

"I just might do that. Thank you so much."

Breanna hung up and hurried back to her car. The station attendant turned to smile at her, giving her windshield one last swipe with a blue towel. "Say, do I know you from someplace?''

"No." *Oh, God.* Breanna opened the passenger door and climbed inside, slamming it behind her. She bent forward so her hair fell over her face. *I don't believe it. They've got an APB out on me. I'm wanted.* A sharp rap on her window made her jump. She looked up to see the attendant peering in at her.

She cracked her window. "Yes?"

"Aren't you Jason's sister?''

"Oh, yes." She laughed with relief. "Do you know him?''

"Yeah, real well. You're Bree, aren't you? Deanna's the married one with the short hair. I didn't use to be able to tell you two apart.''

"Yes, I'm Breanna. And your name is?''

"Jim. Jimbo to Jason. We played basketball together in high school." Tyler walked up just then and the station attendant flashed Breanna a farewell grin, walking to the front of the car. "I filled you up and topped it off. Your oil is fine.''

Tyler handed him a twenty and Breanna's eyes were immediately riveted on it. *Oh, please, don't let it be counterfeit.* The man stepped to the island till and made change, then came back to count it into Tyler's palm. "Thanks. Stop in again. Bye, Bree. Tell Jason I said hi."

"I will," she called.

Tyler slid into his seat and buckled up. "An old friend?"

"Of my brother's."

"Well, we're ready for that treasure hunt." He started the car, shifted into first and pulled into the traffic. "Do you feel okay? You're kinda pale."

"No, I'm fine," she lied.

"Are you sure?"

Breanna pulled back her hair from her cheek, meeting his gaze for an instant. *Counterfeiting*. It was incredible. "Yes, I'm sure."

And she was. She stared straight ahead at the road, amazed at how calm she felt. Two days or a hundred, she would give Tyler the time he requested. She had no choice. She was in love with him.

FROM THE OUTSET of their gold hunt, the detector beeped every time Tyler went near metal of any kind. Since the treasure hunt was his idea, Breanna didn't feel the least guilty when he spent more time digging than he did using the rental equipment.

"Hurrah," she teased. "A bottle cap. If any treasure hunters are watching, this should impress them."

Next they found an old belt buckle.

"Don't laugh," Tyler warned. "I'm getting blisters doing this and we've only just begun."

"Must we?" She squinted into the glaring afternoon sun. "I can think of other things I'd rather do."

His eyes ran appreciatively over her figure. "So can I."

He sighed when the detecting device shrilled another signal. Breanna exchanged tools with him again, then took stock of their surroundings for a more exciting spot to search, preferably one in the shade. "Tyler, if we're going to go through with this stupid charade, shouldn't we be systematic about it?"

"Meaning?"

"Well, if there really were some gold, Uncle John would have buried it near something that he could have used as a marker, not out here in the open."

"Good thinking. Trees, maybe?"

"Or a big boulder, like that one in the upper orchard."

"I'm game," he agreed. "Let's go."

Breanna gasped with amazement when the metal detector went crazy near the rock she had suggested.

Tyler glanced at her, barely suppressing an excited smile. "You don't suppose old Uncle John is whispering clues over your shoulder?"

"Dig! It has to be something big to set the detector off like that."

He stuck the shovel into the dirt. He had removed about eight inches of topsoil in a two-foot circle when the metal blade grated against something. Breanna's body went rigid. He made a wider hole and tested the earth with a chopping motion. The blade still clinked.

"Whatever it is, it's gigantic," he declared in a low voice.

"Could it be a chest?"

He raised an inquisitive eyebrow at her. "I didn't think you believed any of those old stories. Now look at you."

"Well, could it be?"

"It's sure big enough. A good three or four feet long and a couple of feet wide. It's going to be a hell of a strain to lift, if it is a chest."

"Especially if there's gold in it," she added.

The more Tyler dug, the more certain both of them became that they had discovered something significant. The object was large and rectangular.

"I can't believe this," Tyler said. "I think we've really found something."

Breanna knelt beside him, placing her hands on her knees and leaning forward, watching as he cleared away the earth around the iron. "Want me to dig awhile?"

"Sweetheart, I like your hands just the way they are. I'm fine." He stopped digging for a moment to wipe the sweat from his brow with his handkerchief. "Do I get a free dinner out of this?"

She giggled. "If there's gold in there, Mr. Ross, I'll take you to the finest restaurant you can find. Do you know the price per ounce right now?"

"It's up, isn't it?"

"Better than it's been for quite some time."

"You know, if this *is* gold down here," he reflected, "you should have a nugget made into a necklace, as a keepsake. It's not every family that has a history like yours. It would be quite a conversation piece, like having a family crest."

Tyler bent over the shovel again. It seemed to take forever for him to dig out the soil around the buried object so that they could each get a grip on an end and lift it. When the moment arrived, she could barely contain her excitement. Tyler was as anxious to see the contents as she was; she could see it in his eyes. He motioned her into the hole, stepping down when she did.

"Oh, I wish Gran was here to see this, Tyler. She'd be so excited." Coaly jumped into the hole with them, trying to dig, and she shooed him out, bending to grab her end. "Silly dog."

"Ready? Now, if it's too heavy, don't strain to lift it, Bree. I don't want you getting hurt."

"I'm stronger than I look."

"Not that strong. Okay, one, two, three, heave...."

He turned slightly red in the face, but managed to raise his end about a foot. Breanna couldn't budge hers. Panting from the exertion, she said, "You'd think he would have put handles on it."

"You know, I don't see how he even planned to open it. It's welded solid."

"Yeah. Do you suppose it's upside down?"

"I doubt it. Maybe it's just sealed." He placed his hands on its corners again. "Let me try by myself."

"No way, Tyler. You'll hurt your back." She grabbed her handholds and strained upward. No sooner had she done so than something showered on her feet and the iron container grew lighter. Glancing down, she saw that her sneakers were covered with dirt.

Tyler looked at her over his end of the box. "Bree, I just figured out what this is."

"What?" she breathed.

"A trough. We have just spent an hour and a half digging up a damned old water trough."

After all his hard work, she knew she shouldn't laugh, but his expression struck her as so funny that a giggle escaped. To her relief, she saw him grin. A second later, they were both laughing so hard that they'd dropped the trough and sat down on it to catch their breath.

Sitting there beside him, the thought occurred to her that it really wasn't that funny. Their laughter bordered on hysteria; it was an outlet for the tension they had both been under these last two days. Behind her eyelids, Breanna felt tears burning.

"I don't believe this," he told her between chuckles, draping an arm around her shoulders to pull her against him. "I nearly ruptured myself getting this thing out of here. And all that's in it is dirt. Coaly thinks he's finally made a soul mate of me."

Breanna sighed, holding her palm over her aching stomach, smothering another giggle. His arm around her felt so right, the possessive pressure of his hand so good. Her common sense told her to pull away, to keep a wall between them, but another part of her argued that anything so wonderful couldn't be wrong.

"Look at the bright side. There could be some gold in the dirt." Another laugh rippled up her throat. "Now I'm glad Gran wasn't here. She'd never let us live this down. That trough has probably been lying there for years and years, sinking deeper and deeper."

He reached to rub something off her chin, then glanced at his dirty hand. "I think I just made it worse." His eyes rose to meet hers once again. "You know, all the gold I need is right here."

Breanna's chest grew tight with emotion. Even the way he touched her, so lightly, as if she might break, broke down her defenses against him. "Oh, Tyler . . ."

She thought he might kiss her, but her turmoil must have shown in her expression. "I love you," he murmured. "I know I haven't done a good job of showing that I do. But I do love you."

"Love doesn't mix well with secrets."

A shadow crossed his face. "I know. That's me, the fella with bad timing. I guess I've no right to say it, do I?" A humorless smile curved his mouth. "I'm sorry."

"Don't be. I'm glad you said it."

"Maybe when all this is over, we can talk. Until then, I guess we're on hold."

"Not entirely."

"No?"

There was an eagerness in his eyes that made her smile. "I gave you the two days, didn't I?"

"Yes, you did." His hand tightened on her arm. "I guess that should tell me something, shouldn't it?"

"Yeah, that my timing is as rotten as yours."

"We both need a bath," he said, wiping her face again. "You're a mess. What do you say we go down and take one at dusk?"

"Together?"

His mouth claimed hers with an infinite gentleness that told her how much he truly cared. A tender caress, underscored with a hesitancy that erased any lingering doubts about her decision to give him the two days. Breanna leaned into him. There were no answers to the questions that plagued her. Tyler just *was*, and nothing beyond that made any sense.

Chapter Fourteen

On the way back to the cabin from their bath that evening, Breanna and Tyler walked with their arms around one another, hers around his waist, his draped over her shoulders.

"When I was little, I loved it here," she said with a sigh. "At night, Gran would make fudge or hot chocolate and we'd sit around the fire while my grandfather told stories."

Tyler traced circles on her arm, as if he couldn't get enough of touching her, even now. "I make a mean batch of fudge. I like to drop-test it and eat the balls. How about you?"

"Yeah, except that I could eat the whole pan that way before it was done. I have to make a double batch if I expect to get any to keep."

He laughed and tightened his arm around her. As they drew close to the cabin, she heard Coaly whining. Handing Tyler her soiled clothes, she said, "Go on in. I've got to take a walk."

He glanced toward the outhouse, then at his watch. "Okay, but hurry." Giving her a quick kiss, he ran up the steps. "How's about I make some fudge? Sound good? We'll build a fire."

"Sounds great." Breanna smiled as she angled across the drive, pleased that he trusted her enough to let her go alone.

Just as she reached the outhouse, a hand clamped down on her arm. "Bree."

Her heart missed a beat. "Dane, you scared me out of a year's growth."

"I'm sorry," he whispered. "Keep your voice down." He pulled her behind the lean-to, then released her to lean against a corner post. In the moonlight, she could see he was pale. "Breanna, I'm in big trouble, the worst I've ever been in. But this time I'm not gonna drag you down with me. You've gotta get out of here, tonight. You understand? Grab your things, get in the car and go. Right now. Before it's too late."

She put a hand on his arm. "Oh, Dane, what is it? What's happened?"

"I . . . set the fire. I never meant to hurt anybody. I swear to God it was just a prank, Bree. You gotta believe that."

"I do, Dane, I do."

"It was Morrow! Thatcher and a guy named Darren, they were working with him, growing and selling marijuana, and they cheated him somehow." Dane's voice shook. "I didn't know that then. Chuck talked me into setting a small fire, just as a prank. You know how we all hated the hippies. I thought that was why, to scare them. I had no idea, no idea. I swear to God, Bree."

"Go on, Dane." *Darren, Joseph Darren.* He had been killed in a car accident. Breanna remembered the name from the news story Gran had circled. A hippie from San Diego. She was beginning to see the picture now. After ten years, it was all becoming clear.

"I put a gas can by one of their sheds and used a dynamite cap of Gramps's to set the fumes off. It had a long fuse, so it gave me plenty of time to run. And then it blew. But it blew like an atomic bomb. The whole damn mountain went up, Bree. Morrow had stashed more gas all around, in bushes, behind trees. And the explosion just kept setting cans on fire.''

Breanna closed her eyes.

"And I did it!" Her cousin's voice rose to a shrill pitch. "I set the cap off. You and I even bought the gas.''

"You and I?''

"Yeah, two days before that. Remember, when we filled all those cans for Chuck's generator? And we loaded them in Gramps's Jeep?''

Breanna swallowed her nausea. *Oh, God, please no.*

"I bought the gas on Chuck's charge card. He had my signature on the receipts. It was my cap that was used to set the fire. Don't you see? He had evidence against me. He could have sent me up with what he had on me. When Thatcher died, it wasn't just a prank anymore, Bree, it was murder.''

"All right, I understand." Breanna hugged his waist to hold him steady. "Dane, it's okay, it's okay.''

"No, it—it isn't okay. You don't understand. Rob didn't just *happen* to get pinned by that tree! Remember all the wild things he screamed at us? Accusing us? He thought we knew! He thought we knew!''

"Knew what?''

"Chuck drugged him, put something in his beer. Then carried him up there, downed the tree and used the winch on his truck to lift it and pin Rob under it. He murdered him, Breanna, burned him alive. Only he framed me for it, just in case it came out the fire was arson.''

Breanna stood speechless, clinging to Dane, her eyes riveted to his face.

"Morrow used it against me over the years. Just little favors, at first, dirty work, never anything serious. But the deeper I got, the bigger the favors got and the more I was involved, until there didn't seem to be any way out for me. I just did what he said, so he wouldn't ruin my life.''

"Oh, Dane..." She pressed her forehead against his shoulder. "If only you had told me. You should have trusted me. We could have gone to the police. I would have testified for you. Why? Why didn't you tell me?''

"It's too late for that now. Chuck's crazy. I mean really crazy. He's got to make a shipment. You won't leave. He's talking murder, Breanna. You've got to get out of here. I've tried to talk sense to the rest of them, but they won't listen.'' He took in a bracing draught of air. "It was the twenty I dropped that did it, that's what clinched it. Chuck was turning them against me anyway, because I've been getting suspicious. I found out about...well, this girl named Marcy, she did Chuck a few favors, knew too much. And then she had a wreck. I suspected Chuck of tampering with her car. And he's been out after my ass ever since. Some of the money came up missing, counterfeit money. The guys Morrow's tied up with now, they think I stole it. Morrow's set me up again. This time to get rid of *me* because *I* know too much.''

Breanna couldn't stop trembling now. "Oh, God, Dane...''

"He's taken a stash and hidden it. I don't know where. But that twenty I dropped, the one you found, it came from him. He deliberately gave it to me, knowing I'd spend it without realizing it was hot. Only I didn't. I dropped it. And it came over the news that a woman had passed it, a woman who fitted your description. The others put two and two together and figured I gave you the money. You don't screw these guys over and get away with it.''

Breanna groaned. "Dane, they might kill you. You can't go back.''

"If I don't, they'll get suspicious. But you've got to run, Bree." Dane gripped her shoulders and moved her away from him. "You understand? This is my way of making it up...all those things I did to you. I had to come tell you."

"Dane..."

"I know I don't deserve it, but trust me, just once more. Go inside and tell Ross what's happening. He doesn't know things have turned sour and he's got to know it. If he doesn't, I won't be the only one who gets hurt. You understand?"

"Tyler," Breanna whispered. "He's a part of it. I've known for a couple of days."

"God, no! Ross? He's an agent. I wasn't sure at first, not until he moved in with you. He's a G-man with the Treasury Department. Since Morrow pulled that stunt with the scythe down by the creek, Ross has been guarding you."

"No...." Breanna shook her head. "No, Dane, that couldn't be true. He and I...we..." Her voice trailed off and a hundred memories flashed into her mind. Damning memories. "He's been watching me? You mean it was part of his job?"

"Breanna, right now the last thing I'm worried about is your feelings. He's a cop. None of the others know it, but I trailed Ross one afternoon and saw him meet some other fellows in the brush, down by the creek. They're Feds. It stuck out all over them."

Strangely enough, she didn't feel so much frightened now as empty. Just empty, horribly empty. "All right, Dane, I'll go tell him what you've said. But I want you to come with me. This doesn't have to be the end for you. You never meant to hurt Thatcher. You haven't done anything *that* wrong, not yet, not if you stop now."

"I can't. They'll know something's up." Dane cocked his head, then shoved her away from him. "Go! Morrow's coming."

She looked toward the creek. She heard the footsteps, too. "Dane, please..."

"Bree, one more thing! The mine—there's another— Oh, damn, run! Run, Bree. I can see him coming."

Breanna saw a flash of white in the bushes and turned to go, more afraid for Dane than she was for herself. She knew her cousin had committed the unforgivable sin by confiding in her. They'd kill him for sure if they found out.

She reached the cabin and let herself in as quietly as she could. Tyler was wiping the stove when she stepped into the living room, and he turned to smile at her. "My God, what's wrong?"

"Everything."

He clenched the dishcloth in his fist. "What are you talking about?"

"You're with the Treasury Department. Everything, it was all a lie."

"Not everything."

"Oh, yes, everything. Why? Was it a fringe benefit of the job? Do you sleep with every woman you protect?"

Anger flashed in his eyes. "Who the hell have you been talking to?"

"It's true, isn't it? You were assigned to watch me. Weren't you?"

"Yes, but—"

"No buts. When you moved in here, it was part of your job, wasn't it?"

"Breanna..." The guilt on his face answered her question.

"Looking back on it, I think you even thought I was part of it all for a while, didn't you?" She wiped her moist palms on her jeans. "Answer me!"

"Yes," he admitted. "Breanna . . . it hasn't all been a lie. I believed—"

"Just shut up!" she hissed. "You *used* me. You wormed your way into my confidence to learn all you could about Dane, about the hold Morrow had over him. It's all so clear now. How could I have been so stupid? My cousin's going to die, and you don't even care. Anything for your precious investigation!"

"Breanna, you weren't stupid. What you told me that day, I've never repeated. The only thing I told Jones was there was a chance Dane *did* have something to hide and that Morrow might be using it to coerce him. I swear it."

"They're going to murder him. You could have stopped it! Don't tell me you didn't know about Morrow, Thatcher and Darren. You've known. And you stood back, watching Dane go under. Tough luck, right? Well, let me tell you something. Dane's a good person. He's made some mistakes, but only because he didn't have anywhere to turn. Of course, you wouldn't understand that, would you? All you think about is getting the job done."

"You're hysterical. Who's Darren?"

"You're right, I'm hysterical. You did nothing to help Dane. Why? Doesn't a human life count for anything with you people?"

"I'm getting confused here. I began to suspect Dane was being coerced, but—"

"You're confused?" There was an awful stillness in her chest. "You ought to be me, then you'd know what confused is."

"I think you'd better calm down," he said softly.

"I'm calm enough." She blinked tears from her eyes. "Dane told me to tell you we'd better get out of here. Morrow has set him up, stolen some of the money. They..." Her voice faltered, then she regained control and finished Dane's message in a stilted monologue, telling him everything. "I think they're going to kill him."

Breanna lifted her hands in a helpless gesture. "I tried to persuade him to come with me. But Morrow was coming."

She started to cry, softly, brokenly, and Tyler came to her, wrapping both arms around her. "Breanna, it'll turn out okay. It's not as bad as it seems right now. You'll see."

She stiffened and drew away from him, wiping her cheeks. "Get me out of here. Maybe if I'm gone, he'll have the sense to run."

Tyler doused the lantern and strode quickly to the bedroom. As he reentered the living room, he strapped on his shoulder holster and donned a yellow jacket. "Forget packing. Breanna, are you sure Dane's the only one who knows who I am?"

"That's what he said. And I think he's beyond lying."

"I'll notify Jones of that, then. Thank God Dane had sense enough to keep his mouth shut."

"How will you notify anyone?" She no sooner asked the question than she knew the answer. "Oh, on your radio. I was incredibly naive, wasn't I?"

In the fading glow of the lantern she saw him shake his head. "You just trusted. There's no sin in that."

If there wasn't, why did she feel so humiliated? Tyler groped in his jeans pocket for the car keys, then led her onto the porch. Coaly scampered in front of them, down the steps and around the fruit cellar.

Just as they reached the car, Coaly charged off, barking furiously. It was a frenzied, wild sound. Breanna whirled. In the dark, the black dog was scarcely more than a shadow, but she saw him streak up the ramp and into the barn, in hot pursuit of something. *No, not something, someone.*

Almost immediately there came a bout of vicious snarling, then a shrill yelping that ripped nightmarishly across the drive. She sprang into a run. The dog was screaming with pain, and each cry cut clear through her. She saw Tyler coming from the other side of the Honda, also running flat out.

"Bree, no!"

"Coaly? Coaly!"

Breanna was up the ramp in two strides and into the corridor before Tyler could reach her. He clamped his arms around her, dragging her backward. "No, Bree, for God's sake, no!..."

Just then the barn fell deathly quiet. Breanna froze in Tyler's arms, staring into the black bowels of the passageway. "Coaly?"

Tyler's hand swooped down over her mouth and stayed there, pressing so hard that it almost suffocated her. He stepped back with her. She could feel his heart pounding against her shoulder blade and realized, too late, that the counterfeiters were inside the barn with them.

A gun went off and she heard Dane's voice. "No, damn you! Leave her alone!"

The bullet splintered the wood right beside them. Tyler swore under his breath and dived with her toward the door. They rolled partway down the ramp, then thudded off it onto the ground, hitting so hard that Breanna got the wind knocked out of her.

Crouching over her, Tyler whipped out his gun. She heard a click and knew he had pulled back the hammer. When she looked up, she saw he had his right wrist braced against his left palm, arms extended and locked. He remained like that, his eyes riveted above them on the yawning doorway.

"Run," he whispered. "Straight up the drive to the car."

Breanna caught her breath and rose on the balls of her feet. "Tyler, we can't risk the car...not after what Dane said about Darren and the girl."

Tyler thought furiously. She was right. "Cut through the woods to the road. I'll catch up with you. My place. There'll be other agents there to protect you. Tell them to douse the lantern. If no one's there, turn on the radio, leave the frequency where it is and call for help. If I don't make it, someone else will."

If you don't make it? Breanna's heart sank. "But..."

"Go," he ordered, "before you end up getting me killed."

She leaped forward into a full-length run. Behind her, she heard the report of a gun, then another, the shots increasing quickly to a volley.

Never in all her life had she run so hard. All she could think of was reaching the radio to call for help. Nothing would stop her. When her foot hit a chuckhole, sending her into a headlong sprawl, she jumped up again, ignoring the pain of a twisted ankle.

It was her fault, all her fault. Tyler had called out to her, trying to stop her from going into the barn, but she'd run on ahead. *Stupid, stupid, stupid.* If he died back there, it would be her doing, as surely as if she'd held a gun to his temple and pulled the trigger.

Oh, please, God... The unfinished prayer echoed and reechoed in her mind as her legs ate up the distance to Tyler's cabin.

She had reached the last bend in the road before the cutoff, when Tyler caught up with her. He grabbed her hand and dived with her into the ditch alongside the graveled shoulder, covering her body with his. "We need to get out of sight. They're not far behind." She heard him reload his weapon.

"Breanna, I love you. I want to be sure you know that, just in case. I love you, Bree...."

"Oh, Tyler, I'm sorry. They were hurting Coaly and I ran in there without thinking. I'm so sorry...."

"Hush!"

Headlights came around the curve, bathing them in their glare. Tyler ducked his head and shrank closer to her. Breanna held her breath as Morrow's pickup passed them. Then it braked and began backing toward them, coming fast.

"Oh, Lord. Cross the road to the creek, Bree, quick."

A shot whizzed past them. Tyler clasped her arm, dragging her to her feet, then they dashed across the asphalt, Tyler firing off shots to cover them. The next second, Breanna felt open air under her feet, then she was falling. When she hit ground, she landed on her back and slid until her hip collided with a tree trunk. At least the truck couldn't follow them here.

"Damn, it's straight down," he whispered. "Hold on to me."

The rest of the descent was fast and scary. It was so dark that Breanna couldn't see the trees that loomed ahead. She ran into her share of them, scraping her extended arms, and so did Tyler. It was no consolation to hear sharp barks of pain coming from the men who pursued them.

"Who are they? How many are there? It's not just Morrow."

"Counterfeiters, a bunch of them. Dammit, I can't see."

A bunch of them? How many is a bunch?

They broke out of the trees. It was lighter along the creek. Hand in hand, they forded a shallow spot in the stream and raced into the pines on the adjacent hillside. Behind them she heard voices raised in argument, then the splashing of feet following their trail.

Breanna's lungs felt as if they might burst. She had run almost a mile on the road and now they were lunging up a steep hillside. *I can do it,* she told herself. *I can't let him know I'm tiring.* Tyler was getting ahead of her. His arm was outstretched behind him to keep hold of her hand. A couple of times, she felt him slow down so she could catch up. Behind them, she could hear brush cracking. They were losing ground; the men chasing them were getting closer and closer.

Tyler pitched forward. "Oh, damn!" She heard him fall into the brush. Then he bit back a moan of pain.

Frantic, Breanna dropped to her knees, groping blindly to find him. She ran into a tree, bruising her shoulder. She slid down a slight decline into a growth of vines. "Tyler...?"

Her pulse slammed with fear. Where was he? She heard him moan again. She clawed her way on her belly, slapping the air ahead of her with her hands until she touched his boot.

"Bree...my leg...it's bad. Can you find your way out alone?"

Alone? Without him? "No, I..."

"Go to my cabin. Stay in the woods until you're sure you've lost them. You know how to take care of yourself in the brush. You have to get me help."

"But..."

"Get to my cabin and radio for help," he commanded her. "Go! I'm counting on you, Breanna. You've got to make it."

The men below them were drawing closer. She could see the beam of a flashlight bobbing. Tyler squeezed her hand a moment, then gave her a little push. "Go."

Breanna crawled backward. As much as she hated leaving him, if he couldn't run, she had no choice. She sprang to her feet. "Tyler, I—I love you."

"I never doubted it."

Chapter Fifteen

Breanna backtracked and crossed the creek about a quarter mile above Tyler's cabin, then cut into the heavy brush that lined the road. She'd managed to lose her pursuers, but there were lights glowing in the cabin windows, so she hid behind the woodpile. A blond man stood in the kitchen. She could see him over the top tier of logs, pouring a cup of coffee. His shoulder holster, which was similar to Tyler's, and his nonchalant air convinced her he belonged there. She ran to the front door. Glancing behind her, she rapped softly. A moment later she heard footsteps inside.

"Who is it?" a deep voice demanded.

"Breanna Morgan. Let me in, please, let me in."

The door opened a fraction, then swung wide, but there was no one standing there. That struck her as odd. She stepped cautiously across the threshold.

"Freeze!"

The harshly barked order stopped her dead and buckled her knees with fright. The door hit the wall behind her, and movement flashed on both sides. So tense that her neck creaked, she looked first to the right, then to the left. In both directions she gazed into the snubbed barrel of a gun. She had walked right into a trap.

The two men who flanked her crouched in a ready-to-fire stance that made her skin crawl. Their fingers were curled around the triggers of their weapons. She might be shot if she made a wrong move.

"Arms up," the blond man ordered. "That's good. Now step on inside, lady, real slow and easy like."

Breanna's legs felt like wobbly rubber. She moved forward, praying she wouldn't fall. The blond man inched around her, his pistol trained on her chest.

"Frisk her," he told the other man.

Palms slid beneath her arms, moving in a quick motion downward. "I don't like this, Brent, not with a woman."

"Yeah, well, I'd rather be a live bastard than a dead gentleman."

"She's clean."

The fair-haired man still didn't lower his gun. "Start talking, lady, and fast. Name first."

"Breanna Morgan." Her gaze landed on the gun again. It was exactly like Tyler's. *Agents. Thank God.* "Please you've got to listen...."

"Don't move," he barked. "I mean it, lady."

"Please. We're wasting time. Tyler needs help."

"Ross?" the other man asked.

Breanna turned to look at him, taking in his brown hair and features. *The man in the manzanita?* So it *had* been Tyler she had seen that night. "Yes. They have him holed up about a mile from here. He's hurt. He fell on a—"

The back door burst open. A tall, dark man rushed inside. "Ross is in trouble. I just heard gunfire. Sounded like all hell broke loose." His brown eyes riveted on Breanna. "My God, Falson, put your weapon away! That's the Van Patten girl."

"She didn't say Van Patten, she said Morgan." Falson lowered his gun. "I wasn't taking any chances."

The older man strode across the room, jabbing his thumb at the pictures on the closet door. "If you'd done your homework, you'd have known her on sight. I told you to study the layouts."

Breanna's attention flew to the photographs of herself and Coaly, then returned to the older man.

"What's going on with Ross?" he asked her. "Do you know?"

"He's hurt. The counterfeiters were chasing us and he fell. He's on a hillside, and he sent me for help. I only heard gunfire for a while. He either ran out of ammunition or they—"

"Okay, slow down. Can you tell me where he is? I'm Jack Jones, his friend. You can trust me."

A vision of the woods slipped into her mind. Setting them an accurate course through the forest at night would be impossible. "No, but I can take you."

"Too dangerous," he countered.

"Too dangerous? Tyler needs help, don't you understand? I don't care if it's dangerous. Besides, it's my land. I've every right to be in on this."

Jones met her gaze. She had the feeling he was sizing her up. "All right." He stepped to the table, picking up an extra box of ammunition. "Jacobsen, you come with me. Falson, you man the radio. Get more lookouts posted around the entrance to the mine. Call Simonson and Miller and get the roadblocks up. This sucker's coming down tonight."

Both Jones and Jacobsen withdrew their guns from their holsters and ejected the clips to check for bullets. When they shoved them home, the rasp of metal filled the room. Breanna flinched.

Jones glanced up. "You sure you're up to this?"

"I'm sure."

"I won't paint a rosy picture. If there's a confrontation
it could be dangerous. We won't have time to be worryin
about you." They were already moving toward the door.

"I can take care of myself."

He cocked a bushy eyebrow at her.

"I know these mountains," she explained.

"I sure as hell hope so. We don't. That's what Ross wa
for."

"Tyler said to douse the lantern. I don't think anyon
followed me from the creek, but it's better to be safe."

Jones clipped a radio handset to his belt, motioned t
Falson to turn down the light, then spun on his heel to leave.
Breanna followed him out the door, then Jones slowed hi
stride, letting her take the lead. "You're running this show,"
he said.

"Hell," Jacobsen grumbled. "I could get lost out her
five feet off the road."

Breanna pointed toward the peak of Hungry Hill behin
them. "Keep that mountain in sight. If something happen
and we get separated, head directly for it and you'll even
tually hit the road."

Both men pinpointed the location of the hilltop.

"This way," she called over her shoulder, crossing th
road. Jones leaped down the bank behind her. "It gets s
dark down here, you can't see anything," she warned. "Fee
your way and be careful. A sharp branch can go clea
through you."

The descent here wasn't as steep as the one she and Tyle
had tumbled down earlier, but it was every bit as dark.
Breanna heard Jones grunt and knew that he had run head
long into a tree. Jacobsen swore a second later and brush
snapped. When they reached the creek, she turned to wai
for them.

"How far from here?" Jones asked.

"About a half mile. It would be easier to see if we walked along the creek. Is it safe, do you think?"

"Let's keep in the brush," he decided. "If we stay close to the open, we'll have enough light."

Breanna wove her way into the trees. She picked up her pace to match her heartbeat, thud-thud-thud-thud, begrudging every minute, every second that kept them from Tyler. There was no sound ahead of them, only deathly stillness.

"Mr. Jones, do you think . . . they'll kill him?"

"It depends on how much they know."

"Meaning?"

"If they realize who he is, they'll probably hold him as a hostage. If they think he's a civilian who's discovered their operation, they'll dispose of him."

Her throat felt as though a baseball was stuck in it. "Will Tyler tell them, do you think?"

There was a long pause before he replied. "No, he won't tell them."

Now her heart was pounding even faster than her feet could hit the ground. The sound of it filled her head. Was Tyler's still beating? Her breathing became shallow, fast.

"I can't understand what they were doing in my barn," she said, holding back a limb for them.

"Dammit, Jacobsen, keep up with us. *Under* your barn," he corrected, sweeping past her so that Jacobsen could get through. "Ingenious, isn't it? An abandoned mine that isn't even documented." He grunted and she heard a branch crack. "Careful, it's a sharp one."

"So there's a shaft under there? I suspected that! But the entrance has caved in. How do they get in?"

"They boxed in a stairway between the tack room and the next stall. You probably didn't notice, but the interior has been altered. Are we nearly there?"

"A little farther. So that's why the barn seemed smaller," she exclaimed. "They're actually making counterfeit money in *The Crescent Moon*?"

"Enough to break Fort Knox. They have a press run by a portable generator, with a gas motor. How far is it now?"

"We're almost there. It's about five hundred yards upstream. I left him on the hillside."

Breanna's mind reeled. Suddenly so many things made sense, the footsteps she had heard that afternoon in the stall and the low hum of an engine the other night. No wonder each noise had ceased the moment she spoke. They had heard her and shut down until she left.

Jones grasped her arm to stop her, then took his radio from his belt. She saw a tiny red indicator light blinking. He pulled the antenna and flipped a switch. Soft static buzzed. "Yeah, Jones here."

"We got trouble, boss. Ross is down in the mine. And they didn't take him in through the entrance."

"Damn!" Jack grimaced. "What the hell do you mean, Falson?"

"There must be another entrance," was Falson's reply. "Has to be. They have him down in there and they didn't go through the barn."

Breanna turned to Jacobsen and whispered, "How do they know Tyler's in there?"

Jacobsen replied, "Bugs. You know, listening devices?"

"Oh." Breanna squeezed her eyes shut for a moment. Of course. The tiny microphone she had found in the blind! Piece by piece, it was all fitting together. The man in the manzanita, wearing the headphones. Why hadn't she guessed immediately? She remembered Tyler saying her suspicions of counterfeiting were clear into the twilight zone. How true that was. A tremulous smile touched her mouth, and tears brimmed in her eyes. Would she ever laugh like that with Tyler again?

"Son of a . . ." Jones keyed his mike. "Is Ross okay?"

"Sounded okay."

"All right, over and out." Jack clipped the radio back to his belt and put his hands on his hips. "What the hell do we do now? There's another entrance. Morgan, you sure that old entrance is completely closed off?"

"Positive." Fear inched up Breanna's spine, fear for Tyler. If there was another entrance, the counterfeiters could come and go without being seen. Which meant they wouldn't hesitate to kill a hostage. They had escape insurance. "Mr. Jones, we have to find that other entrance. Fast."

"Go to the head of the class," he said with a grim laugh. "Where? That's the question." He pivoted, looking at the woods around them. "God, it's so dark, we'll never find it."

"Oh, yes we will. Come on." Breanna elbowed her way past him, aiming for her cabin.

Jones slipped on a rock trying to catch up. "Hey, slow down! How can we find it? Clue me in."

"I've been studying those old maps. I think I can make an educated guess where another entrance might be, that's all."

"It'll be like finding a needle in a haystack," he said with a snort. "I can't waste time on wild-goose chases, lady."

"And neither can I. Everything that matters to me is in that mine, Mr. Jones. My cousin, my dog and—and Tyler. If there's another entrance, I'll find it." Breanna glanced over at him, unashamed of the tears that had spilled onto her cheeks. "It's my fault Tyler's down there in the first place."

Ten minutes later, Breanna and the two agents crawled into Tyler's blind on their bellies, inching up beside a man with a radio set. Jones elbowed his way to the equipment, listening intently to the radio receiver. "What d'ya got, Jackson? Anything new?"

"Not much. Ross is trying to get them to talk."

Jackson. Breanna stared at the younger agent as Jack introduced them. "Breanna, this is Mike."

Jackson nodded, then looked at his boss. "They've been giving him a ration about her. He doesn't know for sure if she's safe."

A grim smile twisted Jack's mouth. "Ross is tough. He won't run at the mouth unless he doesn't see any other way out. Whoa, listen...."

Voices were coming over the main receiver. *Tyler.* Breanna heard him talking and leaned nearer. The agents had done a good job of installing their hidden microphones. The transmission came over the air with very little static. A knifelike pain twisted through her at the sound of Tyler's voice.

"Cue in on this," Jack whispered to her. "Tyler'll try to tell us where they brought him in if he can."

Breanna moved closer to the radio.

"I should have known something like this was going on here," Tyler said. "I never dreamed—"

"Shut up, unless you wanna say something worth hearing. Quit stalling, Ross. Why wait until they drag the girl in here? I'll be in a foul mood by then. And believe me, you don't want me in a foul mood with your lady."

Jones took Breanna's hand and squeezed it. She clasped his fingers. *Chuck.* Just the thought that Tyler was at Morrow's mercy made her cringe.

"I told you, she's not my lady. How do you think I stayed single all these years? Love 'em and leave 'em, that's my motto."

"Yeah? That's not what it sounded like in town the other day. We'll see what you say when she's here."

Tyler laughed. "I got no beef with you fellas, really I don't. You do your thing and I do mine. Live and let live, you know? I'm telling you, I'm just a photographer. I carry a gun in the woods to protect myself."

"Sure, a nine millimeter semiautomatic? Right, Ross. Got any used cars you wanna sell me?"

"I tell you, Morrow," Tyler said, "you're dead wrong. I gotta hand it to you, though, that back door down there is really something. I'll bet we passed it a dozen times and never even guessed it was there. I should have known...."

"I thought I told you to shut up. You got a bug down here? Is that it?" The click of a gun hammer came over the air. The sound was unmistakable and Breanna stiffened. "You rotten son of a bitch. Answer me! If I find a mike in here, you're gonna be one sorry bastard."

"Hey, easy...easy..."

There was the sound of a scuffle. Breanna's heart shot clear up into her throat and stopped beating. Air came out in a gush when she heard Tyler say, "Whoa...hey, let's not play so rough. I won't say another word."

"Where's Breanna?" Morrow demanded. "I should've known it meant trouble when the little bitch wouldn't leave. Her and that damned dog of hers, sniffing around. It attacked Dane twice, one time in the barn, then out in the drive after that. Smart little sucker. I'm glad Rawlins bashed his skull in. He's been nothing but a thorn in my side ever since he got here. Where is she, Ross? It'll go easier on her if you talk."

There was another scuffle. "Now talk, Ross. Where's that cute little friend of yours, huh? I'll bet you tell me anything I want to know once I've got this gun held to *her* head."

Breanna was shaking. Not even Jones's tight grip was a comfort. *Oh, God, Tyler.* Did Morrow intend to shoot him?

"I don't know where she is. I lost her in the woods. How many times do I have to tell you?"

A long silence followed and then Morrow's low chuckle came over the air, distorted by a spurt of static. "Tell me something. She good in the sack?"

Breanna's stomach heaved. She heard Tyler reply, "What makes you think I've slept with her?"

"You think I was born yesterday?"

"Let's put it this way. If I had slept with her, I sure as hell wouldn't discuss it with scum like you."

"I'll bet she's a firecracker," Morrow mused.

"Just in case you're thinking she means something to me, Morrow, think again. I haven't known her that long. She's a nice woman, but not leverage."

"So you *do* admit you're a Fed."

"I didn't say that."

Morrow snorted. "You don't have to. So . . . she was just part of your job, huh. Didn't mean a thing to you?"

"She's a nice lady," Tyler repeated. "And I wouldn't want to see her hurt."

"Yeah, yeah, you talk a good game. We'll see if you mean it when they drag her in here. They'll find her, you know. And then you'll talk, Ross, you'll talk." Morrow laughed again. "Maybe we'll all have a little fun. A party. You wanna watch us have a party, man? Rawlins here, he's the slickest fella with a knife you've ever seen."

There was a long silence and then Tyler snarled, "Touch her, Morrow, and there won't be a prison on earth that'll keep me from killing you."

"Oh-ho-ho, so the cool cop loses his temper?" Morrow clucked his tongue. "You threatening me, Ross?"

"I'm promising you."

"And the lady means nothing to you? That's interesting."

"It's called common decency. Something a horse's ass like you wouldn't understand."

"Sure is a pretty little gal. Be a shame if her face got all messed up, now wouldn't it? You wouldn't like that, would you?"

Their voices seemed to be getting farther away. Breanna glanced at Jack. "They left the mike," Jack explained. "Damn, I wish he could have said more. The back door down where?"

They had passed it a dozen times, and never even guessed it was there? *Where, Tyler? What were you trying to tell us?*

"Down," she whispered. "Jones, he said *down* there. That means below the barn!"

"But where?" he challenged.

Her pulse was hammering so fast and hard that her ears rang with it. The copse? It had to be. Breanna turned to stare at Jack. "Of course! Down by the bathing hole. It would explain everything. How that man appeared, then vanished into thin air. The footprints in the brush, with none going in or out. Coaly having such a fit every time I went there alone."

Jones looked at her as if she had lost her mind.

"I know where it is. Come on, Jones. Bring a flashlight."

"No flashlights. Jacobsen, you and Jackson stay here while we check this out."

Jones dogged her heels down to the stream, then stood back with a puzzled look on his face while Breanna strode purposefully into the brush. *The grassy bank.* It was dead ahead of her, silvery with patchy moonlight. A chill of understanding shivered into her mind. She remembered how

Coaly had sniffed the sharp incline after her clothes had been stolen.

"So that's why there weren't any footprints. *My* feet sank into the grass. Don't you see? If someone had climbed that bank, he would have left tracks! And tonight, when I was talking to Dane. Morrow came from this direction."

"Would you try to make some sense, please? What are you talking about?"

Breanna took a halting step toward the bank. "It's here. The door, Jones, it has to be here." She extended her arms, searching the tall grass with a patting motion. "Come on, help me. There has to be a..."

Her fingers ran into cold, smooth metal and she froze. Taking a deep, steadying breath, she tried to pry it up. It moved.

"I knew it," she whispered raggedly.

She turned to grin at Jones, so excited that she wanted to shout. Her smile froze on her lips. A man stood behind Jack, moonlight reflecting off the gun he held in his hand.

Chapter Sixteen

"Don't move, mister," the gunman snarled. "So much as twitch and the woman gets it. Understand?"

Jack stiffened and slowly raised his arms. "Hands coming up, friend. Don't get trigger-happy."

"Open the hatch," the man ordered Breanna. "You just couldn't let it be, could you? You should've got the hell outa here while the gettin' was good. But, oh, no, you had to keep snooping around."

Breanna curled her fingers around the metal once more and pulled. A familiar creaking sound filled the air, then a black opening yawned at her feet.

"Three steps," the counterfeiter said. "Fall and you're dead."

Her legs felt quivery and she sent up a silent prayer that they wouldn't give out under her. One.... She groped for something solid to hang on to and her palms met with damp earth walls on either side. Two.... She heard Jack's boot settle on the step behind her. Three....

Searching with her sneakered foot, she found the dirt floor and moved forward. The floor of the tunnel sloped sharply. She felt Jack grip her shoulders. His fingers bit into her flesh. Before her was a blackness so impenetrable that it was like walking into death's arms.

No, Jack, no, she prayed. *No heroics. Just do what he says.* But even as she thought that, she knew Jack would make his move. He was a federal agent. She was a citizen. It was his job to protect her and if they once got down into this shaft, he'd never get her back out of it, not alive.

Breanna expected it when Jack shoved her forward, so she was ready for a headlong dive. She hunched her shoulders for the impact and rolled. She slithered on her belly a few more feet, then sprang into a crouch, staring back at the shaft of moonlight and the silhouettes that were struggling for the gun.

For the life of her, she couldn't tell which figure was Jack. One man grunted and doubled over. The other one dived for him. Their arms were extended upward, etched in stark relief against the silvery backdrop of light. The shape of the revolver wove to and fro as their hands fought for its butt.

In horror, Breanna watched as one combatant slowly gained control, forcing the pistol down. Then the muzzle exploded with a darting tongue of orange fire. The shot reverberated in the tunnel, each echo louder than the last.

"Oh, God..." a voice croaked.

Breanna's stomach lurched. *Jack!*

"Run... Morgan," he moaned. "Oh, Lord..."

Breanna coiled on the balls of her feet to leap forward. She bit back a scream. Jack was sliding down the wall, holding his stomach, his head lolling forward on his chest. And the other man was raising the gun, pointing the barrel at Jack's head.

"No!" Breanna reached out a hand.

"Run!" Jack cried. "Ru—"

A second shot rang out. The timbers above Breanna groaned. Dust and small clods of dirt pelted her face. Then there followed a silence so eerie that the air pulsated. She froze, arm still extended, her lips parted in denial. Jack's silhouette slid to the floor, completely motionless.

The counterfeiter whipped around and ascended the steps to jerk the door shut. Breanna crouched there, too stunned to think. The hinges creaked and total backness swooped over her. She heard the rasp of metal. Dear God, was he locking her in?

Run! her brain commanded. She whirled and stared into the nothingness behind her. She had no idea where the tunnel led, but terror made her legs move. With her arms held wide, she groped blindly, bouncing off one wall, staggering to find the other. It got bigger once you descended the steps, then? Six feet wide, she guessed, more than her arm span. She would have to stay on one side and feel her way along. She chose the left.

Stay calm. Think! Don't run in a panic. Use your head.

Breanna closed her eyes, summoning all her senses. She counted every step she took, forcing herself to measure the length of her stride. She had to know how many paces she took and exactly how long they were.

He knows his way, she thought, *but you have the advantage, Breanna. Keep your head. This is just a mining tunnel, like any of a dozen you've been inside.*

Her left hand met open air. She fanned her arm. It was an opening, about three feet wide. A passage off the main shaft? She felt ahead. Yes, the main corridor that she was in stretched on ahead. Her heart slamming, she turned, praying that she hadn't stepped into a dead-end chamber.

A bright beam of light bounced off the earthen walls of the main passage seconds after she left it. Her knees wobbled with relief. *One, two, three, four...* She hurled herself along the narrow hall, going as fast as she dared, clicking off her steps, trying to keep track. She had gone fourteen strides in the main tunnel; now she had gone sixteen in this one. Seventeen, eighteen, nineteen . . .

"You can't get of here!" the man yelled. "There's no sense hiding! I locked the door. We'll find you!"

Breanna blocked him out, counting as she ran. *Twenty-three.* A faint sliver of light glowed above her and she stopped, throwing back her head. Moonlight. Her eyes focused. An airway?

Her pulse accelerated. She threw up her arms and felt a hole about two and a half feet square. Could she get a grip on the supporting timbers and lift herself into it? Her vision grew more accustomed to the light. Yes, it was an air hole, a vertical tunnel going straight up to ground level, with a grate at the top.

Bending her knees, Breanna tensed her legs. She leaped upward, flailing her arms. Her right palm struck wood and she homed in on its position, dropping back to the ground. The light beam was coming closer and closer. . . .

She hunkered down again. One more try. If she didn't get a handhold this time, she wouldn't have another chance. With all her strength, she pushed off in a desperate leap. Her fingertips grazed wood, curled, gripped frantically. The weight of her body pried her fingernails away from the quick, but she gritted her teeth and didn't let go.

She had never been very good at climbing. That handicap, coupled with near blindness, made her ascent into the air shaft all the more difficult. She pumped her legs to swing, using the momentum of her body to help lift herself. Flinging up her free arm and groping with her palm she found a cross section of wood along one side of the opening. Repeating the pendulum motion, she found another, a rung higher, and pulled herself up until she could get a toehold.

The hole was high and narrow, but it was wide enough for her to fold her body into it, bracing her shoulders against one side and her knees on the other. She leaned her head back, willing her heart to stop pounding.

"You're locked in, lady," the man roared. "I don't have time to play games with you. Come out and save us both a lot of trouble."

Breanna saw the beam of light bouncing around on the floor beneath her. She dropped her chin to her chest. The illuminated figure of the man came into view between her spread legs and she stared at the top of his bald head. *Don't look up.*

"Dammit," he snarled. "Where the hell could she go?"

He turned and stepped out of sight. Breanna felt sweat trickling between her breasts. She waited for total darkness, straining her ears. A cough sounded some distance away. Was he going for help?

She stared down at the blackness under her. It was safe here. She could probably stick tight and never be discovered. The agents outside wouldn't expect any heroics from her. Neither would Tyler. They would want her to hide, wouldn't they?

Perspiration beaded on her forehead now and ran into her eyes. She blinked and swallowed. What could she do to help? Risking her life for no good reason was stupid.

Coward! Think! There has to be something that you can do.

Had the man taken Jack's radio? Breanna mentally replayed the sounds she had heard when she was running. No, surely he hadn't. Right after the gun had gone off, he had closed the door and locked it. He had followed her almost immediately after that. With the radio, she could call the agents above ground, tell them where the back entrance was, and get help for Jack.

With her heart drumming in her chest, Breanna slid down the air shaft and dropped to the ground. She counted her steps as she ran back up the passage and slowed on twenty-two, feeling for the intersecting corridor. One more step and her hand met nothingness. A right turn and fourteen steps. Jack had to be just ahead of her.

She stooped, searching with her arms. Her fingertips ran into something warm and sticky. She gasped and recoiled, then forced herself to reach out again. His midriff. Sliding her hands downward, she found the radio, unclipped it from his belt and keyed the mike. Nothing. With trembling fingers she searched for an on-off switch, and as she traced the outline of the handset, she felt shattered plastic. Jack must have broken it when he fell.

She stood there for a moment at a loss. With no radio, she couldn't contact anyone aboveground. She was locked in. The only other way out was through the main chamber. Her own life, as well as Jack's and Tyler's, depended on her, and she didn't know what to do. *Jack's gun.* The thought slid into her mind and crystallized. Oh, God, she knew nothing about guns. Could she even fire one? And if she could, would she be able to hit her target? There wasn't much time to think about it.

Tossing the radio aside, she ran her hands over Jack's chest, found his gun and pulled it from the holster. Just as she slipped the weapon into the waistband of her jeans, Jack moaned. Breanna dropped to her knees, scarcely believing her own ears. He wasn't dead? Pressing her palms to his midsection, she found one wound. Nausea rolled up her throat when her hand came away wet with his blood.

Moving quickly, she grabbed the hem of her shirt and tried to rip it. It wouldn't tear. She sank her teeth into it and yanked until the cloth split, thanking God it was a T-shirt, so it would stretch to provide double thickness. As soon as she'd wrapped Jack's middle, she tore another strip for his head. It wasn't much in the way of first aid, but it was all that she could do in the dark. She frisked him, finding his extra bullets and stowing them in the pocket of her jeans.

Oh, Jack, hang on. Knowing how badly a head wound could bleed, Breanna propped him in the corner so that the steps and wall braced him in a sitting position to restrict the blood flow. If he fell sideways... No, she wouldn't think about that, couldn't think about that. She rose to her feet, hating to leave him. *Tyler.* He was down here somewhere. He needed help, too. She had to go.... She heard a sound down the corridor.

Fourteen paces back the way she had come, a left turn and twenty-three more. Breanna ran until she stood beneath the air hole again. By the time she had shimmied back up into the narrow space and wedged herself there, she was exhausted.

Only moments later, the main passage was echoing with shouts, and lights were bobbing everywhere. Breanna held her breath, so scared that her whole body quivered.

"Well, she didn't get out. Look at this," Morrow exclaimed.

The familiar rasp of the bald man's voice reverberated in the tunnel. "I'll be damned. Is he alive? Maybe I won't get a murder rap out of this, after all."

"He's a goner," Morrow replied. "You're in up to the neck."

The bald man grunted. "Might as well finish him then."

Breanna clamped a hand over her mouth. *No, no, don't.* She tensed for another shot, smothering sobs. *Animals, nothing but animals.* She envisioned cold metal pressing against Jack's forehead. Hot tears slid down her cheeks.

"You moron, don't fire that thing down here again. You want the whole place caving in?" Morrow gave a snort.

"Use your head, man. He's history. Forget him. Help me find the woman."

Moments later, the men shone their flashlights down the corridor Breanna was in, but didn't enter it, which confirmed that it was a dead end. The sound of their voices passed her.

"Well, if she hits the main chambers, Rawlins and Pope will nail her," Chuck speculated. "I say we try these. I'd bet money she's in one of them. Damn, she's at home in tunnels."

More passageways? Breanna shivered. It was so cold. She had forgotten how chilly it was underground. Where the perspiration was drying, her bare midriff felt icy.

"I'll go left, you go right," she heard them agree.

When their footfalls had died away, Breanna lowered herself from her hiding place. Just in case she needed it, she pulled the gun from her waistband and searched for the safety. Right behind the trigger guard she felt a small, round button. She pressed it. Metal rasped, something hit her stomach, and bounced down her leg. *Thunk.* She cocked her head, running her hands over the weapon. Horror raced through her when her fingers found a square hole in the butt.

She had ejected the ammunition clip.

Frantic, Breanna dropped to her knees, patting the ground all around her. Her breath came in quick little gasps. *Oh, God, please.* Her hand bumped against metal. The clip. With a sob, she picked it up. In one end she felt an inch-long bullet, on the other a sloping surface. She knew the bullet end went first, that the tip of the bullet had to point forward so it could be ejected into the chamber. She squeezed her eyes closed, gritted her teeth and shoved the metal cylinder into the hole, hoping the sound wouldn't carry. The clip grated, hit home and stayed.

She knelt there, holding the gun in her hand, pointed away from her. If it had a safety, she didn't know where it was. She curled her finger around the trigger. She had to see if it would move without pulling it far enough to activate the firing mechanism. Easy, easy. She tightened her grip, pulling back. Nothing. The trigger wouldn't move. It was on safety, and she didn't know how to get it off.

A shudder ran through her. She blinked, gulped air and swallowed, then stood up. She had to find Tyler. There was no choice. And if she had to bluff her way with a gun that didn't work, she'd do that, too. If she could get the gun to him, they had a fighting chance. *Rawlins and Pope.* That gave her two more men to contend with in the main chamber, which she assumed was under her barn. If they had Tyler in there under guard, how would she ever reach him?

Driving all doubts from her mind, Breanna elbowed her way along the wall and turned left into the main corridor. Twenty paces farther, she felt another doorway. One of those being searched?

It seemed to her that she walked at least a mile, even though she knew the barn wasn't that far from the creek bank. One hundred and eleven steps had registered in her mind when she walked face first into dirt. With her right arm extended, she groped until she felt a door. She pressed her ear against it and heard muffled conversation. Gingerly she tried the knob. The door wasn't locked.

Breanna had never jumped into a den of criminals with a gun before, but she had seen how Tyler and the other agents had held theirs and had also watched enough television drama to hope she could do it convincingly. The counterfeiters wouldn't be too frightened of her if they knew she'd never shot a pistol. Especially if they guessed the trigger was locked.

She closed her eyes for a moment, saying a quick prayer, then tried to remember the most recent detective movie that she had watched. One thing she knew for sure, cops always entered rooms with a bang. She was no policewoman, but maybe if she yelled loud enough, no one would notice her knees knocking.

She turned the handle again and eased the door forward so that the latch was free, then stepped back. Raising her left leg, she kicked as hard as she could and jumped into the opening, slapping her gun hand onto her other palm and locking her elbows.

"Freeze!" she yelled.

The sudden pool of bright light blinded her. She blinked to clear her vision, inching sideways, keeping her back protected by the wall. One man was so taken by surprise that he nearly fell off his stool. Another was lounging against the wall to her left, sipping coffee. He slopped the liquid all over his blue shirt and flinched.

Never in all her life had Breanna been so scared. She hoped her voice would stay steady. "One false move, just one, and I'll blast you where you stand."

The man on the stool made a move toward his revolver, which rested on his hip.

"Don't do it, mister."

Their eyes filled with fear.

Breanna shut the door with her foot. "Okay, fellas, real slow and real easy, put your weapons on the floor."

"Lady, be careful with that thing," the man in the blue shirt pleaded. "You might shoot somebody."

"Yes, indeed." Breanna kept the gun weaving from one man to the other. "Fact is, I might shoot *two* somebodies."

"Just stay calm," the man near the stool said smoothly. "We'll do what you say. Just don't accidentally pull that trigger."

Breanna realized her acting hadn't been very convincing, but they seemed frightened of her this way, so that was okay. She didn't care, as long as she got the job done. They put their weapons on the floor. "That's good, very good. Now turn around and step against the wall. Arms up, legs apart. That's the way. Move and you're going to be exceedingly sorry."

Glancing uneasily around her, she got her bearings. It was a large room, filled with machinery. Copying equipment? A press? She spied the huge generator in one corner and marveled that they had ever gotten something that large down here.

With her peripheral vision she saw jean-clad legs stretched out on the floor to her left, bound with rope at the ankles. She whipped her head around and her heart soared with joy. Tyler's slate-blue eyes stared back at her over a band of white cloth. She couldn't see much of his expression, but guessed he was horrified. He wasn't the only one. She hurried over to him, keeping the gun aimed at the other men while she struggled to untie his feet. He leaned forward so she could reach his wrists.

As soon as he could, he ripped off the gag and scrambled for the weapons on the floor, stowing one in his belt, keeping one in his hand. Leaning against a wall, Breanna sighed with relief, more than happy to let him take over. *His leg? He isn't limping!*

"Keep the door covered," he instructed her.

She jerked erect and gave him a bewildered look. He flashed her a quick grin. "Don't quit when you're on a roll, Bree. We've still got the other two to worry about." He kept his gun trained on their prisoners and stepped back, glancing at the paneled ceiling. "Hey, fellas? Coffee break's over up there. We need some help. Send someone down to the creek, too. There's a back exit there, right up from the bathing hole. A sod door in a bank, right there in the brush."

Breanna watched Tyler tie their prisoners with the ropes that had bound him, then edge his way to the opposite side of the door. She remembered how the agents had flanked her earlier when she had entered Tyler's cabin. She could handle that, she thought. All she had to do was keep her arms locked, her gun steady and look shifty-eyed. She took her position, thought of asking Tyler about the gun safety, then discarded the idea. Just in case the criminals got brave, she couldn't risk them knowing she had a weapon that wouldn't fire.

"Bree, don't point it at me!" Tyler snapped.

She moved the barrel tip, shrugging one shoulder. If he expected perfection her first time at this, he could think again. "Sorry."

Just then the door opened. The bald-headed man looked so big when he stepped into the room that she decided to let Tyler take the lead. Her knees were shaking too hard. Morrow walked in and froze. His brown eyes met Breanna's, and he smiled a smile that turned her skin to ice.

"Come on in, gentlemen," Tyler said calmly, motioning them forward. "Guns on the floor, please."

Breanna watched the barrel of her pistol shake and thanked God Tyler had this mess under control. If she could have pulled the trigger, chances were she would have shot her foot off.

"Shut the door, Bree."

Tyler slid the guns out of the criminals' reach with his foot and instructed them to join their cohorts along the wall. His voice was disappointingly conversational, not rough and tough as she'd imagined federal agents would talk. No wonder the counterfeiters hadn't been convinced by her acting. She was lucky she hadn't botched the whole thing.

"Real good. Keep your arms reaching and don't move." Tyler looked totally relaxed, his eyes deadly calm.

Thumping sounds filled the room and Breanna jerked her head around to stare at the closed door to their right. It flew open and three men entered, Jacobsen coming in last. His eyes landed on Breanna and widened in amazement. She dropped her chin and stared. What was left of her blouse was smeared with blood. Her hands were bright red. No wonder Tyler had looked so horrified. She stooped and let the gun slip from her fingers to the floor.

She fixed her gaze on Tyler. He was already shrugging off his jacket, stepping toward her. Smiling, he holstered his gun, stuffed her arms down the overly long sleeves of his windbreaker, zipped it up and hugged her. It wasn't just an ordinary hug, but a tight squeeze; his arms were trembling.

"What happened to your shirt? Are you bleeding? I'm so glad you're safe."

He leaned over and picked up Jack's gun, stared at it for a moment, then flipped a lever on the left side of the hammer. His face grew pale when he pulled back the slide to check for a bullet in the chamber. "My God, you didn't have a bul—" His eyes flew to hers. They stared at one another for a long moment, then he smiled, hefting the weapon on his palm. "You are one helluva lady, Miss Morgan. Who gave you this?"

Breanna's mind froze. *Jack.* Here she was, feeling so relieved, and Jack Jones was badly injured, maybe bleeding to death. "Jack, he's been shot. Oh, Tyler, hurry. Get a light. We have to help him."

Jacobsen heard her and left the prisoners with the other two agents. "I've got a light," he said, flipping it on as he left the room with them, "but the agents coming in the back way should be there by now."

Breanna cried, "Oh, hurry, hurry...!"

To her relief, the wounded man was surrounded by other agents when they reached him. "She got the bleeding slowed down," one said, "...did a fine job of this, for working in the dark. Excellent...."

Tyler's arm tightened around Breanna's shoulders. Someone shouted behind them. "We've got Van Patten back here! Stomach wound. He's bad, real bad." Breanna turned, staggering down the tunnel. There was a lighted opening ahead. She reached it, braced her hands on each side and leaned in. Flashlight beams bounced. She glimpsed blond hair, a gray T-shirt, sprawled legs. *Dane.* Breanna stepped into the room. She felt Tyler grasp her shoulder, give her a pat. Then he was gone.

Confusion broke out. Voices bounced off the walls around her. Men dashed back and forth. She was trapped in a nightmare of blackness and sporadic light, alone, unable to help, numb. She leaned against a wall, registering bits and pieces of what she heard said.

"Lost a lot of blood."

"Get them to a hospital."

"The dog's a goner. Should I finish him off?"

Tyler's voice rang out. "No! Get him to a vet. That mutt's a good buddy of mine."

Silence. Then, "You gonna foot the bill? His head's bashed in."

Tyler swearing. "Yes, I'll foot the bill, Falson. *Take him to a vet, stat.*"

"Okay, okay, don't get so touchy."

Breanna lifted her head. Tyler's silhouette appeared in the doorway. "Bree?"

She tried to speak, but her throat wouldn't work. There was a terrible emptiness inside her. He came to her, his shoulders blocking out the flickers of light behind him. Breanna finally found her voice, but somehow the words evaporated as they hit the air, coming out in soft sobs, soundless, broken. Tyler clasped her behind the head and pulled her snugly against him. "Shh, Breanna, it's all over."

She closed her eyes. Yes, it was all over. Everything. Dane, Coaly, Jack, Tyler, everything.

"Let's get you out of here. Somebody'll give you a lift to town. You'll want to be at the hospital with Dane, won't you?"

She felt his hands massaging her back. The temptation to lean against him, to need him was great. But her pride was greater. He had said *somebody* would drive her to town, not that he would. And he hadn't used "we" referring to the hospital. It was over, just as he had said. She straightened, pressing her palms against his chest to lever her body away from his.

"Yes . . . yes, I'll want to be with Dane."

In a fog, Breanna left the mine with him, gazing sightlessly at the steep stairwell as they ascended into the barn. Agents crowded the corridors. Flashlight beams revealed tall stacks of currency. Exclamations erupted around her. She stepped outdoors and down the ramp, taking deep breaths of fresh air. It helped to clear her head. Several pairs of headlights were bouncing along her drive. Car doors slammed. Feet thudded on the ground.

She turned, arching her neck to see Tyler's shadowy face. "Your leg. It's better? I was afraid you'd broken it or something."

He laughed softly. "Let's just say it mended pretty fast after I knew you were gone."

A smile touched her mouth. "You didn't . . ."

"I had to do something, Bree. They were right behind us and you were exhausted. We had to split up so I could draw their fire, so I tricked you."

She glanced up the ramp at the men in the corridor who were taking the illegal currency as evidence. "All of this was why you wouldn't let me go to the police?"

"You can see how big an operation this has been. Jack didn't want local authorities messing up the bust."

She nodded.

"They wheeled carts right up the ramp, loaded the cash for transport and circulated it, all right from here. One of the most sophisticated operations we've ever run across. Slick, too. Who'd ever guess this ramshackle old barn was being used for something of this scale? Or suspect that the production was all done underground? It took forever to figure it all out."

"No wonder the barn seemed smaller to me. Fake walls. I can't believe it, Tyler. That twenty I found. All of that was on the other side of the wall?"

"These boys are big-time," he assured her. "Your arrival threw a wrench in their fan blades. That's why they tried so hard to scare you off. Given time, they would have gotten mean about it, which was why we put you under protection. The barn is wired with electronic audio devices that are strong enough to pick up conversations in the main chamber below. That's how I knew when you were in the barn that night and got here so fast. I guess they figured we were on to them tonight when they chased us."

"The night I saw the man and followed him in here? It wasn't you? You were in the blind, listening over the transmitter?"

He sighed, hunching his shoulders against the night air. "After that scenario in Wolf Creek, I had proof you weren't involved. I went down to see Jack to get permission to get you out of here. I'm so sorry for all the lies, but I didn't have any choice. Jack had a fit every time I approached him about leveling with you.''

"You mean you did talk to him about telling me?"

Tyler smiled. "When I was sure you weren't involved. I thought I might persuade you to leave until we cleaned things up. But Jack was never sure about you. That's why we staged all the treasure hunting, so my hanging around wouldn't make you suspicious.''

Breanna glanced up at him. Why was he looking at her with so much wanting in his eyes? He stepped closer, closer. His hand touched her cheek. His eyes caught hers, hungry, full of need.

Breanna stepped quickly away. "Do you think—Dane will be okay?" She closed her eyes for an instant, bracing herself.

"He's pretty bad. All we can do is hope. I'm sorry."

"He made his choice, I guess, a long time ago." Breanna shoved her hands into her pants pockets. "The wrong one."

"If he pulls through . . . well, I—uh—can't make any promises, but I think they'll go easy on him when all the facts come out. Especially if he turns federal witness. We still haven't found the plates. Dane probably knows where they are. We were waiting until we were sure those had been brought in to close the trap. Breanna, can't you look at me? Please don't turn away."

She forced herself to face him. "Tyler, I don't want you to feel obligated to—"

"Hey, Ross! We need you down here!" Jacobsen roared from the corridor.

Tyler swore under his breath, then sighed. "I have to get back down there. Breanna, we have to—"

"Ross, dammit, we need help with Jones. What's keeping you?"

Breanna looked at Tyler through a blur of tears. "Go on, Tyler. Do your job."

"I don't want you thinking like you're thinking."

"I'll be fine."

"It'll be a couple of days. We've got the loose ends to tie up. Reports to file." He stepped toward her. "I'd like to come back, Bree, to explain, to talk. I've told you so many half-truths, trying not to lie to you. There's so much left unsaid."

"Sure," she agreed. "We'll talk."

"Ross!" Jacobsen leaned out the barn door. "You comin', or what?"

She dragged a hand out of her pocket to give Tyler a shove. "Would you go?"

He stopped at the ramp to look back at her, his face in shadow. "I'll be back," he promised. Then he disappeared. Breanna waited there for a moment, staring into the darkness, then turned on her heel. An agent stepped out from a nearby vehicle. "Miss Morgan, I'm supposed to give you a ride to town. Do you need anything here before we leave?"

Breanna glanced back at the barn, then shook her head. "No, there's nothing."

She climbed into the back seat of the car and slammed her door, resting her forehead against the glass. Her eyes stayed on the barn as the agent maneuvered the vehicle up the drive. She hoped for one last glimpse of Tyler. Oh, he might come back. She didn't doubt his word. But talking could never put things right between them. A federal agent and a wildlife writer? It seemed such a shame. Apart from their professions, they had been so right for one another. A sad smile touched her mouth. As Gran would have said, better to have loved and lost than never to have— She broke off the thought without finishing it. Gran was wrong. It wasn't better. The losing hurt too much.

Trees whipped by her window. Patches of moonlight fell across her face. Breanna gazed through the trees at the silver ribbon of water that snaked beside the road. She had been right about Tyler from the first. His identity, at least where it involved her, had begun and ended down Graves Creek.

Chapter Seventeen

The sun inched slowly downward, and the soft, subtle whispers of another summer evening settled over Graves Creek. As Breanna walked to the orchard, carrying a shovel, she tipped back her head to gaze at the distant horizon above Mount Reuben. A smile curved her mouth. At last she could look toward *The California Mine* with a sense of peace. Rob Thatcher's ghost was finally laid to rest, his murderer incarcerated. And nicest of all, she and Dane were becoming close again, as they had been as children, no secrets dividing them.

All had ended well....

Sadness caught at her heart. *Almost all.* A week had passed, and there hadn't been a sign of Tyler. He hadn't kept his promise to return. She had narrowly missed seeing him at the hospital a few times when she went to visit Dane. Other than that, there had been no word, nothing.

Sighing, Breanna slowed her pace, approaching the hole she and Tyler had dug to unearth the old water trough. It was too deep to leave. Someone might fall into it. Glancing down at Coaly, she said, "I don't suppose we could reprogram you to dig in reverse, could we?"

The black dog cocked his bandaged head, eyeing the mound of dirt. A single "Woof" and a wag of his tail later, he was in the hole, digging furiously. Breanna groaned, dropped her shovel and leaped in after him.

"You silly old mutt, you. You'll get dirt in your gauze. Out! Out you go." Breanna half lifted her pet from the hole, giving his rump a fond pat as she put a leg up to climb out after him. "Quiet, the vet said, rest and quiet. You can't act like a puppy."

She grabbed the shovel, filled it with dirt, then sighed. Coaly had again descended into the pit. Down she went once more to drag him out.

"I said no, Coaly. Be a good do—" Breanna froze, staring at her dog's dirt-encrusted muzzle. He held something between his teeth. A very dusty something. A leather pouch? She seized it, prying it from his mouth. "What on earth have y—?"

A tingle of premonition zigzagged up her spine. With tense fingers she loosened the drawstring, opened the bag and stuck her hand inside. More leather? Breanna slowly withdrew a folded piece of parchment-dry doeskin. Carefully she opened it—and gaped. It was a note, the letters inscribed with some sort of leather-burning tool so they wouldn't fade. And it was signed and dated: *John Gregor Van Patten, 1903.*

Scarcely able to believe her eyes, Breanna leaned against the wall of dirt behind her, smoothing the leather. The note read: *Below lies my life's work, unearthed and brought forth from The Crescent Moon. Let no man who does not hail to the name Van Patten lay hands upon it.*

The soles of Breanna's feet tingled. She glanced down to see Coaly busily throwing dirt all over her sneakers. His claws scraped metal.

"I don't believe it." Picking up her dog, Breanna lifted him out of the hole, then grabbed her shovel. "It existed. All these years, it really existed. Dane was right."

Bending over the shovel, she began to dig....

One hour and several blisters later, Breanna knelt, holding a rock in her hand, next to the large chest she had unearthed a foot or so below the old trough. With a mighty swing, she clunked the stone against the rusty lock, breaking the hasp. Her arms trembled as she pried open the lid. Then she could only stare. The chest was brimming with nuggets and leather pouches, a horde larger than her wildest imaginings. *John Van Patten's hidden gold.*

She was so excited that she didn't notice the red pickup that had pulled into her driveway behind her Honda, but the slamming of its door woke her from her reverie. She glanced up, did a double take—and again did nothing but stare. Something far more important to her than gold now held her attention. *Tyler.* She abandoned her newly discovered treasure trove, scrambling gracelessly from the hole.

"Tyler?" Her voice squeaked, and she immediately wanted to kick herself. He had probably only come to say goodbye. "Hi there. Long time, no see."

He looked so good, just as she remembered him, comfortably dressed in jeans, an open-necked red shirt and hiking boots. This last week she had envisioned him in a business suit, with a beeper attached to his belt and a gun strapped beneath his arm. Instead, the closest thing to a weapon he carried was a black puppy, which was biting his wrist and squirming, trying to get free.

"This is Snoopy," he said, leaning down to let the pup go. "He's a peace offering. When the prognosis for Coaly didn't look too bright, I stopped by the pound." Straightening, Tyler shrugged. "He looked so much like him, I couldn't resist. Now that Coaly's better, he's sort of surplus, but he grows on you. Maybe he'll keep the old man company?"

Breanna dropped to one knee to rescue her sneaker, which the puppy had attacked with razor-sharp teeth. Laughing, she stroked his wavy black fur. "Oh, Tyler, he's darling. And he *does* look like Coaly. What a stroke of luck that you found him."

"Say that in about a week." Tyler folded his arms over his chest. "He doesn't eat paper like Coaly. He goes for socks and boots."

Her eyes flew to his frayed shoelaces and she burst out laughing. Looking up, she saw a twinkle of humor in Tyler's eyes. Giving the pup a final pat, she stood. Silence settled. An uncomfortable silence. She glanced one way, Tyler another. Then they both looked at each other, their eyes locking.

"I—um—" Breanna shifted her weight from one foot to the other, folding her arms over her chest, too. "I was hoping you'd stop by. Was the puppy your only reason for coming?"

"Yes." His mouth twisted in a grin. "Only it was more like an excuse, not a reason. I'm a devious fellow, you know."

"Yes, I know."

"I figure that Coaly is all the dog you can handle. Two of him, well—that'd be a bit much without someone around to help corral them. Any openings?"

Breanna's face felt stiff. "Oh, Tyler... how can *you* apply for the job? Your commitment to the department—well, that's all-consuming. How could we ever make it work?"

"I'm a little disappointed in you. Seems to me, no matter what my job, if you love me, it wouldn't matter."

"Ah, but you forget, I have a profession, too. And that's a two-way street. You didn't come back, so I figured you couldn't see how your job and mine could mix. Besides, you never asked for a compromise. You just disappea—"

"I'm asking now," he interrupted. "And I didn't disappear. I've been doing my job and Jack's too, getting the loose ends tied up for him. It'll be awhile before he's back on his feet."

Breanna glanced at Hungry Hill, blinking back tears. "And just what is it you're asking?"

"If I had to go to D.C., would you go with me? If I had to live in some city surrounded by miles of concrete, would you live there with me?"

"And give up my work?"

"No. We'd always come back here. You could do your research, then write wherever I'm assigned, couldn't you?"

Breanna looked into his eyes. New York, Chicago, Los Angeles, Washington, D.C., concrete and skyscrapers and smog. It wasn't what she had planned for herself. But without Tyler, all the forests and mountains in the world wouldn't fulfill her. "Yes, I think I could do that. I've done a lot of thinking about my promise to Gran, and I believe her biggest reason for insisting I come here was to force me to face the past. She was a very wise old lady. I think she knew I was running, and it was her way of making me stop." Breanna smiled. "I think she even suspected what Morrow had done. I found the news story about Joe Darren circled. She had to have done that. And she must have felt his death was significant, or she wouldn't have. As long as I keep the assessments done and the claim stays in the Van Patten family, she'll be content."

"We'd have to make sacrifices. Both of us would."

"Yes, both of us. I'm a simple person, Tyler, with plain tastes. Glitz just isn't in me. Putting on airs isn't in me. I'm afraid I'll be a hindrance rather than a help if you're trying to impress your superiors."

He stepped slowly toward her, then cupped her cheek in his hand. Love shone in his eyes as he smiled. "Breanna, you may not be fancy, but you're more beautiful with dirt to your elbows than other women in chiffon and diamonds.

To me, anyway. I'm not asking you to be anything but what you are. I just need to know you'll stick with me, no matter what, that's all.''

"Because of Karen?" She turned her face to press her lips against his palm, her arms still crossed over her chest. "Oh, Tyler. I won't do what Karen did. If you go away, I'll manage. I'll worry, but I have my own thing to do, my own career. And if we have to live in cities sometimes, I'll tough it out until we can come back to the mountains.''

He lifted her chin. "You're sure? You and I are on, no matter what? Even though you hate guns and know what my life can be like?''

"I'm sure.''

He gave a whoop and imprisoned her in a bear hug, lifting her off her feet. "That's the right answer, lady, the only right answer. I love you. Did you know that? I love you so much.''

Breanna wrapped her arms around his neck, pressing her face into the hollow of his shoulder. "And I love you.''

He swung her in a circle, then lowered her feet to the ground. "Lady, I've got news for you. You see that mountain? We don't have to leave it. See that cabin? That's home. No concrete, period. No guns. No job taking me away.''

"What do you mean?''

He set her away from him. "Breanna, remember when I told you I tried never to lie you? Didn't I say that I'd changed professions? I'm not with the department anymore. I helped out with the Graves Creek investigation because I know the terrain so well. I've been retired for almost four years." He lifted an eyebrow. "'Investigation,' look it up. Webster's definition is 'systematic inquiries.' That's what I used to do. Now I'm a photographer.''

"Oh.''

"Oh? That's all you can say?''

"I could say you're rotten for putting me through all that."

"Not rotten, just wanting to be sure." He ran his fingers into her hair. "I'm a little insecure, I guess. I had to know you'd take me however you could get me."

"As long as it's mutual."

"You're a little dirty. But I'll toss you into the creek later."

Breanna broke off in the middle of a laugh, her eyes widening. "Tyler, the dirt. Oh, my, I got so wrapped up in us, I totally forgot to tell you."

"Tell me what?"

"The trough! Coaly dug up a bag in the hole we dug. And then—Tyler, I found the Van Patten gold!"

"The Van Patten gold..." He stared down at her with a blank expression on his face. "What gold?"

"*The* gold." She seized his hand and tugged him along behind her. "See? Isn't it incredible?"

Tyler gaped at the chest, then began to laugh. "Won't Dane do a jig when he sees this? Gosh, it's a shame he can't be here to see it."

"Oh, I wish he could. He'd be over the moon."

"A picture! I'll take a picture so we can give it to him up at the hospital. One of you, standing beside it. Good idea?"

"A great idea!"

He started for his truck, stopped and snapped his fingers. "Damn! My camera's in town at my folks' house."

"I've got one of those instant jobs. We could use that."

Tyler rolled his eyes. "I suppose I can condescend to use it for one picture. Go get it."

A few minutes later, Breanna posed beside the chest, smiling up at Tyler.

"Lift one of the bags and hold it open." He stepped sideways and clicked the shutter. "Another big smile, Bree."

"Get the picture, moron. You're not using your Leica."

Tyler tugged the photo from the slot, tossing it onto the ground. The puppy bounded up. "Nah, get back, you snoopy little mutt." Tyler rescued the picture and held it between his thumb and forefinger while he snapped another. "Okay, lady, climb out and watch yourself appear."

Breanna scrambled from the hole to stand beside him. Peering over his arm, she watched the images darken. "Oh, it's good, don't you think? Not bad for this light."

"An expert took it." Tyler turned the photo, his smile fading. "A little foggy in one corner." He held up the other, handing her the first. "Oh, this one's clear. Dane'll love it. That smile on your face says it all, sweetheart."

Breanna wasn't looking at her smile. She stared at the corner of the picture, at the foggy spot Tyler had seen, which was now becoming more sharply defined. A frown pleated her brow. "Tyler, who's that man?"

What man?"

"This man, the one behind me in the picture!"

He glanced over, then did a double take. His eyes riveted on the corner of the photo. "That isn't—well, it *looks* sort of like a man, but it's just a bad exposure."

Breanna's mouth went dry. "It looks like a—" She licked her lips. "It's a miner, Tyler. You can see his slickers. And his headlamp."

Tyler leaned closer. "Sure can, can't you?" His gaze moved to her pale face. "Honey, it's just a trick of the light. You know how you can see things in clouds if you look? It's the same principle."

Breanna studied the blurred image for a long moment, then lifted her gaze to the treasure chest. Coaly was off to the right, sniffing the foundation of the barn, the puppy on his heels. A shiver ran up her spine. "Tyler, you don't think it could be—?"

"No ma'am, I don't." He took her firmly by the arm. "Talk about clear out into the twilight zone! That's crazy. John Van Patten's ghost? Come on, get real."

"Nobody believed in his treasure, either. And there it is!"

"It's just a bad photo, taken with a cheap camera. Come on, let's get that gold stowed someplace and take the pictures in to Dane."

Breanna took one more look at the photo, then sighed. "It *is* just a patch of blur when you look close, isn't it?"

"Yup, and that's all it is."

As the words trailed off Tyler's lips, he glanced at the barn. Coaly barked, wagged his tail, then sat on his haunches to emit a long, mournful howl.

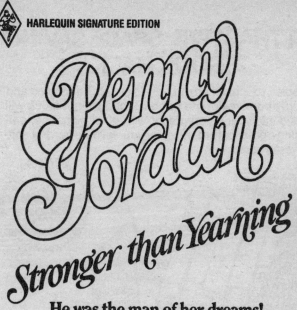

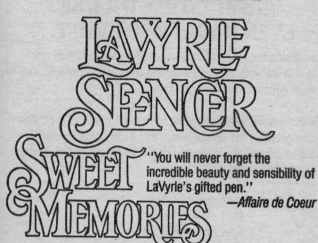

Temptation™

TEMPTATION WILL BE
EVEN HARDER TO RESIST...

In September, Temptation is presenting a sophisticated new face to the world. A fresh look that truly brings Harlequin's most intimate romances into focus.

What's more, all-time favorite authors Barbara Delinsky, Rita Clay Estrada, Jayne Ann Krentz and Vicki Lewis Thompson will join forces to help us celebrate. The result? A very special quartet of Temptations...

- **Four striking covers**
- **Four stellar authors**
- **Four sensual love stories**
- **Four variations on one spellbinding theme**

All in one great month! Give in to Temptation in September.

TDESIGN-1